The Meat Market

Mashiul Alam is a writer and translator who was born in northern Bangladesh in 1968. He studied journalism at the Peoples' Friendship University in Moscow during the late eighties and early nineties. A journalist by profession, he worked at *Prothom Alo*, a leading Bengali daily in Bangladesh, for many years. He is the author of over a dozen books, including *Tonushreer Shongey Ditiyo Raat*, *Ghora Masud*, *Mangsher Karbar* and *Pakistan*. He has also translated Fyodor Dostoevsky and Bertrand Russell's works into Bengali.

Alam was awarded the debut Sylhet Mirror Prize for Literature (2019), the IFIC Bank Literature Prize (2020) for his fiction and the Panjeri-BTF Literary Translation Award (2024) for his translation of Dostoevsky's *Notes From Underground*. His short story 'Doodh', translated as 'Milk' by Shabnam Nadiya, was awarded the 2019 Himal Southasian Short Story Prize, and Shabnam Nadiya's translation of his work entitled *The Meat Market and Other Stories* was awarded a 2020 PEN/Heim Translation Grant. He was also a Resident Fellow at the International Writing Program at the University of Iowa. He is currently working on *Laal Akash*, a novel set in the Soviet Union during Perestroika.

Shabnam Nadiya is a Bangladeshi writer and translator settled in Philadelphia. A graduate of the Iowa Writers' Workshop, she is the recipient of the Steinbeck Fellowship at the San Jose State University (2019) for her novel-in-progress *Unwanted*, a PEN/Heim Translation Fund Grant (2020) for her translation of Mashiul Alam's short fiction, *The Meat Market and Other Stories*, and a PEN Presents (2022) grant for her translation-in-progress of Wasi Ahmed's novel *Borofkol* (The Ice Machine). Her translation of Mashiul Alam's story 'Doodh' (Milk) won the 2019 Himal Southasian Short Story Prize. Nadiya's published translations include Leesa Gazi's novel *Hellfire*, Moinul Ahsan Saber's novel *The Mercenary* and Shaheen Akhtar's novel *Beloved Rongomala*. Her translations and writing have been widely published in journals and anthologies, including the W.W. Norton collection *Flash Fiction International*, *The Best Asian Poetry 2021-22*, the New York Public Library's *Pocket Poems* series, *The Offing*, *Joyland Magazine*, *Amazon's Day One*, *Gulf Coast* and *Copper Nickel*.

TRANSLATED FROM THE BENGALI
BY SHABNAM NADIYA

MASHIUL ALAM

The Meat Market

TEN STORIES
AND A NOVELLA

eka

eka

First published in English in 2024 by Eka, an imprint of Westland Books, a division of Nasadiya Technologies Private Limited

No. 269/2B, First Floor, 'Irai Arul', Vimalraj Street, Nethaji Nagar, Alapakkam Main Road, Maduravoyal, Chennai 600095

Westland, the Westland logo, Eka and the Eka logo are the trademarks of Nasadiya Technologies Private Limited, or its affiliates.

This translation was supported by the PEN/Heim Translation Fund Grant from PEN America.

The following stories were published in journals:

'Milk', 2019 *Himal Southasian*, 2020

'Horse', *Shuddhashar/Free Voice*, Issue 32, 2023

'The Underpass', *The Aleph Review*, Vol. 4, 2020

'The Cuckoo Keeps Calling', *South Asian Avant Garde* (SAAG), Vol. 1, 2020

'An Indian Citizen Came to Our Town', *Words Without Borders*, 2013

'The Meat Market', *Asymptote*, Winter 2019

ISBN: 9789360459352

10 9 8 7 6 5 4 3 2 1

Typeset by Jojy Philip, New Delhi

Printed at Nutech Print Services, India

Contents

Milk

Once there was a severe flood in the month of Magh.

—Local saying

1

Salimuddi's wife Julekha did deliver the baby, but barely two months had passed when her breastmilk dried up. What was the baby supposed to survive on? There was no answer to Julekha's brutal question. He who was the Master of the land and the skies was also the Master of Julekha's breastmilk; this, Julekha believed. But now it seemed to her that the Divine Master had His lips pursed in a smirk when He saw the distressing situation Julekha and her baby were in. It made her very angry. God was exceedingly whimsical: these words continued to beat in her heart. Unable to bear it, one day she held her baby away from her breast, looked up to the sky and blurted out, 'This wasn't a good thing you did, Allah.'

But within this Julekha's heart lived another Julekha. That Julekha raised her forefinger and said, 'Do not try to comprehend the mysteries of Allah.' It was enough to terrify her; she spat on her chest and said *tauba* in repentance. Nevertheless, she received no forgiveness and came down with a terrible bout of stomach flu. She flooded the house and the yard with her piss, shit and vomit.

But the people of Modhupur knew that the Master of the land and the skies was infinitely kind, extremely forgiving. He sent the nonprofit worker Aminul Islam to Julekha's bedside, bearing packets of oral saline, and thus, ordered the angel of death, Azrael, to go back this time around.

2

Julekha was no emperor's daughter. She was a farmhand bound in year-round employment at the Talukdar farmstead of Modhupur village. Her husband Salimuddi was the same. (There is no difference between a bound farmhand and a bound cow.)

Julekha was twenty-four years old. Her skin was the colour of a shabby, old black umbrella; her body suffered a scarcity of flesh. Joint-ridden and thin as a cane, her body jutted out every which way, angular and long. Her nose was bony and high, her jaw at the ready. Her eyes were narrow; below them lay shaded hollows. They were like a pair of rusted black sickles. Julekha's breasts were not as large as a woman's should be. Her waist was flat and narrow. Her buttocks, disappointing.

3

There was no milk in Julekha's breasts. But, through Allah's grace, her son didn't die due to lack of breastmilk. He was quite well, growing. After all, rice-water wasn't a rare commodity in a farming household. Besides, people had seen him eat clods of earth. Meaning that Julekha's son was growing up on a diet of rice-water and dirt. This was not a problem. He had begun to crawl and could even stand, grabbing onto this and that. This crawling pup advanced along the yard, the verandas, the stove-side and the barns of the Talukdar farmstead with ease. He wedged his red tongue against the back of his two just-grown teeth and cooed, *toh toh toh*. There was no one in Modhupur to pick up the child gently, or rock him a little, or make him chuckle or cry. It made no difference to him. He kept to himself, crawled here and there, grabbed this and that, played with the lambs and the baby goats, and laughed aloud whenever he felt like it.

4

In the evenings during the month of Poush, winter winds blew across the northern lake of Modhupur, baring their teeth, laughing and gnawing at the entire village. Cold dew dripped from the black sky onto the tin roofs, the straw thatches, the leaves, the haystacks, the supine paddies, the dusty roads and the hardened fields. In the Talukdar's barns, the cows shivered with cold, and mosquitoes and gadflies swelled from sucking their blood. At some point, an owl poked out its grotesque face from a hole in a tree and gazed at the misty dawn. The elderly muezzin chanted the *azaan* from the village mosque in a trembling voice, and in one of the many barns owned by the Talukdar family, a black dog eased her distended belly by bringing five puppies into the world. Still, there was no sign of the sun in the eastern sky. Still, adjacent to the Talukdar household, inside the tin-roofed shed spread thickly with straw, a group of dark-skinned people breathed noisily in their sleep.

5

The black dog's pups couldn't open their eyes yet. They couldn't bear the light of the world. They squealed and constantly tripped over each other. They couldn't even locate their mother's teats.

The mother's teats were bursting with milk. But her belly burned with hunger. She filled her babies' bellies and went out. She needed food. Crossing the hay-filled barn into the yard, and along the bank of the pond and the grove of bamboo where leaves fell, swaying her milk-filled teats, she went in search of food.

6

A muscular male dog showed up in front of the barn. His drooping ears pricked up. His nostrils began to expand and contract. Inside the barn, there was indistinct squealing. The dog, sinewy like a wolf, slipped into the barn. In a moment, he shot out like an arrow. The white puppy dangling from his mouth was clearly visible in the bright light of midday. Bright red blood dripped onto the dry earth. The earth sucked in all the blood but the stain didn't disappear.

The dog, with the puppy in its maw, disappeared. Then, for a while, there was absolute silence everywhere. All the men and women of Modhupur were frantically busy with cutting, threshing, boiling and husking the rice harvest. In a short while, a pack of monstrous dogs showed up in front of the barn and, within seconds, the black dog's hideaway became empty. Only drops of blood creating patterns remained on the white, hard soil of the month of Poush. The parched, thirsty soil had absorbed the blood, but still couldn't remove all the signs.

The mother returned from the bamboo grove. She didn't waste time anywhere and quickly slipped into the barn. But her home inside the barn was empty. She writhed in distress. She clawed apart the piles of straw with her paws. Then she clawed at the earth, searched in the hay, and began running from one end of the barn to the other, distraught. She came out and raised her front paws to the sky, moaning. She clawed the earth again, rolled around on the ground, panted, and again raised her front paws to the sky, crying, and continuing to cry.

The people of Modhupur didn't see any of this. They had much more important things to do in this world.

7

Julekha's son crawled everywhere, through the house, the yard, the outer yards. In Modhupur, the rice harvest continued: the fields grew empty as the farmers' homes filled up with rice and hay.

During the day, Julekha dried the unhusked rice in the red yard dabbed with cow-dung; she walked in circles amidst the spread-out unhusked rice, sifting it with her feet. In the afternoon, when the sunlight began to redden and die, she pulled the rice into piles with a *paura*. She covered the piles with polythene fertiliser bags and sacking so the rice wouldn't be dampened by the night's dew. When night descended, she boiled the unhusked rice in large brass pots on a five-mouthed stove. She tossed some chaff into the fire; it crackled and burned.

Salimuddi reaped the paddy with the other labourers, carried back paddy sheaves in baskets and arranged them in the outer yard. At night, he laid out empty barrels and wooden planks to flail the bundles of paddy or threshed them by walking a cow or water-buffalo in a circle.

During this time of massive toil, Julekha's son was quite neglected; he wandered around on his own.

The dog with the lost puppies sat by herself in front of the barn. Her face was streaked with tears.

Julekha's son crawled over to the dog. The dog wagged her tail. She stretched out her neck and sniffed the human child.

8

One afternoon, Abdul, the servant of the Mondal household next door, was heard shouting. Then, he began to jump up and down, slapping both cheeks of his ass, telling everyone, 'What a strange thing, brother, what a strange thing! Julekha's son is feeding on dog's milk!'

Everyone was stunned. They dropped whatever they were doing and rushed over to the Talukdar's outer yard. There they found Julekha's son and the dog that had lost her puppies next to a pile of straw; the two were playing together in safety, in harmony. Nobody could see a hint of Abdul's aspersion in their simple play. Someone smacked Abdul on the back of his neck and said, '*Shalla*, you've become a detective now, have you?' Abdul touched the soil to swear on his mother, to swear on Allah, and said, 'But I saw it with my own eyes!' When another smack seemed impending, he grew dejected and said, 'One day you'll see it with your own eyes and know that I'm not lying.'

9

Abdul vowed to himself that if he could show no one else, he would at least show Julekha and Salimuddi that astonishing scene. He remained vigilant from then onwards. After investigating for several days, he noticed that when the labourers left for the fields to reap the harvest after their breakfast of watered rice, when the women workers and the other women of the farmstead were engrossed in cooking and other chores, Julekha's son cooed *toh toh toh* and crawled across threshold after threshold, making for the outer yard. There, amidst the countless piles of straw and maze of haystacks, Julekha's son and the dog missing her pups found each other.

One day, Abdul begged and pleaded and brought Salimuddi, Julekha and three other labourers to the outer yard. They stood behind a high haystack and watched.

Julekha's son was crawling, the carpet-like straw crackling under him. Around him, heavy with milk, danced the dog. She was exulting, clawing at the straw, wagging her tail and emitting a strange squeal. Whenever the boy wanted to pet the dog, she pretended to move away, but the next moment, she was back, wagging her tail, calling to him and shaking her head. Julekha's son giggled and reached out to grab her, but again she moved away.

Thus, their play and pretending went on for a while. Then, gradually, the dog grew calm. The boy cooed *toh toh toh* and went up to her. The dog splayed out her legs and stood still. Julekha's son pulled his little legs together and then extended them sideways under the dog's belly, balancing himself on his hands. He craned his neck, raising his face upwards, and attached his mouth to one of the milk-filled nipples.

Salimuddi slid out from behind the haystack. He gripped hard the hoe resting on his shoulder and raised it above his head, arching his spine like a bow, poised to strike. The dog ran in terror but, impeded by another haystack, it changed direction trying to run a different way, when Salimuddi opened his mouth expelling his breath, and landed the heavy back of the hoe right in the middle of the dog's head. There was a noise like the thick shell of a ripe velvet apple cracking open and, trembling and biting down on its tongue, the dog fell.

Salimuddi saw millions of fireflies jumping and circling around him, sparking impossibly in the midday sun. While everyone stared wide-eyed at the dog thrashing on the ground in the last moments of its life, the hoe slipped from Salimuddi's slackened fist and dropped almost silently onto the hay. Watching the shimmer of the hostile fireflies circling his head for just a few seconds made his eyelids droop, and when his body lurched slightly and fell, like a tree trunk, the other farm workers turned to look at him. As Salimuddi's body tumbled like the trunk of a banana tree chopped at the base, they caught him. When Julekha witnessed the moment and began to howl, three crows began screeching in chorus from the mango tree by the pond, and Julekha's son forgot his own tears and gazed in wonder at the crows.

10

Salimuddi regained consciousness after cold water from the wintry pond was poured over his head for a little while. At first, he glanced this way and that, looked at the branches and boughs of the trees in surprise. Once he was able to locate himself, he began to look more normal.

He lay there comfortably for about an hour and then, proclaiming, 'Ah, nothing happened,' he stood up. He glopped a fistful of mustard oil on his head and kneaded it onto his crown before smoothly walking to the pond with his lungi and towel slung across his shoulder and ducking himself into the water before coming back.

Then, with the sweet heat of the southbound winter sun warming his back, he sat in the yard with the other labourers and ate rice till his belly was stuffed; after the meal, like any other day, he chugged down gallons of water. As he stroked his belly, now round and tight like a watermelon, he lit up a *bidi*. He took a long drag and chatted with the others.

When their brief post-lunch break was over, Salimuddi accompanied the other labourers to cut paddy just as he was supposed to.

11

Then, the winter sun grew tired and quickly sagged in the western horizon. The men's shadows grew longer and longer in the golden fields until finally they faded and disappeared. The dry straw grew damp from dew, and from the northern expanse, with its teeth bared in laughter, winter arrived to sink its fangs into the skin and bones of the people. Winter's terror had silenced the fields and the houses. The echoes of the azaan shivered their way from the minarets of the mosque into the winter sky. The labourers had returned with the rice. Neither the rice nor the house belonged to them. Every year, during the harvest, these dark-skinned people came from Rangpur, Roumari, Kurigram, Nilphamari, Gaibandha, Gobindaganj, looking for work. They reaped the rice crop in the fields belonging to the householders; they slept on straw spread out in the tin-roofed shacks erected on the outer yards of the farmsteads; they ate white rice with *kheshari-kalai* legumes and green chillies; they harvested the rice; they threshed it. In moonlight, as well as in the utter darkness of the new moon, they got wet with dew as they threshed the rice and sang.

12

The labourers sat in a row in the yard eating rice. They devoured tub after tub, as if there was no end to their hunger. As if they would be happy if they could eat into eternity. They didn't want to stop, they just wanted to eat, eat, and eat.

Dew dripped onto their heads from the black sky. They thought about the sky sometimes; they called it *asmaan* instead of *akash*. They usually only looked at the sky to check for rain or storms. Very rarely did they think of the sky as having any different significance: where it was the throne of He who possessed both worlds; where, even if the Master, although He was infinitely kind, nevertheless brought forth terrible disasters and calamities, and it was beyond humans to comprehend His mysteries.

The labourers ate rice and drank water and inhaled tobacco smoke and transformed their bellies into watermelons; they groaned *ahh* to indicate their satiation and sat together chatting. Then, they tied their cotton towels around their ears and heads and laid out empty barrels and wooden planks and *thipish thipish thopash thopash* they beat sheaves of rice against the planks.

Thus, the night deepened even further. The dew thickened and collected on the tin roof, the haystacks, the bamboo grove and the leaves of trees. Owls hooted, from afar floated the baying of foxes, dogs howled at the mouth of the pathway.

Finally, it was time for Julekha to leave the side of the stove. The rice chaff still sat inside the stove's belly, smouldering to the colour of egg yolk. Salimuddi left his companions and returned home. As the farmhand employed year-round by this household, he and his family had a separate room allotted to them. Although there was no cot in the room, there was bedding made out of woven date-palm fronds, and now, since that bedding had been spread out over a layer of thick straw, it felt as if they had an actual warm and springy mattress.

Their son lay asleep on that mattress. Salimuddi and Julekha finished their work, returned to their room, latched the door and fell asleep. The moon rose in the sky. The land

and the sky grew enigmatic in the moonlight. A mysterious, ruthless creature spread frost everywhere. There was no sound anywhere in Modhupur. No hooting owls, no baying foxes, no howling dogs.

Trapped in an endless silence within a profound chill, Modhupur shivered.

13

When the night ended, the people of Modhupur awoke shouting. The moonlit land and sky shifted, rocked by the solemn sound coming from afar. People stood in their homes, at their doors, their verandas and yards, and watched an all-encompassing deluge approach. The flood inundated the surrounding plains and surged and grew. As they watched, the flood swelled and submerged the bamboo grove, the dock by the pond, the alleyways. It overwhelmed the yards and entered houses. People began to climb up the haystacks, the mounds of rice, and to the rooftops.

They saw that the world was flooded with milk. The land and the sky were inundated with white moonlight and milk. They looked at each other in surprise, they understood nothing, they felt a helpless and wretched desire to understand the profound machinations of the Master of the land and the sky. Their hearts trembled, they felt apprehensive. They stood atop the mounds of rice, the rooftops, the highest points of the haystacks and the treetops, and they looked around, and they searched for Salimuddi in their minds, they remembered his son and felt a keen curiosity to see him.

Suddenly, the sound of laughter, like never before, reached their ears. In the silent milk-flooded plains, they heard a child's numinous laughter echoing and re-echoing in a way that moved beyond all their experiences. Then they saw that the village paths and walkways, the yards, the banks of the pond and the bamboo grove were inundated by milk; the fog-ridden moonlight and the steam from the milk curled their way up towards the sky.

Against this never-before-seen white backdrop, the people of Modhupur saw—Salimuddi's son was swimming in the moonlit milk-sea in infinite joy; beside him, like a queen, swam the dog, her swollen teats swaying in the rippling waves of milk.

Horse

I used to dream of a white horse that had wings. This horse didn't gallop; it flew.

Before I ever saw an actual horse in real life, an image of a horse had grown within my mind. I was never able to figure out how that had happened, no matter how much I thought about it.

When I was studying at university, I used to listen to Mr Plato's utterances. He had once said, 'There is only one true horse, which is in the heavens. What you see here are merely the shadows of that true horse.'

I had asked him, 'Sir, does the true horse have wings?'

In response, Plato nodded and said he had never seen the horse of the heavens. When reminded of Pegasus, he smiled like an English gentleman of modern times, and in the manner of an administrator, he said. 'In an ideal state, there will be no space for poets and artists.' In my intense youth, I had journeyed across the Caucasus mountains on the back of a white horse, to the place where Prometheus had been imprisoned for stealing fire from the heavens; but even that horse hadn't had wings. It was a profound question: how did the image of a winged horse form in my mind?

There might have been some connection with my paternal grandmother, because in my childhood she had told me many weird stories. Her bizarre tales might have included mentions of winged horses. But by the time it occurred to me to ascertain the origins of this idea, my old Dadi was no longer alive.

Before she died, my Dadi had most probably fallen in love with my maternal cousin's maternal grandfather. My paternal grandfather and my maternal cousin's maternal grandfather (I called him Nana) had been cousins of a sort. Nana, my cousin's maternal grandfather, was an LMF doctor. My Dadi said Doctor Nana used to own a horse. He used to ride it when he went around the villages, visiting his patients. Nana would wear a pith helmet on his head, Dadi said, and he even had a pistol, and he used to wear pantaloons, and he would tuck his pistol into his pantaloon's waistband, and when he rode off to distant villages to see his patients, he looked very *pretty* (perhaps Dadi had meant 'handsome'). Dadi's husband was a farmer who owned two hundred bighas of land, while the doctor had a pith helmet, a pistol and a horse.

But that horse didn't have wings either. If it had, surely Dadi would have told me that detail before telling me anything else. So how did the idea of a winged horse form in my mind?

Much later my father told me this: At the age when static objects, such as trees, had no value to you, wings were your only attraction. As a child, you chased after birds for days on end. Later you discovered that the word 'pakhi', bird, had been derived from 'pakha', wings.

But this eternal verity, that real horses didn't have wings, I learnt first in the village of my paternal grandfather. When, for the first time in my life I saw a real horse in the flesh, I was very disappointed, because people had turned these horses into donkey-like beasts of burden.

People loaded up their sacks of rice on the horses' backs; the horses trudged along the dusty paths of our village, their gait slow and non-equine. We chanted:

O ghora, tor payer toley ki?
Nora
Der thyang khora!

Hey, horsey, what's beneath your hooves?
Pegs,
And one and a half lame legs!

Once, the rice traders stopped at my grandfather's grain yard with three horses. They gathered beside the barn where rice was stored and bought the unhusked rice for forty-five takas per maund. When the sacks of rice had been loaded onto the horses' backs, my grandfather touched the tip of his finger to his tongue and counted out the many soiled banknotes that the traders had pulled out of their waist pouches.

I said, 'Dadu, go and buy watermelons with this money.'

The watermelons were black and impossibly round, as if they were footballs. There were countless seeds in them. My Dadi pointed at the watermelons and told me, 'These are horse eggs.'

Dadi hid the watermelons in her room, under her bed. I used to think one day those eggs would hatch into foals.

But one day we left those horse eggs under Dadi's cot in her room and we left Dadu's village and went to the town; my father had built a house there. We started living in that house. I was admitted to Ramdeo Bajla Government High School.

Then one day I saw a horse standing in a corner of the school's playground. This one didn't have wings either; instead, this too was like those laughable donkeys, the ones that bore rice sacks on their backs along the dusty roads of my Dadu's village, headed for the Moslemganj marketplace. On this horse sat, not a sack, but a ludicrous leaf-thin man, with a wooden box in front of him. He stuffed *gool*-tobacco into his mouth with the tip of his index finger and raised the lid of the wooden box, slamming it down with a thwack, and yelled out in a grating voice, i-i-i-c-e-c-r-e-e-a-m!

On hot days, we bought bright red ice-lollies on sticks and slurped them with gusto; the ice cream vendor said that ice cream kept your brain cool, and with a cool brain, you could focus more on schoolwork, etcetera.

One day I told him: I want to ride your horse just once. But he wouldn't agree. I tempted him: 'Just one lap around this field, you'll get one taka.'

He said yes out of greed. He stretched out his hand to me: 'The money first.'

I gave him a taka. He took the ice cream box from the horse's back and placed it on the ground. Then he hoisted me on his shoulders and sat me on the horse's back. But he kept hold of the reins. I wanted the reins in my hands. He said, 'You won't be able to; if you fall and break your bones, I'll be the one who's blamed.'

And then he jumped onto the horse, behind me. He dug his ankles into the horse's ribs. He yanked the reins and made noises with his mouth, '*Hoot, hoot!* Go, go!'

But the horse didn't go, didn't move. When the man dug his heels further into its ribs, it splayed its hind legs further apart and stood stubbornly unmoving.

I was quite embarrassed. Because all the boys from my school were watching me and laughing. I loathed that horse; I jumped off its back and threw a curse at it, 'Fucking mule!'

Then one day I saw the leaf-thin man ride his horse to the northwestern corner of the school playground and stop there. He pulled out his gool-tobacco pot, excavated gool with the tip of his index finger and stuffed it into his mouth, raised the lid of his wooden box and slammed it down, shouting out, 'i-c-e-c-r-e-a-m!' And immediately the horse collapsed to the ground. The gool-guzzling leaf-thin fellow fell flat on his face with his ice cream box, and the horse began to foam at the mouth. Our eyes bulged in surprise and terror.

After that, I never told anyone that I used to dream of a winged horse.

2

My son told me he had dreamt of a horse. Apparently, the horse had a pair of wings; it was flying over the National Parliament House of Bangladesh, which is located in Sher-e-Bangla Nagar, Dhaka.

My son is only eight, but he talks like an octogenarian. He wanted to define his own dream as unrealistic and outlandish using this logic: 'A horse is not a bird; why should a horse have wings!'

Then one day he showed me a hand-drawn and coloured illustration and said, 'Baba, look, they've drawn wings on a horse. Isn't it crazy?'

I worry; my son is growing up to be a hardheaded realist.

But he wasn't like this. At two and a half, he would tell us this story: 'Someone was ringing the doorbell. I knew it was a ghost. So I took a stick and went to the door and asked, "Who's there?" He said, "Open the door." I opened the door and hit the ghost on the head with my stick and his head cracked open, and then so many cockroaches whooomed out of his head!'

That same son of mine was now looking at an image of a winged horse and considering the artist crazy. This was worrying.

I told my son, 'Horses used to have wings; they used to fly through the clouds.'

My son laughed and said, 'Baba, you're mad.'

I asked him, 'If horses didn't have wings, how did you dream of a winged horse?'

My son made a serious face and said, 'Are dreams ever real?'

'Of course, they are. You'll see, one day a white, winged horse will show up at our house.'

My son started shouting, 'Ma, Ma, come quick, Baba has gone completely mad.'

His mother shouted back from the next room, 'That didn't happen today—your father went mad long before you were even born.'

The mother was fourteen times more a truth-teller compared to her son. Other than Allah, the *fereshtas* and the djinns who had been mentioned in the Holy Quran, she considered truth to be only what was visible in reality. Everything else, to her, were lies, imaginary, the mad imaginings of those who were mad.

The mother had taught the son arithmetic: two plus two always make four; they never make three or five. I called my son close and told him, 'Listen, my son, two plus two make twenty-two.'

My son pulled a sombre face and said, 'You want me to flunk my test, don't you?'

I told him, 'When the winged horse shows up, you can ask him how much two plus two makes.'

My son pursed his lips and said in an acerbic manner, 'So horses talk as well?'

'Of course, they do. The winged horse will tell you why the wings of horses can no longer be seen.'

'Why don't you tell me why they can no longer be seen?'

I said, 'Humans have told them, hey, horses, you're not birds. You're not allowed wings. If you don't get rid of your wings, we'll shoot you down like birds. Then we'll carve you up and cook you and eat you. Since then, horses hide their wings because they're scared of people. But they can spread their wings whenever they want. But they only do it at night, especially on nights with a full moon, when the entire world is filled with moonlight.'

My son wasn't confused in the slightest. Instead, he looked at me and smirked like a know-it-all old man and said, 'You think I'm still a little boy, don't you?'

The next morning, he had school. The driver came to me and said, 'Saar, the car isn't starting. I think the battery's down.'

I was annoyed. The battery had been replaced just last month.

My son said, 'Baba, you should return the car to your office. Then, a horse should be bought. I'll go to school on horseback. You'll also go to work on the horse. There will be no need for oil or gas and the horse won't break down.'

I marvelled and said, 'After the longest time you've finally said something worthwhile.'

But on the way to school in a rickshaw, my son said, just to disappoint me, 'The problem is where will you keep the horse, what will you feed it? The landlady won't allow you to keep a horse in the garage. The horse will pee and poop … isn't that a problem?'

I kept quiet.

The rickshaw crossed Mohammadpur bus stand and drove onto Shaat Masjid Road. Every single day, around this time, there would be a terrible traffic jam on this road. Today the entire street was empty; other than our rickshaw, there was no sign of other vehicles or other people. I was surprised, but my son was unperturbed.

I asked him, 'Your school isn't closed today, is it?'

He said in a confident voice, 'No.'

'But do you see how empty the road is?'

My son said like a citizen in the know, 'For sure some VIP is going to go through here.'

'But VIPs don't take this road.'

My son nodded and said, 'They do, they do. Nobody can say which road VIPs will take, or when, or why.'

Suddenly, from behind us came a rhythmic metallic sound—clip clop, clip clop …

Before I even had time to turn around to take a look, a red horse sped like an arrow towards us, an army man in uniform astride its back. It crossed us to the right and galloped ahead.

My eyeballs were about to explode. As he stared at the galloping, disappearing horse and its rider, my son smiled a know-it-all smile and said, 'Didn't I say some VIP will be passing through?'

The red horse and its rider clip-clopped their way across the silent, empty Shaat Mosjid Road that lay flat straight ahead. My son said, 'This horse came from India. Now the alliance between the two nations will deepen. However, there's a problem, there might be some conflict …'

My son continued saying terrible things; his words broke through the mystical silence of the empty street like the hoofbeats of a herd of horses; and soon, from behind us, six more muscular horses hurtled through, six generals astride their backs. They galloped beside us and sped towards Pilkhana.

My son watched them, and suddenly he began to laugh and chant a rhyme:

Hey, horsey, what's beneath your hooves?
Pegs,
And one and a half lame legs.

Then, when the herd of galloping horses and the sound of their hooves had disappeared, to keep me on my toes, my son said, 'But horses have no wings. Mind it, Baba.'

When we reached the school, as I was paying the rickshaw driver, I suffered a gentle jab from my son's elbow. He pointed to a corner of the school building, where the *chotpoti*, *fuchka*, *jhalmuri*, peanut, chickpea sellers were usually crowded. Now, none of them were there; there was only a horse, on its back a man as thin as a leaf, and in front of him, a wooden box. He pulled out some gool-tobacco from a pot with the tip of his index finger and stuffed it into his mouth, raised the lid of his wooden box and slammed it down, shouting, 'i-c-e-c-r-e-a-m!'

I thought my son would want some ice cream now. I would buy him a red ice-lolly; he would slurp it up and I would watch him, and this scene would bring me great joy.

But he didn't even bring up ice cream. Instead, in the manner of a wise old man opening my eyes, he said to me, 'Look, even this horse doesn't have wings.'

He slid his arms swiftly through the straps of the schoolbag bursting with textbooks and notebooks and, carrying it like a mountain climber's pack, he shrugged his shoulders a couple of times, directed a polite smile at me, waved goodbye, and marched off towards the main entrance of the school building.

The Hands of the Man of Light

Evening was descending. The spring sky overhung the canal next to the road. Legions of bats flew back and forth from the mahua tree on the other side of the canal. And on this side, Khoybor Ali's ten-year-old son Khobir stood on the elevated highway, pissing into the canal. His pee spurted noisily onto the water.

Kalimuddi was walking back from the marketplace that way. When he saw the boy, he said, 'You son of the devil, you're pissing in the water? Your dick hole's going to close off, I'm telling you.'

Khobir had forgotten that *fereshtas,* Allah's angels, lived in the water. He had drunk a pot of water late in the afternoon. His entire afternoon had gone by without any food. In the evening, that pot of water turned into piss and created pressure in his lower belly, and so he stood by the canal and pulled his short pants down to his knees and was pissing when Kalimuddi saw him and told him this, so now fear had entered Khobir's thoughts. Ten years old, and he didn't know Allah's book or His words. He didn't know how to say tauba and repent. He looked skywards, searching for Allah. If he found Him, he would say, Allah, forgive me, I'll never do it again. But Allah wasn't in the sky. The iron-hued sky remained silent. So Khobir spoke aloud as if telling himself, 'It's not so bad if it's small young folks pissing in the water.'

'Whose son are you, eh?'

Startled, Khobir looked behind. A fair-skinned man, wearing a *panjabi* as white as milk, was grinning with his very white teeth.

'Whose son are you? What are you doing by the canal in the evening?'

'Khoybor's.' Khobir responded tersely and looked the man over. He had never seen a person who looked like this in his entire life. He hadn't come out from the bottom of the canal, had he? He wasn't a water fereshta, was he?

'Khoybor's? Which Khoybor is your father? What does he do?'

'Doesn't do anything.'

'Doesn't do anything? Then what do you eat?'

'Nothing.'

The man came forward and took hold of Khobir's hand. 'Your wrists are like sticks. What do you eat?'

'Nothing.'

The man pushed his tongue against the base of his teeth and clucked.

Khobir thrust his neck forward like an egret and asked, 'Who're you?'

'A person.'

Suspicion leapt in Khobir's mind. For a moment he thought he should just make a run for it. But the man was holding his hand.

'Hey, why are you shaking? Don't be afraid, I'm not a kidnapper.' The man pulled out a banknote from the pocket of his panjabi and gave it to him, saying, 'Give this to your father.'

Khobir, son of Khoybor, the boy who believed that small children pissing in water wasn't a sin, and to ask for Allah's forgiveness without sinning counted as a virtue, grasped the note with all his fingers. He hid it in his fist and waited with bated breath for the man to let go of his hand.

The man delayed no longer; Khobir shut his eyes and took to his heels. He was terrified that by the time he reached home, the money would no longer be money, it would turn into blank paper. He tripped three times on the way, but it didn't discourage him. He kept running, and he kept on running. His short pants kept slipping down to his knees, and he kept pulling it back up with one hand. As soon as he entered his home, panting, he ran towards the lamp. He held his breath and smoothed out the crumpled note in the light of the lamp.

'Hey, where did you find that money?' His father pounced on him and grabbed the note. 'Fifty takas! Where did you find this, my son?'

'The fereshta gave it to me.'

Khoybor Ali narrowed his eyes, his brows knotted. He looked at his son and then he held out the note this way and that in front of the lamp, examining it. He looked at his son's face in surprise and said, 'Which fereshta? Why did he give this to you?'

Khobir said, 'I was standing straight, right on the bank of the canal, and then a bright white fereshta came down from the sky. Said, you're poor so here's fifty takas, I'm giving it to you. You can buy some sweets. Said, don't give it to anyone though.'

'You don't need this much money to buy sweets. I'll buy you some sweets tomorrow.' Khoybor Ali tucked the note into his waist.

His son began wailing. 'No, no, that is my money! The fereshta gave it to me and told me, don't give it to anyone. If you do, the money's going to turn into blank paper!' He rolled around in the dirt, his wailing like a song. 'Give me my money.

Why should you take it? The fereshta didn't give it to you, they gave it to me.'

It felt as if his father had become his enemy. He thought, if only he was a little taller and a little heftier, he could fight his father right now. He would throw the horrible man flat on his back in the yard, and then climb onto his chest, and then he would break all his fingers, crack crack crack, when he snatched the money from him.

'Why didn't the fereshta give me that strength,' Khobir asked himself. 'Koromali from that other neighbourhood rammed a shovel right into the chest of his own father, was that for nothing? Fathers are very bad people.'

Khoybor Ali was running. The heat of the money was making him rush to the subdistrict town. There, in a tin-roof shack, people of all kinds gambled together. That's where Khoybor Ali was headed. Even when he spotted an unusual crowd flocking at the entrance to the alleyway, he didn't have the patience to stop for a moment. As he zipped past, he overheard some of their conversation:

'Yes, yes, a new leader. Does business in Khulna.'

'What kind of business? How much money does he have?'

'Who knows what business, they say there's no end to his money.'

'It's jute. They say he exports jute abroad.'

'Why is he running on the boat symbol? This year all the votes are going to go to the sheaf of rice.'

Khoybor Ali muttered, 'I get it now, now it's clear who Khobir's fereshta was.' His pace quickened.

His father had gone off to gamble. Khobir felt extremely resentful. He was thinking, people were right in calling his father a gambler. His father was not a good person. Khobir decided that when he grew up, he would beat his father morning and night.

His father had left to gamble, and Khobir sat by himself in the yard, staring at the sky and weeping. After he had cried for a long time, his mother came home. She had brought back a plate of rice from the Mondal household after finishing her day's work there. Mother and son sat down to eat. As they ate, Khobir said, 'Oh, Ma, a fereshta gave me some money. Abba snatched it from me and went off to gamble.'

His mother wrinkled her brow and asked, 'What fereshta?'

Khobir told her the evening's story. His mother didn't believe him.

'You stole the money, right?' his mother said.

'I swear by Allah, Ma, the fereshta gave it to me! Said, you're poor, so here, take fifty takas. Buy some sweets, but don't give it to anyone. If you do, the money won't stay money, it'll turn into blank paper.'

'Sure, fereshtas have nothing better to do. Tell me who really gave you the money.' She started to interrogate her son. He kept repeating his story. But she didn't believe any of it. She thought, however, such a small child wouldn't steal; somebody must have taken pity on him and given him the money. Which was a good thing, but that the father had snatched it from the son and gone off to gamble was not a good thing. The mother's heart turned bitter.

'O, Ma, why does Abba gamble?'

'How do I know?'

'He's your meal ticket man and you don't know?'

'Shut up, you bastard. Does your father feed me that he's my meal ticket?'

'Your meal ticket man isn't a good person, Ma.'

The mother slapped the son. The son hissed, 'Your meal ticket's going to die.'

He received another slap on the same cheek. 'He'll die, he'll die!'

The mother got up and began whacking her son on his back and said, 'Your father's going to die, so you die too, you bastard!'

It was very late at night. Khobir lay beside his mother; his heart felt hollow every other moment. His father didn't love him; why was his father such a bad one? Why had he taken the money away like that? Was there no tenderness, no fondness in his father's heart?

Khobir whimpered now and then. He felt wretched about his mother because she hadn't consoled him at all. A mother who could leave her son with such sorrow and sleep so unconcernedly was not a good mother. The thought made him even sadder. His heart pulsed with hurt.

He began thinking about Allah. Allah was the only good one. Allah would judge them for sure.

He couldn't tell how late it got as he pondered all these things. Gradually, their yard brimmed with a strange illumination. A man made of light came down from the sky and stood in their yard. Then, as if floating, he walked into their home. Immediately the entire room was flooded with an orange light. The man of light came close, and closer still.

Then Khobir saw his mother right next to the man of light. She was smiling.

A man of light and a skin-and-bones woman were gesturing with their hands, smiling, nodding their heads and whispering together.

The man kissed the woman on her forehead, and Khobir saw that in the blink of an eye, his mother became as beautiful as the women on television.

His beautiful mother was now laughing loudly, and shiny, bright coins dropped from her mouth like pearls. *Shiki*, *adhuli*, *taka*—different denominations poured out onto the ground, rolling around the room like the wheels of a car.

A large coin, quite large, as big as a bicycle wheel, suddenly rolled out into the yard. It rolled beyond the yard into the alley, and then kept going. Khobir ran after it. The silver coin, or the divine bicycle wheel, kept rolling, and he followed it like mad. His short pants kept slipping down to his feet and tripping him up.

The coin as big as a bicycle wheel continued along the road and then suddenly—shloomp—jumped into the canal. And Khobir, who had stopped in his tracks by the canal, felt his belly swell up and bloat. He pulled his pants down to his knees and pointed his penis towards the water and said '…'eady, one two three …' with immense force—oh, no, there was no force! His flow was stymied.

'So what's going to happen now, Khoybor's son?'

'What'll happen? Will I die?'

'Hold it, why die now? Oh, look, there's Abedali, headed towards the marketplace, carrying his sewing machine on his shoulder to sew lungi seams. Call him, call him!'

'Oh, Abedali bhai, you have a needle, don't you?'

'I do, why?'

'The hole in my wee wee is closed, will you open it up for me?'

'Sure, I will, why wouldn't I?'

Abedali wielded his needle and settled himself in front of Khobir's penis. Khobir thrust his hips forward and held out his penis. 'Do it, bhai, do it!'

As soon as the needle touched the tip of Khobir's penis, the tiny organ turned into the hosepipe of a firetruck. A great surge of liquid silver emerged with immense force and swept Abedali into the canal. Gleeful, Khobir clapped as he noticed that there wasn't a single drop of water in the canal; instead of water, there was money, bright red bank notes. It was now a stream of money, and a man was drowning in it, dying.

Khoybor Ali left the gambling den at the subdistrict town and stood on the road. He saw that the rice fields of the month of Ashwin were flooded with moonlight. His waist pouch stuffed with cash, he dreamt as he began to walk homewards: one day, I'm going to buy all this land in this field. This Khoybor Ali will be the owner of five or even seven hundred bighas of land. Possible? Must be. Only possible by gambling, not in any other way. All those rich people are gamblers, or perhaps their fathers or grandfathers or great grandfathers were gamblers. Of course, of course. What other way could there be to get rich?

He ruminated as he walked home. His waist tingled with the heat of cash. Suddenly, a pair of ghosts emerged from behind a tree. They waylaid him.

'Give us a share, you bastard.' One of the ghosts sounded hoarse.

'A share!' echoed the other ghost.

'What share? I won it, it's my money. What share?' Khoybor Ali's attachment to his money was stronger than his fear of ghosts.

'Want to share or die?' the first ghost threatened.

'Want to share or die?' the second ghost threatened.

'Won't share, won't die, do what you can!' Khoybor took a stand with his feet apart.

The attack wasn't unexpected; in fact, Khoybor was getting ready to fend them off. But it happened in such a way, meaning, before he was prepared, a long strip of *gamchha* wrapped around his neck so suddenly, with first a yank, and then, without letting up for a single moment, growing tighter and tighter, turning into a noose, Khoybor Ali had no choice but to have his eyes bulge out, his tongue protrude like a turtle trapped under a rock, foaming at his mouth, as he glimpsed the eternal darkness with his eyes.

Field Report from Roop Nagar

1

We left the book festival and walked to Shahbag before climbing onto a bus. I got off at Bangla Motor and continued towards my home in Eskaton; Shagar went back to work. Our office is in Karwan Bazaar. We work at a daily newspaper. I'm in the editorial department; Shagar is in the video section of the web version. My work is usually done by six or seven in the evening, but he has to stay in the office until eleven.

At eleven thirty, I got a call from Shagar. 'Jamil, the office just told me there's no need for me to come in from tomorrow.'

I wasn't too surprised. News media has drastically lost advertising revenue under the onslaught of non-journalistic platforms like Google, Facebook and YouTube; media houses have started to sack employees in an attempt to curb expenditure.

I said, 'You're having to leave before me?'

I heard laughter at the other end. Among the coworkers I was friends with, Shagar Sengupta was the most even tempered. He wasn't upset by anything; at least I hadn't seen it. It had never seemed to me that he harboured hatred or resentment against anyone. Our office had just fired him, bam, without any due notice, yet he didn't say a single word against them. I never saw him grow angry at anything ever; never heard him complain about anyone. Forget quarrels, I never even heard him get into an argument with anyone. I felt wonder whenever I watched him bear a major injustice without any protest. At times, I reproached him. 'What kind of a person are you? Why are you so meh about everything?'

He never said anything in response. He just smiled.

There are many people in the world who are meek and goody-two-shoes due to a lack of intelligence; Shagar wasn't one of them. His all-knowing, gentle smile told me that. He had a sharp intellect. His bright eyes shone with that light. He had studied Fine Arts and worked as a journalist, but there was no subject matter—including mathematics, quantum mechanics, cognitive science, semiotics, history, philosophy—on which he couldn't expound without pause for a couple of hours. None of us knew English the way he did. He had taught himself German, who knows how that is even possible. He had translated stories by Kafka and Peter Bichsel from the original. He had finished reading serious literature from around the entire globe. He was a wonderful writer too. But his was not the kind of writing that won the Nobel Prize. He wrote science fiction, psychological thrillers, mystery, horror, weird fiction—stuff like that. Perhaps it was because he was so involved in all these weird things that he lacked emotional expression.

2

I'd gone to bed at three in the morning. It was about three thirty when sleep finally arrived. When the phone rang right next to my pillow, it disrupted my sleep so badly that I swore out loud. It was four thirty. And the call was from my childhood friend Abdul Gafur. Surprise was added to my annoyance.

'What's going on, Gafur? Calling so late?'

'Dosto, but you don't go to sleep before dawn …'

I felt annoyed. Just because I go to bed late, does it mean you can call me at four thirty in the morning? I wanted to yell at Gafur and hang up. But he was a beloved childhood friend. He loved me twice as much as I loved him. I asked him, 'Where are you right now?'

'Roop Nagar.'

'Why aren't you asleep?'

'Listen, don't be annoyed …'

'I've got a headache. I'll call you in the morning, now go to sleep.'

'Wait, wait. Listen. Mehedi and I got off the bus and saw that there wasn't a peep from anyone anywhere. The people at the bus counter were all fast asleep. In front of Panchu's hotel, on a bench, the night guard was bleating in his sleep. The dog at the foot of the bench was also asleep. We went to buy cigarettes and found the shopkeeper snoring away. There are no rickshaws on the streets, no EZ Bikes, no nothing. Mehedi said, "Well, it's already time for the *Fazr* prayers, we might as well say our prayers at the mosque." We went to the mosque and there were six or seven of the faithful keeled over here and there, unconscious. The muezzin was all crumpled up near the *mimbar* where the Imam usually stands to deliver the sermon. He was passed out too. We didn't get to say our prayers; we left the mosque. So now we're headed home. We're having to walk. Mehedi's house is quite far. He said, "Dosto, I'm scared. Walk me home." But if I walk him to his house, then how am I supposed to come all the way back on my own, you tell me?'

Abdul Gafur and Mehedi Iqbal were close childhood friends of mine. They taught at a private college in Roop Nagar. Gafur was the principal of the college; he had come to Dhaka with Mehedi to take care of some administrative work. Last evening, I had spent some time with the two of them at the book festival. They had known that I had a new book out. After they were done with their errands at the Ministry of Education building, they called me up in the afternoon and said, 'Come to the book festival. We'll buy your book, and you can autograph our copies.'

I went; we spent a couple of hours at the festival and then they left. Their return bus to Roop Nagar was at 8 p.m.

It was after saying goodbye to them that I had run into Shagar.

3

When I woke up at nine thirty, I remembered Gafur and Mehedi. I felt curious. I called Gafur, but his phone just rang and rang. I disconnected and called Mehedi. His phone also just kept ringing. I figured they'd been traveling all night, so they must be sleeping now.

I went to work, sat in the editorial meeting, and forgot about them. It was when I sat down to write the editorial after the meeting that I thought of them again. I called Gafur. The phone rang, but he didn't pick up. I called Mehedi and heard: *This line cannot be reached.*

I finished writing my editorial around one thirty and called Gafur again. This time his phone was turned off. So was Mehedi's.

I was born in Roop Nagar. The first days of my childhood, my adolescence and my youth had been spent in that small town in northern Bengal, two hundred and fifty kilometres away from the capital city of Dhaka. That is where I spent my years of school and college. Now my parents lived there as well as both my brothers and their families. First, I called my father. The phone rang, but he didn't pick up. I called my eldest brother. The phone didn't even ring. I called my second brother. The phone rang, but he didn't pick up. I called my eldest sister-in-law's number. The phone was turned off. My other sister-in-law's phone was also turned off.

My second brother's son Shoumik was studying at Mymensingh Medical College. I called him. But he disconnected the call. A little later, I got a text from his number, 'Chachu, I'm in class. Will call when I'm done.'

I called the Roop Nagar correspondent for our newspaper. The phone rang and rang; he didn't pick up. I called again after a few minutes. He still didn't pick up. I instructed the office phone operator to connect me to the Roop Nagar correspondent's number. A while later, she told me, 'It keeps ringing, but he doesn't pick up.'

I said, 'Try again. Keep trying until he picks up. It's extremely urgent.'

I called the National Desk Chief, explained the situation to him in detail and told him I desperately needed to get in touch with our Roop Nagar correspondent.

He called a little later to tell me, 'He's not picking up.'

The executive editor of the *Daily Voice* of the *Times* was a friend of mine. I called him up and said, 'Dosto, I desperately need to talk to your Roop Nagar correspondent. Send me his number.' He texted me the number. I called right away. The phone rang and rang, but nobody picked up at the other end.

One by one, I called every single relative or friend whose number I had in my contact list. Some of their phones were switched off, others didn't pick up.

I started feeling hot even though I was in an air-conditioned room. I went to the bathroom to piss and noticed that my forehead was beaded with sweat. I splashed water on my face and returned to my desk. A coworker asked, 'You're looking kind of off. Are you okay?'

I said, 'I'm fine.'

My colleague wasn't convinced. He said, 'Check your blood pressure.'

My coworkers in this section know that I suffer from hypertension. I said, 'No, it's okay.'

Other coworkers also remarked that I wasn't looking normal. In the end, I was forced to tell them that my father, mother, brother, sister-in-law—nobody was picking up their phones. I couldn't reach anyone in Roop Nagar by phone.

One of my colleagues rang up the head of the Crime Desk. He called the officer-in-charge at the Roop Nagar Police Station. When he couldn't reach the OC, he called the police super. When he couldn't reach the police super, he called the Roop Nagar district commissioner. It was all useless. Nobody picked up.

My nephew called from Mymensingh. 'Chachu, what's up?'

'Call your parents.'

'Why? What's happened?'

'Nobody at home is picking up when I call. You try.'

My nephew called me back in ten minutes. 'Nobody's receiving my calls either. What's going on, Chachu?'

'I don't understand any of this.'

Bogra was the district closest to Roop Nagar. I called Parvez, our Bogra correspondent. As soon as he picked up, he said, 'Jamil Bhai, have you forgotten me?'

'Parvez, I'm extremely worried. I can't contact anyone back home. Nobody's responding to any calls.'

'Why, Bhai? What's happened?'

Parvez wasn't merely a colleague, he was also a distant relative. He had often visited our house at Roop Nagar. I explained the situation in detail. He heard me out and said, 'I'm heading out to Roop Nagar right away. I'll give you a call when I reach your parents' house.'

'Go quickly.'

My father's only brother lived about twelve miles away from Roop Nagar, in my grandfather's village. I rang him and, explaining what was going on in some detail, said, 'Please, send someone to Roop Nagar right away. Please, get me some news from there as soon as you can.'

My uncle said, 'Hey, young man, why so impatient?'

If he hadn't been my elder, I would have told him straight up, 'Nobody is as callous as you folks in this entire world.'

I couldn't rely on my uncle, so I waited, counting the hours until our Bogra correspondent, Parvez, would call. I didn't tell my wife any of this. For a moment, I thought of ringing up Khurshid Uncle to tell him. This uncle was the singer Khurshid Alam, my wife's maternal uncle. His village home was about ten miles from Roop Nagar. He had close relationships with all the important people there. But I was afraid that if I called him, he would call my wife and tell her everything, so I abandoned the idea.

Suddenly, I recalled the member of parliament from Roop Nagar—he lived in Dhaka with his family. I called him up and told him everything. He said, 'Bhai, I've not been able to get in touch with anyone either since morning. My father's ninety years old. My mother's dead. I suffer from high blood pressure and diabetes on top of that. I can't control my anxiety. I'm headed to the airport right now to catch a plane. I'll fly to Syedpur and then who knows how long it will take to reach Roop Nagar. Pray for me.'

I had no appetite for lunch. My belly felt bloated with gas. I waited and waited for Parvez to call until it was four forty-five. Then I called him myself. His phone rang, but he didn't pick up.

I felt sick. I told my coworkers, 'I'm going home.'

My department chief said in a kindly voice, 'Keep your phone switched on.'

4

Shumona opened the door, took one look at my face, turned pale and said, 'What's happened? Why do you look like that?'

'I think my pressure's gone up,' I said as I entered the house. I went straight to the bathroom, and as soon as I went in, vomit spewed out of me. Shumona's worried voice shot through the bathroom door. '*Ei*! What's wrong? Why are you throwing up?'

'No reason, just gas.'

'Why? What did you have for lunch?'

'Nothing. Wait, I'm coming out.'

'Why are you throwing up?' The banging on the door began. 'Why have you locked the door? Unlock it, right now.'

'Oh, come on, nothing's happened. Why are you so agitated?'

'Do you have a problem unlocking the door?'

Surges of vomit choked my voice. Shumona's banging on the door changed to frequent shoving.

I felt a little better after I was done vomiting. I rinsed my mouth and splashed some water on my face before exiting the bathroom. Our eyes met; Shumona's were filled with worry.

'It's nothing. It was just some gas that had built up. It's better that I vomited it out.'

Shumona stared at me in surprise. I grabbed a bottle of water from the fridge and glued my lips directly to the bottle, chugging the water. My stomach felt settled.

The phone rang in my pocket. My nephew Shoumik from Mymensingh. With his voice breaking, he said, 'Chachu, both my parents' phones are turned off. What am I going to do now?'

'Wait.'

'You couldn't connect with anyone either?'

'No. I'm trying. Don't worry.'

'But I'm feeling so anxious.'

'There's no need to be overly worried about it. Just wait.'

As soon as I finished talking to my nephew, Shumona wanted to know who I'd been talking to, why were they tense, and what did I tell them to wait for?

I realised that I couldn't hide it from her any longer. I told her briefly about the situation. Shumona began calling relatives one after another.

I changed out of my work clothes and lay down in bed. Straightaway, I began thinking of my mother: when was the last time I had talked to her on the phone? How was the pain in her knee? Could she manage to go to the bathroom by herself?

5

Around seven in the evening, I got a call from Shagar. 'Jamil, what's all this going on with your Roop Nagar?'

'You've heard about it too?'

'The entire capital is in turmoil. All the television channels are weeping and wailing about Roop Nagar …'

'How? Have they been able to send any reporters there?'

'They sent them; everyone's dispatched reporters, photographers, videographers there, but nobody's come back. They sent a helicopter to Roop Nagar from the Police HQ, and there's no news of that either. Even the Prime Minister's Office is completely at sea. It sounds like the government's about to fall.'

'It sounds like you would be happy if that happened.'

'Makes no difference to me. Listen, there's a video clip in your inbox.'

'What video?'

'The TV channels can't really show anything from Roop Nagar ...'

I jumped up immediately and turned on my desktop. I opened my inbox, downloaded the video file Shagar had sent, and started watching.

Several young men were slitting open a young woman's throat.

My heart stopped. I couldn't breathe and my eyes shut themselves. Gasping, I shut my computer down. Shumona entered the room and said, 'Nobody's picking up. What could be going on there?'

'I don't know.'

'You're not even trying to find out.'

'There's nothing that I've not tried.'

The phone rang. Shumona rushed over and said, 'Give it to me! Give it to me!'

'*Arrey*, it's Shagar.'

When I took the call, I heard Shagar's voice. 'Jamil, did you watch the video?'

'What did you send me? Is it possible for a normal, sane human being to watch something like that?'

'Hey, *mia*, aren't you a journalist? You're going to have that kind of solid evidence right in your hands and not watch it?'

'Where did you get this video?'

'I didn't fake it. It's one hundred per cent authentic as a document.'

'So, I get it, a girl's been murdered in Roop Nagar ...'

'Not just murder—she's been slaughtered. When the boys abducted her at eleven this morning from the road outside the entrance to Roop Nagar College, there were many people present. Everyone just watched. Nobody made a single sound.'

'Even the police don't do anything, what are regular people supposed to do? Don't regular people love their lives? Those boys have got to be cadres for the ruling party.'

'According to those boys, the girl had a bad character. She pretended to be in love and ruined the lives of many boys. They picked her up to punish her. The girl thought they were going to gang-rape her. So she told them, "You don't have to rape me. Just come one by one."'

'Shagar, you're making jokes in the middle of all this?'

'But the boys didn't rape the girl. How far did you watch the video?'

'Not even thirty seconds. It's not possible to watch something like that.'

'Okay, there will be an audio clip in your inbox in a little while. Listen to that.'

'I don't feel like listening to anything. I'm extremely tired.'

Shagar hung up. I lay down in bed. I was exhausted. But I could find no peace of mind. I had absolutely no news of my parents. How was I going to get through the night?

I hadn't noticed when Shumona had left the room. She came back to tell me that Khurshid Uncle was going to take the night bus to Roop Nagar. I sat up. Why hadn't I thought of that all this time? Why hadn't I already started for Roop Nagar? I called Khurshid Uncle and said, 'Uncle, I'm coming with you.'

'But how, son? There's no transportation. I called Hanif Transport. They said all communication with Roop Nagar was cut off. Not a single bus that went to Roop Nagar from Dhaka has returned. So, they've just closed off that route altogether. Not just Hanif, none of the bus companies are sending buses to Roop Nagar. Roop Nagar is totally out of communication.'

'Have you contacted anyone in Bogra?'

'Yes, I called a friend. He sent someone from Bogra to Roop Nagar. That man went there and hasn't been heard from since. He's not picking up his phone. I requested the director general of the Rapid Action Battalion to try and get some news from Roop Nagar. They couldn't contact anyone either.'

Before he was done talking, a call came through from Shagar's number. I took the call and heard, not Shagar, but a robotic sounding male voice.

'First, with a delicate trilling, a narrow spurt of blood sped like an arrow onto the wall about two metres away; a bright red pattern was traced on a snow-white background. Then, as if playing with a water-sprayer filled with colors, the faces and bodies of the boys were spattered with blood. A rumbling arose from the foaming blood and the air exiting the foam.

'The young woman with the slit throat was thrashing on the floor like a fish. The young men grabbed her flailing limbs and pinned them against the ground. The young woman's entire body trembled under the force of their hands and their knees; her spine bucked and twisted under the pressure.'

'What the hell are you listening to?' Shumona screamed.

'Shagar sent it.'

'That horror writer friend of yours is truly sick. And how the hell can you listen to this stuff at a time like this?' Shumona was furious. She stomped out of the room.

On my phone, the robotic voice continued.

'The floor was submerged in blood, it was flooded; streams of blood snaked through the door, rushing towards the drawing room, but the bleeding still wouldn't stop. The foam that had collected in the slit-open maw of the young woman's throat was now emitting a strange sound. By the time it took for her limbs to stop moving completely, the floor of the room was completely swamped in blood. One young man asked, "How's all this blood going to be cleaned up?" Another yanked the bedsheet onto the floor. The cotton sheet immediately grew heavy with blood, but it didn't reduce the amount of blood on the floor even a little. The young man picked up the blood-soaked sheet and started to wring it out above a bucket. The other young men followed suit, grabbed whatever fabric they could find and busied themselves cleaning up the blood in the same way. When the bucket brimmed over with blood and foam, one of the young men carried it to the bathroom and emptied it out.

'Then they carried the young woman's dead body to the kitchen. To make it easier to carve her up, she was disrobed entirely, and she was utterly naked. First, her head was separated from her body. Very easily, because the young woman's throat had already been cut open more than halfway through.

'Then, like skilled and experienced butchers, the young men wielded knives on her shoulder blades and separated the arms. They began to use knives and cleavers along her pelvic bone to separate her legs. Then they placed the major joints and bones of the young woman's body on a chopping block and used an axe. Then they worked fast to separate the flesh from the bones and began to saw the meat into smaller pieces suitable for cooking.

'The kitchen did not have a large pot. The homeowner's son went into the next room and soon returned with two large brass cooking pots. There was already enough flesh chopped up to fill everyone's bellies, but they did not stop. They continued carving up her body. At one point, they encountered some difficulty with the young woman's thigh bones. They were so dense and hard that even the axes couldn't go through them. Resigned, they scraped the flesh off from the bones. Then they leaned the bright white bones against the wall to one side.

'The young woman's decapitated head stared at the ceiling with eyes wide open.

'Her full head of hair, thickened and weighted with blood, had clotted into dreadlocks and lay splayed out on the ground.

'"What to do with the head?"

'"Brain tastes real good. Let there be fried brains."

'The skull was cracked open with the axes. Some of the brain matter splattered here and there. One of them gathered it all together and placed it in a frying pan.

'The two big brass pots were filled with meat. Soybean oil was poured in. Thinly sliced onions, garlic, ginger and green chillies were added. Then cardamoms, cloves, whole black pepper and other warm spices. The gas cylinder was switched on, the burner knob turned, and the match lit for the fire. In a little while, an appetising aroma permeated the kitchen.

'In the meantime, one by one, the young men showered, and refreshed, they sat down. Their hunger peaked even more.

'Rice had been set to cook in another big pot. Now the rice was boiling, and the steam was pushing its way out, dislodging the lid.

'When the cooking was done, the young men sat in a circle on the floor. First they served themselves from the big pot of rice, ladling steaming hot rice on to their plates. Then they took the perfectly cooked meat and began to devour it all. They chatted as they ate. They talked about many things. One said, he could finish off one *seer* of rice in one sitting. Another said, not rice, right now they should only eat meat. Because it was going to be a long time before the next

Qurbani Eid was here. One commented that the meat lacked heat. Another nodded in agreement. One said, a masterplan should be drawn up, to pick up all the girls of bad character in Roop Nagar, and one by one, they should all be slaughtered and eaten like this. The others nodded and said "yeah, yeah!" in support of his proposal.

'Soon they had finished all the meat in the first pot and reached for the next. One of them grew furious because the pot of rice was empty. The others said, why did they need rice when there was so much meat left?

'The young men grew tired of eating. Their tongues, gums and jaws grew stiff and numb. They had no space left in their bellies. Each of them gulped down some water and began to belch. Their bodies grew heavy; they couldn't rise from the floor. Sleep descended heavy on their eyes; their arms and legs slackened where they sat, and soon they were immersed in deep slumber.'

The robotic voice stopped. I heard Shagar. 'Jamil, are you there?'

'Where did you find this?'

'Don't ask any questions. Listen to what I tell you.'

'Okay, tell me.'

'When those boys fell asleep, all the people of Roop Nagar began to weave and sway, feeling drowsy. By the time evening came, every single person in the town was unconscious, asleep. Now, nobody's awake. Not a single person. The Khulna to Parbatipur train has stopped running. Because to pass through Roop Nagar, they have to receive the line clear signal. But no signals are coming through from Roop Nagar station. The station master's phone is switched off. None of the buses from Roop Nagar are reaching Dhaka. The buses that went from Dhaka to Roop Nagar—as soon as they entered the town, the drivers, the bus helpers, the conductors ... everyone just began falling asleep ...'

'How do you know any of this?'

'I'm in Roop Nagar right now.'

'What!'

'But don't share this information with anybody.'

'How did you get to Roop Nagar?'

'Don't ask any questions. Just listen to what I tell you. That is all you will get.'

'You're really in Roop Nagar right now?'

'I don't lie.'

Shagar doesn't lie. That had been my impression all this time. But what were these things he was telling me today?

I started getting dressed to go to his house. Shumona asked me in surprise, 'Where are you going?'

'To Shagar's house.'

'Why, suddenly?'

'An urgent matter.'

'When are you coming back?'

Shagar lives in Kathal Bagan. It's about a fifteen-minute walk from my house. 'Soon. I'll just go there and come back.'

'Fine, just don't sit down with that pervert and start boozing.'

6

About fifteen minutes later, I rang the doorbell at Shagar's house. I heard his wife Nishi's voice from the other side of the door. 'Who is it?'

'It's me, Jamil.'

The door opened and, with a smile, Nishi said, 'Come on in.'

I went in and asked, 'Where's Shagar?'

'Sit down, I'll go get him.'

I sat down on their living room sofa. Nishi turned the ceiling fan on and went inside. Shagar came out.

'Well, mia? Aren't you in Roop Nagar right now?'

Shagar laughed silently and sat down on the sofa across from me. He didn't say anything. I said, 'That audio fiction of yours turned a bit extreme.'

'That wasn't fiction.'

'What was it then?'

'The audio version of a field report.'

'Really? You sent it in from Roop Nagar?'

'I'm still in Roop Nagar. The only person who is awake in a slumbering small town. Walking around like a phantom.'

'Shagar, how can you joke with me at a time like this? I've not been able to trace any news of my parents; do you understand how I'm feeling?'

'Don't you believe I'm in Roop Nagar right now?'

'I'm leaving.' I stood up in annoyance.

Just then, my phone rang in my pocket. I pulled it out and saw Shagar Sengupta's name floating on the screen. As soon as I received the call, Shagar's voice rang out on the other side, 'Don't disturb the people of Roop Nagar, Jamil. They're all asleep.'

The Underpass

The children chanted the Quran like a melody. Their musical recitation spiralled and spread in the air like the smoke rising from mosquito coil repellants. As he left his home to the sounds of the chanting, the face of his six-month-old daughter surfaced in Kabirul's mind.

But as he took the stairs down from his fourth-floor apartment, he forgot about his beloved child. The sound of the chanting disappeared like the tail of a fleeing snake. He bent over as he exited the small door embedded in the iron gate. He raised his head when he was out. His spine straightened.

It was nine past eleven in the morning. Sunny. His eyes felt tight. From the Bou Bazaar turning to the Green Supermarket corner, two rows of rickshaws stood motionless. Completely still. The foreheads of each of the drivers were shiny mirrors. The passengers dozed. They yawned. Their lazy, impassive eyes saw nothing. Kabirul looked for a way through. There was no path. He worked up a sweat zigzagging his way through the gaps between the immobile rickshaws. Then he began walking along the left side of the road. He felt the sun hard.

Kabirul imagined: the sky had descended, and it was gleaming like an overturned wok just one and a half hand's breadth above his head. People's brains were melting and dripping out of their ears on either side. It was *roz kiyamat*, doomsday. People were travelling towards the *hashr-er moydan*, the Plain of Assembly. But, midway, they got caught in a terrible traffic jam and were waiting there stock-still.

Suddenly, three men appeared out of nowhere. One called to him, 'Come.' The same command was repeated in the eyes of the other two.

He asked, 'Where?'

In response came a muted reprimand. 'Come.' One man ahead of him, one behind. Behind the second man walked another. They zigzagged through, stopping every now and then.

In a rickshaw, a baby held in the lap of a borkha began wailing. The borkha patted the baby's back with a black-gloved hand. 'Oh, oh, oh!'

The rickshaw driver swivelled his neck to look. His eyes were bloodshot. His mouth smiled. 'Feed him your tit.'

Kabirul didn't get the chance to observe whether the borkha gave the baby her tit or not. He had to keep moving. One man walked ahead of him, one behind. Behind that man walked another.

To the left of the road, inside the boundary walls of a residential area, rose the noise of children. A white Toyota Corolla stood at the iron gate, with half its head sticking out. The driver dozed with his head against the steering wheel. In the seat behind him, a middle-aged lady professor sat in profound meditation.

Across the street from Popular Meat Sales Centre, a dung-smeared Indian ox sat impassively, tied to the lamppost and chewing its cud. Its large eyes were vacant and indolent. It made no difference to the ox whether the world stopped or not.

The man in front of Kabirul clambered onto an empty rickshaw to cross the street. He followed him. The two men behind him followed him. At the corner, under the lamppost stood the pineapple seller, a middle-aged man with a sad face. He raised his hand to his forehead and silently salaamed him. Kabirul too responded silently. This happened every day. It suddenly occurred to him that he had never asked the man his name. How many children did he have? Standing under the lamppost all day long, selling pineapples today, papayas tomorrow, and grapefruits the day after—how much did he make? How did his household survive?

The front wheel of a rickshaw had climbed onto the flat backside of a rickshaw-van.

'Oh, that bull has mounted the cow,' someone joked. Some people laughed at that, some were humourless.

From the southside of Green Road, a hot wind blew towards the north. A gnarl of rickshaws had created quite the jumble at the point where the Raja Bazaar alley met Green Road. There wasn't even space to put one's foot down. The man ahead of Kabirul began to walk southwards, in front of the row of shops to the right side of the street. The man behind Kabirul nudged him in the back. He followed the man before him and forged ahead. The other two followed behind.

A long, black car stood with its head peeking out of the depths of an apartment building. A beautiful young woman's face hung in one of the windows. Kabirul's wife had been just as beautiful about five years ago. In the past, when he spotted a pretty girl, his spirits would lift; now he grew sad. Pretty girls didn't stay pretty. The film star Babita had become terribly fat. He felt sad when he saw a fat woman, he felt pity. The poor things were so defenceless!

A young woman who had been unable to perform her namaz was singing of her remorse on the loudspeaker of a shop. Kabirul knew that the girl who was lamenting with such melody had never performed prayers in her life. It seemed to him that the man who had written the song was trying to hoodwink Allah into accepting that he was helpless, that he couldn't perform his namaz because of household duties. But he wouldn't be spared. Just as Allah was eternally merciful, He was also the supreme punisher. Was it for nothing that He had created seven hells?

'Amin Bhai, where are you going?' Someone called out to Kabirul Amin in front of Banoful sweetshop. He seemed familiar, but Kabirul couldn't place the man. Instead of responding to his pleasantries, he immersed himself in trying to remember him. At that moment, the man behind him shoved him in the back. Then he took the chance to cross over an empty rickshaw to their left. But immediately he got stuck between a cab and two rickshaws carrying passengers.

Kabirul climbed onto the empty rickshaw and sat down. The man behind him also climbed on and sat beside him, placing a hand on his shoulder, as if they had been friends forever. The last man stood beside them and his eyeballs began to spin. The cab next to them stirred. The first man slipped right into that gap. The man sitting beside Kabirul jabbed his elbow into his ribs. Kabirul descended from the rickshaw and followed the first man. The man next to him followed him. The third man was lost.

The first man crossed the road onto the sidewalk and began walking in the opposite direction. The second man shoved Kabirul on his back and ordered him to follow the first. A man was wielding a tyre pump in front of the River Research Institute, injecting air into his rickshaw tyres. Somebody said, 'Do it, do it, do it hard.'

A large leaf fell from a teak tree. Woodworms never infested teak. But the teak bed that Kabirul had bought for seven thousand takas after his marriage was now bored through by woodworms. They had infested the display cabinet, the wardrobe, the bookshelf and every single door panel and doorsill. His wife alleged that woodworms had even gotten into their Ariston refrigerator. As soon as she'd open the door, woodworm droppings crumbled and fell out. When he said, whatever else woodworms ate, they couldn't possibly eat iron, his wife grew angry and snapped, 'You're just blind.'

A man held an aluminium bowl near Kabirul's chest. There was a pair of red cavities under his brow where his eyes were supposed to be. Kabirul dropped a coin in his bowl. The bowl clanged its thank you. Right next to him, a shirtless man in a lungi sat pissing at the base of the wall, his dark thighs bared. His piss was foaming yellow; he had jaundice for sure. Kabirul once had jaundice. At the time, he had drunk a lot of sugarcane juice. If you added a little salt to sugarcane juice and some green chilli paste, it tasted quite nice. But the vendors selling sugarcane juice across from the entrance to the Kazipara alleyway were adding neither salt nor green chilli paste.

The man ahead of him walked through the Kazipara alleyway. The man behind him shepherded Kabir into the same. The alleyway was being dug up. There were mountains of loose dirt. This dig had been going on for ten years. The labourers dug up the earth, then filled it back in. They dug it up again and filled it back in again. They had grown old while working on this job. Kabirul was growing old too. Ten years ago, he had been twenty-five. Back then, not a single strand of his hair had gone grey. Now, ten years later, half his head was grey. Not a single one of the crows whose raucous cawing at dawn broke his sleep ten years ago were alive now. The crow perched on the telephone wire right now, conspiring to shit on the heads of the men digging away beneath it, wouldn't be here in ten years. Kabirul might be here; then he would be forty-five years old. How many years after that? Ten? Ten more? Here, he could count it on his fingers. Perhaps twenty years passed by quicker than the time it took to count from one to ten.

But why count the years? Who knows who would die when? Kabirul thought today, tomorrow or the day after, he was going to die.

But at the mouth of the alleyway sat that old woman with a tin plate set out in front of her. Kabirul had passed by this street on many days thinking that perhaps he would not see the old woman the next time. But the next day, he would see her again, sitting the same way, in silence, with her plate, with not the slightest sign of decay. It occurred to him that one day this old woman would no longer hear his footsteps in this alley.

Singaras were being fried in a wok full of oil. The oil had burnt completely black; the singaras were taking on a brown hue like congealed blood. Kabirul liked singaras. However, these singaras could give you cancer. His father had died from cancer. He never ate singaras. He didn't eat betel leaf or *zarda*, and he didn't smoke either. He would eat a small amount of rice. He loved spinach and small fish. His favourites were mola and kachki fish. He would wake very early. He would perform the fazr prayers and go out to take a walk in the open air. He didn't have high blood pressure, or diabetes, or stomach problems. The light in his eyes was undimmed. That's why he got cancer. Death needs an excuse. One day, scientists will know what causes cancer. One day, a cure for cancer will be discovered. Still, people will die. If the cure for every single disease were to be discovered, people would still die.

A beehive hung from the mango branch arching over the drugstore. Kabirul needed to buy honey for his daughter today. She was prone to colds. If she took honey, she didn't catch a cold or fever so frequently. But where was pure honey to be found? Dabur, S & W, none of those companies could be trusted.

A kitchen market had been set up right beside the street side wall. A seller sat staining a carp's gills with *sindoor*, vermillion. Blue flies were buzzing around. The cucumbers in the vegetable shop were yellowed. The tomatoes were pus-filled blisters. The Malabar spinach was black. Maggots squirmed out of the ridge gourds and the eggplants. A shopkeeper bared his teeth in a grimace while he scratched his thigh. Another pressed his finger down on one nostril and noisily blew snot out of the other. Right beside his vegetable basket sat a pat of cow dung. Across from him, on the other side, three naked children sat in a row by the wall, pissing.

A thick, twisted bamboo pole had been plonked down sideways to close off the street. An efficient group of workers were nailing wooden planks to each other, knocking together a stage. Next to it, a red banner hung off a shack with the words *Holy Urs Mubarak,* Holy Blessed Death Anniversary, written on it. Beside it stood a hut with a signboard. The word "Earth" was written below the word "Bangladesh", and below that, it said: Ward No. 32. Alongside Emperor Aurangzeb's, some Liaqat's name was being announced. On the next wall, it said in large, red painted letters: "Long live the Lilliputian King! Public announcement by Sikandar Jonathan Swift."

Grapefruits were heaped on a rickshaw-van. 'Take a grapefruit, sir, these are good.'

You could use grapefruit peel to make a pretend set of scales and sell dirt. The wholesale price for dirt was forty-one takas per maund. It cost a lot of potsherds to buy a maund of dirt. If you pressed the grapefruit peel, it squirted fluid, and if that fluid got in your eyes, it burnt. But it didn't harm your eyes; instead, it cleaned your eyes.

The man behind him shoved Kabirul beside the grapefruit van. The man ahead of him looked back and started moving again. An electric generator near the steps of a restaurant made such a noise that all other sounds were crushed beneath it.

Beyond the other side of the street, in the distance, rose the green minaret of the Kawran Bazaar *jam-e mosque*. The man ahead moved towards the underpass. The collapsible gates to the underpass were shut. Blue-shirted policemen stood there with rifles and rubber batons.

'The President will be going through.'

'The Prime Minister will be coming through.'

'How far is the Prime Minister now?'

'How much longer will it take?'

'She will come, she will come, she will come any minute.'

A majestic motorbike shot from the south to the north with a heartrending whistle. Then the empty highway was quiet again.

'Coming! The bugger on the bike just gave us advance notice.'

'Yeah, they're all ministers and prime ministers now, and we're just a bunch of pubes hanging from a dick.'

'Well, you all are dick pubes.'

'And you're all pube-dropping policemen.'

The constable laughed. As he cocked his rifle, he said to his colleague beside him, 'Suleman, should I just drop a pube?' And he fired a shot. A man, shot, was jolted six feet away and fell.

'What happened?'

'I just dropped a pube.' The constable laughed.

The prime minister's motorcade passed by with a delicate sound. The people pulled open the collapsible scissor gates to the underpass. The man ahead of Kabirul glanced back once. Then he began to climb down the steps into the underpass. The third man showed up again. He came and stood to Kabirul's left. The second man was on Kabirul's right. The two of them guarded him and took him towards the underpass stairs. The underpass could be accessed by two sets of steps across from each other. He was taken towards the staircase on the left. As soon as he placed his foot on the first step, a white light streaked across the tunnel from the other flight of stairs. There was darkness at his feet. Light in the distance. As he descended, buildings, shops, people disappeared. All that was left for his eyes to see was a piece of sky. Gradually, even that was lost.

As soon as he stepped onto the last stair, darkness surged downwards. He closed his eyes and stopped abruptly. The two men on either side of him slipped their arms into his. From the distant corner of the dark tunnel, the sad melody of the Quran being recited floated towards them.

Kabirul opened his eyes. The deep darkness lightened. To the right, an impenetrable wall; to the left, utter darkness. The man ahead of him pranced forward into the darkness. The two men slid their arms out from under his armpit and moved towards the left.

Thick pillars stood on either side. There were several kiosks in between the pillars: rows of shops. 'Nakhalpara Flea Picking Centre' to the right; to the left, 'Barbershop'.

Several monkeys were industriously slapping the heads of men sitting on stools in two rows. The men emitted 'ahs' and 'oohs'; Kabirul couldn't tell whether in pain or satisfaction.

A very small man emerged from the Bhagyakul Goat Reproduction Centre. His ears were long like a goat's, drooping onto his shoulders. His bare torso emitted a fetid smell. His enormous testicle had pushed aside his loincloth and was sticking out against his right thigh. Kabirul's companions laughed. Kabirul didn't.

The short man said, 'George Orwell's sitting over there.'

Kabirul replied, 'Convey my salaam to him.'

The short man said, 'The Prime Minister's political secretary's there too.'

The man on Kabirul's left said, 'Hey, give him a glass of goat milk to drink.'

Suddenly, the short man clapped and shouted, 'Bahadur, grab that guy!'

Like magic, two jumbo-sized police constables appeared. The short man instructed them, 'Rip the bastard apart by his legs.'

The big bruisers gripped the man's legs on either side. Then they hauled him into the air and started pulling him in opposite directions. A ripping noise was heard, blood began to drip, and camera flashes began going off around them repeatedly.

'Hey, hey! The sons-of-bitches are taking photos!'

The short man untucked his loincloth and, pulling out his goat's penis, he aimed it at the photojournalists and, like the hosepipe of a firetruck, began pissing in a circular motion. The photojournalists fled in a rush. The two bruisers hauled the two halves of the ripped-apart man on their shoulders and lumbered off into the darkness.

The other man grabbed Kabirul by his collar and yanked him along. The first man backtracked and joined them.

When they had walked a few steps forward, to their left was the Sales Centre for the Spirit of the Liberation War. A ghost sat at the front desk with its mouth agape.

'How's business?'

'It's doing okay.'

'Don't fib, man. Just close up shop and go home.'

'The three million martyrs, the honour of two hundred thousand of our mothers and sisters!'

'Forget it, man.'

'Oh, Allah the divine being! Has every son-of-a-bitch turned into a *razakar*, a collaborator?'

The passerby jumped up and slapped the ghost's bony cheek hard.

A man, long and thin like a bamboo, stood shouting beside a pile of booklets heaped around the base of a pillar. 'Come, brothers. Get your pocket-sized constitution right here at an affordable price. Regular retail price, fifteen takas. Special discount due to the upcoming sacred elections: ten takas, ten takas, ten takas. Inside this constitution, you will find information on how many months before a baby's teeth begin to grow. Which colour, if chosen for carpets by the wife of the chief advisor of the interim government, leads to disasters for the nation. Whether MPs should or shouldn't spend nights with females at the MP Hostel. The devil does not enter any of the Parliament chambers. What punishment should be meted out to the speaker of the Parliament should he allow opposition MPs to speak. Come, come! Pick up your pocket-sized constitution at an affordable price!'

One of the kiosks sported a sign written in strange English letters: GЯOꓕESQUE. Inside the kiosk, on a screen spread across a wall, several shadowy figures were walking in a line on a tightrope. Beneath the tightrope, a fire raged. More shadowy figures were adding fuel in the form of bamboo and wood.

A bat flew overhead. It was followed by the sound of its flapping wings. In a little while, the sound returned. Kabirul spotted a bat overhead again. Its eyes were balls of flame. It dove towards his forehead and pretended to nip him before flying off again. It circled overhead. Then it was lost in the darkness ahead. Suddenly, a fox darted from right to left, like a loosened arrow. A dog chased behind it. After a few moments, howling could be heard nearby, followed by a dog's bark.

After walking for a while longer, the two men stood beside an open space. Kabirul stopped too. The darkness wasn't deep in that spot, which was like a high, smooth plinth. There was a cool shadow like twilight. Beyond it was open space. In the distance, sat a gloomy field, low and silent. In the middle of the plinth lay a smooth plank, a foot and a half wide and six feet long. Another piece of wood, about four inches wide, lay on the end of the plank that was closer to the field. An arm's length away, a woman sat on a three-legged stool, with her back towards the field. An infant played in her lap, about six months old. Its arms waved, it cooed *ta ta da da*.

'Your last wish?'

Kabirul didn't respond.

'Would you like a cigarette?'

Kabirul didn't answer.

'Do you want to cuddle your child?'

Kabirul didn't speak. In silence, he walked to the plank in slow steps and lay down flat on his back. On the smaller piece of wood, he placed the back of his neck, not his head. So, his neck was stretched taut and his head bent back at such an angle that the upside-down image of the woman with the baby, an arm's length away, swayed in front of his eyes. But when one of the two men kneeled beside his head, the sight of the woman and the child was hidden from his view. The man grasped his forehead hard, pushing it downwards; Kabirul's head rubbed against the cold, damp earth beyond the plank. The man used his hands to shove his head even harder against the ground. Kabirul saw that the first man was standing to the right side of his head. He had grown massively tall; his head touched the sky. Kabirul couldn't see his face clearly in the shadowy gloom.

He held a shiny knife in his right hand. That too was as long as a sword. When the man leant forward, lowering himself, his impassive, dutiful face grew clearer. He kneeled beside Kabirul's right ear. He clasped Kabirul's chin, pushing it down, and Kabirul's throat spread even tauter. He gripped his long blade tighter in his right hand and bent his arm at the elbow.

Kabirul closed his eyes.

From a distance came the sound of a weeping child and the melody of the Quran being chanted.

The Cuckoo Keeps Calling

Modhu wakes up at dawn and says to his wife, 'Say goodbye.'

Modina clasps her husband's hand and says, 'Not today. Go tomorrow.'

The cuckoo trills from the branches of the koroi tree. Modhu doesn't know what it means when the cuckoo calls on a spring dawn. He lies back again. Now comfortable, he goes back to sleep.

The next day at dawn, Modhu again asks his wife to bid him farewell. Again, his wife says, 'Not today, tomorrow.' Modhu again lies down like a good boy. Sleeps comfortably. The cuckoo calls from the tree. Modhu doesn't hear it. He is sound asleep. The cuckoo grows increasingly desperate. *Coo. Coo-oo. Coo-oo-oo*. Modhu sleeps, he doesn't hear. His wife Modina lies awake; she doesn't hear either.

But Mofiz hears the cuckoo trilling on this spring dawn. He is not unromantic. He breaks into song: *Oh, why do you call to me so early in the morning, oh, little cuckoo of my life?*

Modina doesn't hear Mofiz's song. Mofiz leaves his home, and gazes at the three-way intersection, the road that people take to reach town. Mofiz doesn't see anybody taking that road. He walks. He places his foot on the threshold of Modina's yard and, in a subdued voice, calls out, 'Brother, Modhu, have you gone to Dhaka?'

Modina comes out of Modhu's home. She stands on her stoop and rolls her eyes at Mofiz. Mofiz feels bewildered; with teary eyes, he asks, 'Gone?'

Modina shoos cows. *'Hyat! Hyat, hyat!'*

'Hey, girl, why are you shooing me away?'

Modina picks up a wooden stool and throws it at Mofiz. Mofiz sniggers like a jackal and leaves. As he departs, he says to himself, 'No matter how many times you cut me, or hit me …'

2

Modhu wakes up hungry. Modina serves him rice and eats as well. Not freshly cooked, steaming rice. Old rice, with water added to it. As he eats, Modhu asks, 'Isn't there anymore panta-rice left?'

Modina bites her tongue in shame. Which means that there is no more watered rice left.

No more, meaning that in Modina's judgment, because she herself has eaten too much, the panta is finished before her man's hunger has abated. Hence, the shame; hence, her biting of the tongue.

'Now I need to go to Dhaka.'

Modina asks, 'Isn't it hard to drive a rickshaw?'

Modhu knows that this is Modina being tender. Modina knows that driving a rickshaw in Dhaka city is gruelling. But working the fields was hellish torment, and the wages were poor—merely sixty takas a day. One day in the month of Joishthya, Modhu had almost died while weeding the jute fields belonging to the Mondals. There was no water in the fields, there were no clouds in the sky. Modhu's back was burning to ashes from the sun, his throat was parched wood. He was desperately thirsty, he was running for water, the solitary plains had become the deserts of Karbala, and in the distance, Bacchu Mondal's new tin-shed glinted in the sunlight. There was a new tube-well near the outer yard of the house, Modhu was running towards it, stumbling on the clods of earth in the hoed field, shouting 'a drop of water, please!' But before he reached the tube-well, he tumbled onto the ground, his eyes rolled back into his head, he foamed at the mouth. Modhu almost died that day.

So, Modhu travelled beyond Kalai, Mokamtala, Bogra, Sirajganj, across the Jamuna Bridge, to the city of Dhaka, two hundred miles away. There he pulls a rickshaw, earns a hundred takas a day, counts that money each night again and again. He can't settle on one place where he can hide this money.

This is how, day after day, for fifteen straight days, Modhu drives a rickshaw. In Kawran Bazaar, twelve of these drivers live in a windowless room; with them live twelve thousand mosquitoes. The mosquitoes sing, suck the blood of all the Modhus, and yet the Modhus all sleep like the dead. At the crack of dawn, when the tired mosquitoes are each an immobile drop of blood, the Modhus wake up; nature calls them. They not only feel the thunderclouds rumbling in their bellies, they hear them as well. They go out in a group, pull the *tabans* covering their asses over their heads, and they display their naked dark asses in a row as they hunker down at the edge of the Kazi Nazrul Islam Avenue, or some of them in front of the Hotel Sonargaon gate. They wipe their asses with newspapers because there is no water; not only do they lack water to clean themselves, the Modhus don't have water to bathe in. For fifteen straight days, Modhu doesn't wash himself; sometimes the odour of his own body makes him want to vomit, especially when the sun is strong and Dhaka's skies and air cease to be.

This is how it is, day after day, night after night. But what happiness, what success! When Modhu returns to Modina after fifteen straight days, there is at least fifteen hundred takas in his waist pouch. Which means that for at least a month, he neither thinks of Dhaka, nor speaks of it.

3

Modhu goes to Dhaka city. The watered rice is finished, there is no more rice left in the house, Modina sits empty-handed by the derelict stove. A cuckoo trills in a tree; Modina doesn't hear it, but Mofiz does. It has never happened that a cuckoo sings and Mofiz doesn't hear it.

When Modhu crosses the three-way intersection of the highway and heads for the subdistrict town, Mofiz peeks from behind the house. He spots Modina sitting by the stove doing nothing, and he begins to joke around. 'Bhai, Modhu, are you off to Dhaka?'

Modina turns her head.

Joyous, Mofiz says, 'What's up, Modina?'

'What's your deal?' Modina scolds Mofiz in a solemn manner. 'You're hankering for a beating?'

'If you beat me with your own hands,' Mofiz says as he grins with all his teeth and fearlessly comes forward, 'my life would be a treasure.'

'Go home.' Modina is even more serious.

'Do you want a job, Modina?' Mofiz coaxes her.

Modina isn't willing to listen to anything. She threatens Mofiz, 'I'm telling you, leave.'

Mofiz tries to sound angry and says, 'I'm here to do you a favour without being asked, and you want to shoo me off like a cow?'

Modina asks in a sombre tone, 'What favour?'

Mofiz responds in a mysterious tone. 'You'll get money, wheat. Want a job?'

'What job?'

'Shooing goats,' Mofiz says and chuckles. Although he hadn't intended to laugh.

Modina is furious. 'Go away, you bastard. You can't find someone else to joke with?'

Mofiz moves fast to try to control the damage and speaks in a very businesslike manner. 'Not a joke, Modina, for real! No actual work involved, just shooing cows and goats.'

'Explain clearly, what sort of job is this then?'

'Have you seen the trees planted on either side of the highway? Those trees need to be guarded, so that cows and goats don't chew them up. That's the job. They'll pay in cash, they'll also pay with wheat. You sell the wheat to buy rice. And with the money, you buy beef, tilapia ...'

'Stop, stop.' Suspicion rolls across Modina's eyes and face. She narrows her eyes, creases her forehead and interrogates him. 'Why would anyone give me this job when there are so many people around?'

'Why, I'll arrange it for you. I'll grab the chairman's hands and feet and I'll beg ...' Mofiz pauses for no reason. He can't find anything else to say.

But his plan and his words are quite clear. Still, Modina wants to hear more about this job of guarding trees and the means to get it even more clearly. 'Go on, why did you stop?'

Mofiz laughs and says, 'I will grab the chairman's hands and feet and beg: Uncle, give this job to Modina, you won't find a girl as nice as Modina even if you search and search ...'

Modina howls with laughter. A cool breeze wafts across the ditch and disappears. From the branches of the koroi tree, a cuckoo calls. Mofiz glances at the tree and spots the cuckoo. Then he gazes at Modina's face and says in a melancholy manner, 'Do you know what the cuckoo is saying?'

'What?' There is a smile on Modina's face; she knows what Mofiz is about to say.

He says, 'The cuckoo is crying. It's crying and asking, where did my own little cuckoo bird go?'

Modina laughs again. Her laughter enrages the cuckoo in the koroi tree. Mofiz speaks the cuckoo's mind, 'Why do you laugh like that, Modina?'

'What is it to you if I laugh?' Modina asks, cocking her eyebrow like a flirt.

'My ribs shatter to bits and my soul wants to fly away,' he says.

Modina laughs, shimmying her whole body. Mofiz looks at the tree, but the cuckoo is gone.

4

It has been raining all day in Dhaka; Modhu pretty much took a shower as he pedalled his rickshaw. After getting drenched all day, all the warmth had left his body, and Modhu cannot fathom where his body is finding so much heat from now. He feels cold, his head hurts, and soon he begins to shiver. He rolls around on the floor in the dark room, and like a child, he moans, calling out to his mother.

It isn't raining in the village of Modhupur; the moon is visible in the sky and a cuckoo is singing in the branches of the koroi tree. Mofiz stands by Modina's window, grasping the grille and whispering, 'Modina! Oh, Modina!'

Scared, Modina scrambles into a sitting position, and spits on her own chest to dissipate her fear. Mofiz whistles in the air, saying, 'It's me, Mofiz!'

The power has gone out in Dhaka city. In the box-like room where Modhu rolls on the ground by himself, shivering and moaning, the darkness of hell has descended: Modhu thinks he is dying.

In the village of Modhupur, through the gaps in the branches of the koroi tree, slivers of moonlight land on Modina's window; outside stands Mofiz, like a ghost, and inside is Modina. Her teeth look white in the shadow of moonlight, her eyes are shining, and she is pretending to be angry with Mofiz, telling him she is going to complain to Modhu when he returns, and that Modhu will grind Mofiz's bones to powder and apply it to his body. Modina purses her lips in laughter as she talks, and Mofiz says that Modhu isn't coming back to Modhupur anymore, he is going to die in Dhaka. Mofiz tells Modina, 'Our fortunes were written together. You have no choice but me, Modina.'

Modina slides her arm through the window grille and punches Mofiz in the chest. 'Go home, you stray cow.'

Mofiz grabs Modina's hand in the blink of an eye and says, 'You don't know this, but I know it for sure, Modina. I have you written in my fate and you have me.'

Modina thinks that Mofiz has lost his head.

As Mofiz returns to his own house, he dreams that Modhu has died in Dhaka. 'He's dead, that bastard Modhu is dead,' says Mofiz, willing Modina's husband to die as he walks home.

Right then, in Kawran Bazaar, Dhaka, Modhu is freezing and shivering, and he is calling out to Allah, saying, 'Don't take my life, *Khoda*. Let me live this time around. I'll never come back to Dhaka in this lifetime.' The next morning, Modhu recovers from his fever; he sees that there is no more rain, the sky is a shining blue, and the buildings are all smiling. Modhu forgets his promise to Allah, and that very afternoon he goes out again with his rickshaw. He recalls the bone-rattling fever from the night before and laughs to himself.

That morning, Mofiz places his foot on the threshold of Modhu's yard and calls out in a low voice, 'Bhai Modhu, are you back from Dhaka?' But Mofiz knows very well that if Modhu is supposed to be back every two weeks, there are still three more days to go.

Two days before Modhu is supposed to return to Modhupur, he drops off a passenger on the inner side of Gulshan-2 and goes to grab a cup of tea at a roadside stall. He takes two sips of his tea and turns around to find his rickshaw gone. At first, Modhu doesn't believe it. He thinks someone has hidden his rickshaw nearby as a prank. But no, it isn't that simple. The rickshaw has actually disappeared.

Modhu goes to the rickshaw owner and apprises him of the situation. The owner points towards Modhu and orders his people, 'Tie that fool up.' Before the ones under order begin the work, the owner himself lands a kick on Modhu's belly. 'You fucking nobody, where's my rickshaw?'

A grunt emerges from Modhu, he doubles over and grabs his mouth with one hand. One of the owner's followers runs over and, almost astride Modhu's shoulders, he grabs his hair, shakes his head and demands, 'Say it, you son-of-a-bitch, to which of your fathers did you sell off the boss's rickshaw?'

The boss screams, 'First, do him over real good.'

Modhu is turned almost into a corpse, and thirteen hundred and twenty-five takas, which means all his earnings, are taken away from him before he is handed over to the police. The police take Modhu to the station and hit him some more in the hope of getting some money, but they quickly realise that not only will no one show up with any money for his release, the owner and his men have already beat him so much that he could very well die in the police station. In which case, the newspapers will start writing about deaths in police custody, and all those poor-loving human rights organisation folks will drum up a furore.

The police think about all this hassle and push Modhu out of the station. Modhu can't walk; he falls onto the street in front of the police station and moans. The police feel inconvenienced and annoyed at this; they load Modhu into the back of a pickup truck, and drive around the city, along this street and that, and they focus their flashlights here and there, looking for a convenient spot in which to dump him.

As they search, one of them has an idea. 'Well, then,' he says to his colleagues, 'whose fault is it that we're going through all this trouble?' They drive the pickup truck with Modhu in the back to the Begunbari house-cum-garage of the rickshaw owner and roar at him, 'You, pal, have murdered the suspect before handing him over to the police!'

The rickshaw owner doesn't seem perturbed by the roaring police; he goes inside and quickly returns with ten thousand takas. He tucks it into the hand of one of the policemen and says, 'There's no more cash in the house, saar. Just manage the thing, please.'

One of the policemen grows angry. 'Is this a joke!' The rickshaw owner doesn't quite understand what his anger means; still, out of habit, he goes back inside and returns with another ten thousand takas. Then he gets a louder scolding, and a policeman even utters the words, 'under arrest'. Therefore, the rickshaw owner goes back inside again, and when he is late in coming back out, the policemen look at each other with suspicion. But before they lose their patience, the rickshaw owner re-emerges with a leaf from his cheque book. He says,

'Saars, it was an accident. It is my fault, but I didn't want the guy to die. Here, I've written out one hundred thousand.'

The policeman stops him midway and says, 'Pal, if you want to survive, show up at the station tomorrow morning with five hundred thousand in cash. We don't do cheques-feques.'

The rickshaw owner says, 'What arrangements for the body?'

A policeman answers, 'That's the big trouble right now. What to do with this dead body? We've been going around all night, pal. That five hundred thousand won't cut it. We'll have to take care of the journalists; we'll have to take care of the human rights people. Make it six lakh and be at the station by 9 a.m.'

But Modhu isn't a dead body yet. On the floor in the back of the pickup truck, he lies flat on his back with his neck at an angle, peering at them like a weak, sick kitten. There is still a spark of life in his dying eyes.

It is the end of the night when Modhu is carried out of the police pickup truck and carefully laid down behind a bush in a corner of the Suhrawardy Gardens. Silence descends once the mechanical noise of the pickup truck disappears in the distance. It reigns for a few moments; then suddenly, someone blows into the mosque microphone, and in a voice deep like thunder, begins the chant of Allahu Akbar. When the quivering notes of the azaan float over to Modhu's nearly numb ears, his eyes open a slit. In the distance, he sees a quivering light. He tries to move one of his hands but can't. He tries to move his legs but can't. Modhu tries to make a noise with his mouth; he forces himself to say, Allah! But his voice doesn't echo in the wind.

5

Modhu will die and Mofiz will have Modina forever—this is what is written in Modina and Mofiz's destinies. Modina doesn't believe it, but there isn't an ounce of doubt in Mofiz's faith. But why Mofiz counts the days till Modhu's return is something only he knows.

Two days before Modhu is supposed to return, which is fifteen days after his departure, Mofiz stands by Modina's window once again and says that Modhu will not return. He is going to die in Dhaka; and when the poor die that far away, their bodies never make it back. Modina will never see Modhu again.

When Mofiz is telling Modina all this, Modhu is rolling back and forth between consciousness and unconsciousness on the floor of the pickup truck in the streets of Dhaka. Modina protests the ill-omened, cruel words from Mofiz by scratching his chest and neck until he bleeds. But when Mofiz groans in pain, she covers his mouth with her hand and says, 'Oh, does it burn?' When Mofiz sulks and wants to leave, Modina grabs his shoulder again and says, 'Come tomorrow! The day after, he'll be back home!'

The next night, before the cuckoo in the koroi tree begins to sing, three ghosts come to Modina's house. They whispered to each other as they came down the road that Modhu is gone. 'Let's go and eat Modhu's wife.'

These ghosts only eat females; from age eight to fifty-eight, wherever they find a girl or a woman at an opportune moment, they eat her. These famous ghosts live in the subdistrict town; they have come to the village of Modhupur after verifying and ascertaining the information that Modhu is absent, and truly they find Modina by herself in Modhu's house, and when they find her, they begin to eat her. They take turns at eating Modina. After the first ghost, the second ghost, then the third ghost, then the first ghost again.

While they are eating Modina by turns, Mofiz shows up. Modina sees Mofiz and whimpers in the hope of getting some help, but one of the ghosts grabs hold of her nose and mouth so hard that not only any noise, even her breath cannot emerge from her. In addition, another ghost grasps her throat with five plus five, ten fingers; Modina thrashes around, groans, her tongue lolls out, her eyes bulge. Seeing which, Mofiz, a single person, attacks the three ghosts. Two of them pick him up and slam him onto the ground; a grunt emerges from Mofiz's throat and his eyes go dark. The third ghost picks up a half-brick and smashes it on Mofiz's head; his skull opens up with a crack, which enthuses the ghost, so he begins smashing the brick into Mofiz's skull again and again.

Right then, the cuckoo trills in the koroi tree.

Ghosts don't know what it means when a cuckoo sings on a spring evening.

An Indian Citizen Came to Our Town

An Indian citizen arrived in our town. This wasn't really news. The Indian border is very close to our town and many people cross over every day. They are ours; they belong to this land. Most of them are smugglers. Although bona fide businessmen and people visiting relatives aren't small in number either. This coming and going happens every day. Although not too many people from that country come to ours, we don't have the same interest in them as we have in people from other countries. And because West Bengalis do not have white skin or a different language, they don't seem like foreigners to us like Europeans do. Therefore, nothing about an Indian citizen visiting our town should have given rise to curiosity or surprise. Until we found out that the gentleman had come here to die. Never in our lives had we heard of such a thing.

When our friend Tapan Kumar Kha informed us of this astonishing fact, we exclaimed, 'Wonderful!' We were excited, because not much that is unusual, or fun, happens in this humdrum township. The people here were quite humourless. If anyone made jokes, they were deemed frivolous. A person with a sense of humour was neither prized nor respected. This was probably why boys and girls practised seriousness from primary school onwards. Those who lacked seriousness, whose innate temperaments tended towards jokes and laughter, were not valued in this town. Their parents cursed their own fates more than they decried the frivolous nature of their offspring.

In such a humourless town then, the few of us who had been overtaken by laughter turned gleeful when we heard of the madness of Tapan Kha's seventy-three-year-old uncle, and we thought to ourselves, finally, a man of humour emerges. We couldn't keep still when we heard that the man had declared the day and hour of his death, that he would make his death an event worth attending. We rushed to meet him. Our curiosity was: what's the story, why this strange oath? But we were unable to see him. He would leave the house while it was barely dawn and return late. And because by then he got weary and listless, Tapan's mother allowed no visitors. We heard from the gentleman's young travel companion, his grandson Avijit, that the old man had become mentally unbalanced. His constant harping of *Bangladesh-Bangladesh-Bangladesh* had driven his children and grandchildren to distraction. Finally, one afternoon, he had dreamt of his dear departed mother and decided he was coming to Bangladesh. He took leave of his family and friends and informed them that he would not be returning to India. The ancient cremation ghat on the shores of the Tulshiganga in Bangladesh was where his mother had been cremated; his funeral pyre would burn at the same place.

Avijit informed us that every morning since his arrival, his Dadu had been gulping down some flattened or puffed rice, shoving a handful of coconut *naru* in his pocket, and leaving Tapan's house. He walked around looking at fields, ponds, lakes, trees, and searched the villages for this person or that. Those he sought were no longer there; they had all died. But this didn't dampen his spirits; he had to find at least one of his old friends. How could it be that everyone had already died, leaving him behind?

We heard of his doings from Avijit and Tapan, and our desire to see him grew. Such a man, who joked this way about death—to have him here in our town and not meet him, we couldn't allow that. No matter how, we were going to capture him, even if it were 11 p.m., even if Tapan's mother scolded us.

But that very afternoon the gentleman appeared of his own accord at our hangout. Our *adda* usually gathers in the field beside the Shaheed Minar, the memorial to the martyrs. The spot is a little bit away from the main road, where the light from the streetlamps doesn't reach. We couldn't see his face clearly in the semi-darkness. We only noticed his glinting eyes. He was tall, but his body had not bent with age, and his spine was surprisingly straight. We stood up from the grass to greet him. We touched our foreheads and said, '*Adaab.*' One of us, a bit of a clown, said, '*Salamaleikum.*' (The poet Nirmalendu Goon once visited here and this clown said Salamaleikum to him, too. His explanation for this, which isn't really relevant here, was: people's speech should be in accordance with who they are. For instance, Hindus never said Salamaleikum to Muslims, they greeted us with Adaab. But we greeted Hindus with Adaab, we didn't say Salamaleikum to them either. Why? He thought this was because Muslims felt inferior, etc.)

The gentleman nodded in response to our Adaab and Salaam and sat down on the grass. Tapan introduced us. His uncle told us his name was Nabin Chandra Chowdhury, and he announced, as if making a proclamation, that he had returned. We asked him precisely what he meant by saying he had returned. He told us that he had returned to the land of his birth and that he was never going back to India. Displaying no interest in our response, he said that after spending fifty years in a foreign land (it seemed to us that he placed an undue emphasis on the phrase 'foreign land'), he had finally returned to his homeland at seventy-three, and this was his final return.

One of us jokingly told Tapan's uncle that 'homeland' and 'land of birth' were not the same things. No one would deny that Bangladesh was his land of birth, but he could no longer claim Bangladesh as his homeland.

We scolded our friend into silence, advising him to give up intellectual pretensions. Another friend asked how many days the government of Bangladesh had allowed him on his visa. He said, fifteen. We noticed that the uncle's garrulity from minutes ago had disappeared. Perhaps he was hurt by our friend's words. But what could be done?

We asked him the next question. How was he going to remain in this country once his visa expired?

He said that by then his lifespan would also have expired. We found it truly funny. But we concealed that and, instead, expressed surprise, asking him how he knew. He said that he had acquired divine knowledge on this topic. Someone at the back of our group made a sudden exclamation, one that was clearly in mockery. Even in that mix of light and darkness, Tapan's uncle could probably see our disbelieving smiles. Perhaps he wanted to intensify that disbelief. He said, 'I can see the beginning and the end of my life now.'

We concealed our disbelief and asked him to explain. He stated in a quiet but firm voice—he was born on 15 August 1924 and he was going to die on 28 October of this year [1997]. He could clearly see his entire life of seventy-three years, two months and thirteen days. We thought he had crossed into the realm of humour, and if we joked with him a little, surely it wouldn't be unfair or disrespectful. We challenged his claim to supernatural ability. 'Can you tell us what will happen tomorrow?'

But he didn't accept our challenge. Surprising us, smiling gently as if he was surrendering, he said, 'No.'

'Then why are you saying you know? Can't you really see it all?'

Our question sounded brusque. He withdrew and apologised in a low voice for his ill-considered comment. Moments later he pronounced in a clear voice, pausing before every word, 'I don't know anything.'

We now agreed with Avijit about his Dadu's mental state. We were no longer well-behaved boys; mischief raised its head within us. We lined up questions, one after another, with which we were going to goad him for our entertainment.

Some of us identified this as incitement. Our Hindu friends, including Tapan, protested—the conversation was taking a communal turn. One of us, a stubborn guy, against whom you could never win an argument, said, 'We're already living with communalism, we don't need to be pushed that way.'

When we scolded him, he erupted, 'Why do Hindus on this side die when the Babri Mosque on that side is demolished? Let them do whatever they want in their country, why do we kill each other? Does that mean that we're still the same country? That's the question that needs to be resolved.' Tapan and our other Hindu friends kept quiet. Accepting the silence as support, he felt encouraged. 'The Christians in Bosnia are destroying Muslims; why don't we run to slit Christian throats here? But if anything happens to Muslims in India, we run to slaughter *maulanas* in this country. Why? Because there has been no resolution yet between these communities. Because the Hindus are our brothers, we have no happiness if we don't squabble with them.'

'Will you stop with your jawing, or are you looking to get punched?' An older friend scolded our stubborn Hindu-loving friend into silence. This friend used to be a hardcore communist; at heart he still was. We had many Hindu friends because of our communist politics. We still believed that India had been partitioned because of the Muslims, a belief we probably got from the Communist Party. We grew up clasping the hands of Hindu comrades. Hindu-Muslim wasn't the real concern, the real issue was the inequality between the rich and the poor—apart from this lesson, we also got from the Party, our discerning taste in music, literature, art and culture. Although our fathers or grandfathers expressed no disgust about Hindus, they weren't above saying things like, Hindus were too dominating back in the day. The residents of the red buildings, which now stood skeletal on either side of our only main street, had never allowed our fathers or grandfathers to buy the biggest fish in the market. Apparently, the fishermen wouldn't let any Muslim even touch the big fish. If anyone even tried to approach, they would holler, 'Don't touch, don't touch, that's for the Babu.' But telling us these stories had been useless. Our fathers and uncles hadn't succeeded in sowing any hatred for Hindus in our hearts. Although most of the Hindus had left for the other side, we still had a good number of Hindu friends. They had access to the inner sanctums of our households. Some of them even ate beef with us. We observed Saraswati puja with them. Our fathers and uncles all performed namaz five times a day, and fasted, but they had no influence on us—we didn't go near the mosque unless it was a Friday.

But one could count how many of us there were on the fingers of one hand. And it's not like we remained the same. Our current political realisation was that all Hindus supported the Awami League. Even those involved in the Communist

Party voted for the symbol of the boat. After the fall of the communist movement, we discerned a change within ourselves. Now the Hindu communists talked like the BJP-wallahs. We noticed that the Hindutva ethos had grown central within them. Now when we looked back, we could see that our Hindu comrades in the party had demanded atheism only of us; they themselves had remained religious to their cores. But we did not let this bother us. We were moving away from politics; we *had* moved away. Our politics was now limited to mere talk. Now our focus was on cricket. Except now and then we felt that if nothing else, the failure of communist politics had left the secular sensibility damaged. The Awami League was turning into the Muslim League; otherwise, it wouldn't get any votes. The Awami League didn't want to undertake the risk of saving the Hindus, although they did want the Hindu vote. How fortunate that the Awami League didn't have to ask for the Hindu vote; they got it anyway. What they had to work for was the Muslim vote. To get Muslims to vote for them, they had to prove that they were not a Hindu party, that they were not irreligious, that they were not toadies of India. They had to prove that they were more religious than the opposition, the BNP, that they were zealous Hindu-haters.

Anyway, we didn't really worry our heads over these things anymore. Our relationship with our Hindu friends was more a function of habit, nothing to do with politics-shmolitics. There was no Party, no politics, but we were here. We played cricket together, played cards, smoked weed, got involved with the Rotary Club. Of course, occasionally we were saddened, such as when one morning we heard that a friend who had finished his medical studies at Rajshahi Medical College had left for India. Not too many, just two of our friends had left. We were hurt; we cursed them in our hearts: they studied medicine on Bangladesh's dime and then went off to India? Couldn't they have left earlier? Look, this was also an aspect of our relationship with them: the buggers didn't feel reassured. Why? Who was going to attack you? Let them go. We will see if their necks were brave enough to carry more than one head. You never truly thought of this country as your own … that's what we thought. Then we also thought, why *weren't* they thinking of the land of their birth as their own? Was the fault theirs or ours? They feared us. The Awami League that they voted for was the same Awami League whose people seized their lands, pressured them to sell at low prices. Why *shouldn't* they leave? This is also what we thought. Not always though, only when somebody left, or when someone's sister had to suffer the leering gaze of some thug, or when there was some conflict over someone's shop. Of course, that sort of thing didn't happen very often. We hadn't even noticed it for many years—for they left quietly, in silence, in secret, in the darkness of night.

'Are you going to die with this wound, that the Muslims exiled you?' Our friends jabbed at the gentleman. Before we could yell at our friends, the gentleman replied, 'Fate! Fate is to blame.'

'Fate! Not your community? It's because of the Hindus that the country was partitioned. You don't want to remember that Hindus split the country because they couldn't abide by the rule of the brute majority?'

'Our fault! Our …'

One of us shouted, 'You son of a bitch, talking like a *Jamaati*! Why did you come here? Go crawl up Abbas Ali Khan's ass!'

'I'm telling you, watch your mouth! Does your father own this field …?'

We scolded the two stubborn fellows, but they paid no attention to us and swore at each other while rolling up their sleeves. When our older friend threatened to kick them out, they calmed down, but the hissing inside them continued. An uncomfortable silence reigned. Among us, Abbas Ali Khan had no disciple, and never had. The one against whom this allegation had been levelled had not been talking like a Jamaati. But it seemed that by pulling in the sins of history and by harbouring erroneous notions of history, we had messed it all up. So, the Hindu-Muslim relationship in Bangladesh wasn't a stagnant thing. The Hindus were becoming more Hindu, and we were becoming more Muslim. We had heard that in India they thought of Bangladesh as a Muslim state. In West Bengal, Bangladeshi literature meant the work of Bangladeshi Muslim writers; apparently our Hindu writers didn't represent us. They thought that Bangladesh was a Muslim country and India was for Hindus. We wanted to verify these notions with Tapan's uncle. But then the Hindu-Muslim issue turned tedious and dangerous.

We said, 'Kaka Babu will now tell us stories from his childhood.'

He said in a broken, hoarse voice, 'I left my home, my land, at twenty-four to live in a foreign country and I have now returned at seventy-three. That's my story, one that everyone knows. What can I say that is new?'

We discovered that we didn't like him very much anymore. We didn't like such mawkishness. We didn't like this talk of sorrow or pain. Our books, plays, cinema were strewn with sorrow. Our everyday family lives too were weighed down by sorrow. We couldn't stand all this talk of sorrow anymore. It annoyed us. We didn't need to be told that this man's life was filled with the pain of exile. We feared him: he was planning to foist his own sorrow on us, he was designing sad sentences in his mind, attempting to bring tears to our eyes. He was going to tell us his tragic tale of exile, about his endless love for his motherland. We did not like this cheap display of sentiment.

We did not give the old man any chances, and as soon as the microphone next door blared the azaan for the *Isha* prayers, we broke up our adda.

The episode with the Indian gentleman no longer interested us. We organised a teen cricket tournament. That excitement lasted for a week. Then the topic of the Indian gentleman came up again when we were hanging out. We remembered that it was Friday, 28 October. The day his visa was supposed to expire. We asked Tapan about his uncle. We asked whether there were any signs of his impending death. Tapan didn't mind our cruel curiosity; he was one of us and he laughed and told us that his Indian uncle had become revitalised from walking around in the pure air of dawn and sleeping well at night. Forget about a natural death, now it would be hard for even three or four young men like us to try and kill him. We reminded Tapan of his uncle's visa dates and asked whether he had had the date extended.

Tapan informed us that he had told his uncle several times to go and extend the visa, but each time his uncle said that the dates could not be extended, that no one had the power to do it. We told Tapan he should tell his uncle that if there was a run-in with the police, it was Tapan and his family who would get into trouble. Tapan grew anxious. He proposed that we all visit his house that evening and ask his uncle to get his visa extended.

In the afternoon, we went to the central mosque for the Jumma prayer. (Yes, these days we go to the mosque on Fridays, because Friday afternoons, when every man of age in the town prostrates himself at the mosque, we can find nowhere to hide. After all, we live in a society and we don't want people to loathe us.) We left as soon as we had completed the *farz* or mandatory part of the prayers; we weren't greedy for the extra *sunnat* blessings. Outside, in the near-empty streets, we saw two cycle-vans pulling firewood, and behind them was Tapan's uncle. He was clad in a blinding white panjabi and *dhuti*, and he was walking behind the cycle-vans with his spine ramrod straight. Soon we spotted Avijit and our friend Tapan trailing behind him. They seemed so annoyed that they looked as if they were about to cry. Tapan gestured towards us, and we immediately followed them.

A little later, we noticed that there were many people following us. As they exited the mosque, instead of going their different ways, they fell in behind us. Not a word on their lips, as if they were all in a silent rally. We took the main street and walked westwards: at the front were the two cycle-vans carrying firewood, then Nabin Chandra Chowdhury, silent and firm of will with his head held high, behind him were Tapan, Avijit and a few of us, and behind us a long, silent procession. We couldn't tell when the streets became a sea of people. We were surprised to see that the townspeople were just as prone as we were to passing fancies, and they had no questions about our childish curiosity. The farther we walked, the longer and denser the procession grew. From the windows and balconies, from the rooftops on either side of the streets, women, children and the elderly watched us with curious eyes. We swarmed behind the Indian gentleman as if in a trance.

The thin stream of the Tulshiganga river divided the wide, sandy shores. On the other side, a forest of shaal trees began at the end of the riverbank. On this side, we waited. We were uncountable in number. There was not a word on our lips.

Meanwhile, the news had spread: an Indian citizen was killing himself on the shore of the Tulshiganga. The district administrator arrived with the police. He stood in an open jeep and shouted into a megaphone, 'What a nuisance! What a nuisance! You want to kill yourself, go to your own country, why here? Arrest him. Take him to the station!'

The police rushed over to surround Tapan's uncle. He was oblivious, his spine straight. His head raised, he turned to face the people. The people shouted in one voice, 'No!'

'Arrest him!'

We protested, 'For what crime? His visa hasn't expired yet.'

'If it's a spectacle you want, go back to your own country and do it there. Hey, what's going on? Get him!' The district administrator's hands trembled.

'No!' The people shouted in one voice.

The van-drivers finished laying out the pyre.

'Why are you just standing there? Get him!'

'No!'

'All right, then. Search him. See if he's carrying matches or a lighter. Search closely, you idiots!'

Four policemen surrounded Nabin Chandra Chowdhury, as if they were tickling him. He pushed the policemen off like pieces of straw in the wind with his long, hard, twisted, bony arms. He took off the panjabi he was wearing and tossed it in the wind. Then he untied the knot holding his dhuti together. The white fabric fell on the sand. His thin, naked body stepped over the fallen clothing to the pyre. He held his arms aloft, his fingers stretched out, and gestured strangely towards the people. He strode to the pyre and lay down straight. We gawked with bated breath.

We hadn't noticed the thick black clouds piling up in the autumnal afternoon sky. We hadn't noticed that there was no sun, that all the world had darkened. We looked to the sky and saw flocks of white geese flying away. Hundreds and thousands of dragonflies, butterflies and other insects whose names we didn't know were covering the sky. We were stunned; our pounding hearts stopped our breaths. Our eyes wanted to explode; we were speechless, we stared unblinkingly at the Indian gentleman atop the funeral pyre.

Suddenly, a flash sparked from the northeastern horizon, a noise ripped asunder the sky, and the funeral pyre burst into flames. In the fire, the long, stretched-out body of the Indian gentleman glittered like a lump of gold. Then the golden figure transformed into a subtle, thin spear of flame, and gradually disappeared into the sky.

The pyre was doused when the cold autumn rain started to pour. At the district administrator's order, the policemen rushed over and searched for the body of the Indian citizen amidst the heaps of damp ash, coal and charred planks of wood. We were annoyed at their idiocy and started for our homes.

But the return journey to our town never ended. We grew weary as we walked. The afternoon faded into the darkness of evening, and yet we could not reach our town; nowhere could we see a single sign of our houses. The shores of the Tulshiganga surrounded us. In the stretched-out barren wild, we kept searching for home.

Jamila

When he heard the caged rooster crow from the next-door rooftop, Jamila's son bellowed for his mother. 'Amma,' the noise sliced through the dawn air. Before Jamila's belly wrenched in hunger, her heart skipped a beat for her son.

But Mofiz, nearly dead from fever for the last three days, didn't stir.

Jamila thought he probably wasn't dead. Although it would have been better if he were.

She stretched her neck out taut, leant forward lowering her head, and exhaled so hard that all the dust around her blew away. Then the air rang with a crash as if a small bomb had just exploded. The noise made the nearly dead Mofiz open his eyes; with a dejected gaze, he watched as Jamila exited the house like a tornado.

Jamila's son also saw the tornado, because he had been watching his mother from the beginning.

When his mother left through the yard entrance like a storm, the cry 'Amma' emerged from the child's throat. In the silent, solitary dawn, the cry followed Jamila for quite a long way.

Once she crossed Mansurabad, she was on the main road for Baitul Aman Housing Society; she ran along this road and that street, left the genteel environs of the housing society behind her, crossed the old alleys and byways of the old neighborhood and ran onto Ring Road at the corner of Adabor Market where she stopped. She stood there, panting and looking this way and that. But she could see nothing; her eyes were blank. All this running and jumping had made her hunger grow five times fiercer.

Jamila realised her insides were burning to ashes. She walked along the right side of Ring Road for a while and slipped into Tikkapara, the neighborhood to her left. After walking along the twisting, turning, rough street for a while, she saw a flourishing papaya tree, almost touching the wall of a house. It wasn't too high; all the leaves were well within her reach. As soon as Jamila thrust her face close to it, a grim shout blasted through the window. 'Hey, who's there?'

Jamila turned her face away and began walking again. But she couldn't decide which way to go. On either side of the curving street within the Tikkapara neighborhood, narrow alleyways struck off frequently even farther inwards. Those alleys seemed dangerous to her, so she kept to the main road. She had to stop after a little while because the road branched off in three different directions. She couldn't decide which one to take, so she stood still for a while. Then, without thinking about it, she veered to the right and started walking again.

After a few steps, she spotted a mosque on the right, surrounded by a belly-high wall. Within the compound, in the yard-like space, a goat's throat was being slit open. When Jamila saw the blood spurting out, she closed her eyes and began to run.

She went along Thana Road, the street that ran past the southern boundary wall of Residential Model School and headed east, merging into Mirpur Road. Alongside the long wall to her left, various kinds of seedlings were for sale. Jamila glanced at the seedlings as she moved forward. The seedlings, with their varied looks and their varied natures, watched Jamila in silence. One of the men in charge of their safety-maintenance-sales said to the other, '*Mamu*, check out the size of those udders.'

Jamila's ears burned. She walked fast, moving almost at a trot. The men and women who were headed towards Chandrima Garden in a bid to salvage their health slowed down, some even stopped, to swivel their necks to get a look at her. They too made obscene remarks about her, especially about the size of her mammaries. Jamila sped up as she listened to them. But she didn't run; she was afraid that it might disturb the public peace on this calm morning, that it might worsen the law-and-order situation.

She had to stop at the crossroads where Thana Road merged into Mirpur Road. Big buses, trucks, private cars and other automated vehicles were moving so densely, it was almost impossible to find a gap or a chance to cross the road. People who were bound for Chandrima Garden had also halted by the side of the road, waiting for the traffic lights to turn red. In a little while, the green light turned amber, and the amber turned red, but the cars and buses didn't stop for a second; they kept going just as they had before.

This went on for a long time. Then the red light first turned amber, then green. When the cars still didn't stop, a traffic policeman raised his baton, blew his whistle and shouted at the cars, cursing them. By then, the men and women waiting on the sidewalk had grown slightly rebellious and they began to cross the road, forcing the vehicles to stop. Jamila crossed Mirpur Road at a run and kept going straight, farther east. She stopped running when she crossed the road; she walked along the street that lay to the south of Gana Bhaban, the prime minister's official residence, which was adjacent to Crescent Lake, and later joined up with Bijoy Sarani.

Every ten feet along the high, red wall of Gana Bhaban stood a uniformed sentry. Some of them stood resting their weight on their right leg, some on the left. None of them were using both legs to stand on. After guarding the prime minister all night long, their eyelids were droopy, their lips dry. Jamila watched them yawn prodigiously. The number, shape and weight of the men and women who were walking past the sentries on their way to Chandrima Garden were bigger than that of the men and women from Thana Road. Their eyes and their faces reflected their vulgar humour and curiosity about Jamila. They discussed her breasts while they walked. Jamila felt furious, but she was forgiving of these people. Because she knew that the filth of their minds was less monstrous than the cruelty of their actions.

Just before the path to the entrance to Chandrima Garden began, where the boundary wall of Gana Bhaban ended, a street branched off to the south. It merged onto the pathway that led to the western entrance to the National Parliament. At the entrance of that branched-off street, a bamboo barricade painted red and white had been erected. To the left of the barricade stood several uniformed sentries, some sitting, some standing; some carried batons, some had rifles slung across their backs; and each man had eyes that were swollen with gunk accrued in the corners.

As soon as Jamila raised a leg to climb over the barricade, a uniformed sentry yelled at her in a rough voice, 'Hey, you slut, where do you think you're going?'

'Beat it!' The sentries tried to get rid of her. She stared at the field; it was a sanctuary for grass; it grew there unimpeded. Even the ancestors of this grass had forgotten what the aggression of the sickle army felt like.

She raised her leg again to climb past the barricade. The guards roared again, 'Watch it!' They pointed towards the Gana Bhaban across the street. 'The Prime Minister is sleeping.'

Then they turned back to the field and stared diagonally across: 'The great, holy parliament.' One of the guards gazed at two red houses standing side by side in the western corner of the field and said, 'The Shpeaker and the Deputy Shpeaker sirs are all asleep.'

Jamila told them, 'I'll just eat some grass quietly for an hour and leave.'

'This slut talks too much!'

'This slut talks back!'

'Go on, get out right now!'

Thus, the three rifle- and baton-wielding members of the law enforcement agency verbally abused her. She bore it all; she had no choice. Her belly was burning with hunger. She told them she had been starving for three days because Mofiz was sick with fever and hadn't fed her. She told them that if she was to live, she had to eat something straightaway. Let her be granted permission to eat grass for just one hour.

'I beg you,' she pleaded.

But her pleading made the members of the law enforcement agencies angrier. One of them raised his stick and rushed at her saying, 'You've come this early in the day just to stir up some trouble. I'm going to give this whore a good one ...'

Before he was done, another uniformed, stick-wielding man stepped forward and said, 'Why all this "going to" business? Just give it to her.' He brought his stick down between her horns.

Jamila's skull clanged, a tremendous wail emerged from her throat and she lowered her head and jerked it up suddenly, and in the blink of an eye, the members of the law enforcement agencies saw the body of one of their colleagues gored by the tips of Jamila's curved horns. When Jamila's head dragged upwards from left to right, the men in uniform saw their colleague against the backdrop of a blue sky. Then, when he crashed back onto the ground, a grunt was expelled from his throat and they saw that his belly had ripped open and his intestines were spilling out through the gap created by ripped-off buttons.

As Jamila did an about face and began to flee, the rifle in the hands of a colleague of the gored sentry roared; two bullets hit Jamila, one in each of her ass cheeks. Still she ran, but then another bullet ripped through an artery in her right hind leg and she collapsed to the ground. She mooed, calling out to her son.

The next day, the newspapers carried the story of the 'tragic' death, caused by Jamila's horns, of a member of the law enforcement agency while he was carrying out his duties in the National Parliament area and of Jamila's subsequent shooting at the hands of his colleagues.

The home minister was devastated by the death of the member of the law enforcement agency and declared that the dead man's family would be granted compensation of one lakh takas. He affirmed that a one-member investigative committee, led by the chief of the Detective Branch, had been convened to appropriately investigate the incident. This committee would submit its report within one week to the home minister. The home minister also promised that no matter who was responsible for this incident, severe legal steps would be taken against them.

The speaker of Parliament expressed sadness regarding the fact that such a tragic incident had unfolded a mere two hundred yards from his residence.

The opposition leader of Parliament expressed his condemnation of the incident and demanded proper medical treatment for the injured Jamila. He termed the death of the member of the law enforcement agency unwarranted and tragic and stated that the grass in the Parliament building area was a gift of nature, and it was the constitutional right of every citizen of the liberated, autonomous state of the People's Republic of Bangladesh to eat that grass.

The general secretary of the ruling party stated that this tragic event, which had been triggered by a grass-eating incident in the Parliament building area, was clearly the result of a deep conspiracy hatched by vested interests against the nation, the people and democracy itself.

The general secretary of the opposition party termed the incident tragic and shameful and said that the ruling party behaved as though all the grass in the vicinity of the National Parliament was owned by their fathers; they had monopolised eating all that grass from day one of grabbing power through a scam election.

Three environmental organisations released a joint statement saying the denial of grass to starving Jamila and the assault by hitting her on the head with a stick was a clear representation of the utter lack of sensitivity among the law enforcement agencies with regard to the existential struggle of all beings.

The following day, after the news reports, all the national dailies published op-eds on the subject. Most of these op-eds called the death of the law enforcement agency man tragic but lay the blame on the 'overly aggressive' actions of law enforcement forces. A popular online journal published a blog post by someone under the pen name of Dilbor Taus with the headline: 'A Death Vs. Jamila's Right to Eat Grass'.

2

Written in formal, archaic Bengali, this was Dilbor Taus' blog post:

'Eighteen-year-old Jamila is an acquaintance of mine. Her owner Syed Abdul Mutkadir is an old friend. Once upon a time he served as the chairman of the National Revenue Board. I say this not because he is my friend, but because all who know him also know that he is a person of profound integrity, and he never accepted a single paisa as a bribe in his entire life. In 1990, using all his life savings, he purchased a plot of land, measuring five *katthas*, in the Adabor area of the capital city. Since then, the plots surrounding his have been populated with houses, mansions and such. It is only the plot possessed by my friend which remains empty. He has not managed to build a house. How could he? The entirety of his life savings, saved throughout the entirety of his life, was depleted by procuring that plot of land. After his retirement he had returned to his father's abode in Kaliakoir due to lack of money. My friend was fortunate that his father had built a house there.

'Afraid of losing that five-kattha plot in the Mansurabad residential area of the capital's Adabor neighbourhood to encroachers, Abdul Muktadir brought an impecunious young man named Mofiz from his village and built him a tin shack on the plot of land. He considered the question of how Mofiz would survive in Dhaka, and purchased a rickshaw for him, thus ensuring a mode of income for the man. One rainy afternoon, while driving the rickshaw, Mofiz met a young woman; she was walking by the side of the road, getting drenched by the rain. Mofiz asked her, "Why are you getting wet? Hop into my car." The woman in wet clothes smiled and replied that she had no money. Mofiz sang to the tune of a song, "I will not take any payment from you." The young woman cocked an eyebrow and swayed in laughter, but she did not respond to Mofiz's invitation by climbing into his rickshaw. She shimmied her buttocks and continued on her way. Mofiz did not let her go; he followed her in his rickshaw as he watched her shimmying rump. As the young woman went her way, she looked back at Mofiz once and smiled. When Mofiz asked her name, she said her name was Jamila.

'Reader, you must comprehend what is about to occur between Jamila and Mofiz. I have, forthwith, reached old age; it is no longer seemly for me to pen love stories. And furthermore, the subject matter of today's blogpost is not of joy, rather it is of sorrow. Bullets have been fired; Jamila has bled. No, before that, the intestines belonging to a law enforcement officer have been expelled and his life lost. In such a situation, it is inappropriate to put forth a saga of romance or love. I shall abstain from the usage of romantic language while bringing to light the necessary information about Mofiz and Jamila. I shall recount, very briefly, only that which is essential to know.

'Mofiz went to Kaliakoir and said to Syed Abdul Muktadir, "Uncle, I want to get married." Abdul Muktadir is a man of pragmatic sense, so he said, "Go ahead." He took into consideration the expenses for a wedding and Mofiz's poverty, and even gave him some money. Mofiz accepted the money, returned to Dhaka, wedded Jamila and set up their household in that tin-roof shack. He no longer wanted to drive his rickshaw; a kingdom's worth of laziness arrived from somewhere and settled over his body and his mind. He rented out his rickshaw and was thus promoted from rickshaw driver to rickshaw owner. Subsequently, the man he had rented the rickshaw to absconded with said vehicle, and then a few days later, Jamila too disappeared. Mofiz wept, returned to Kaliakoir and, describing the whole situation to Abdul Muktadir, he said, "Uncle, this is the situation. What can be done?"

'Abdul Muktadir said, "There is nothing else to be done. Just come back to the village. I'll arrange to sell off the land."

'Right then, one night, an accident occurred on the Dhaka-Tangail highway: a head-on collision between a truck and a bus. The truck was packed with cows being brought in from India. In that collision between a bus carrying human passengers and a truck carrying cows, eleven people died, but none of the cows; they fell off the truck and fled helter-skelter in different directions, while a few were befuddled and continued to create a commotion among themselves.

'Mofiz ran into one of the fleeing cows when he was rushing to the crash site. When the cow was in front of Mofiz, it stopped suddenly and said, "Bhai, save me." Mofiz comforted the cow and he took her to Abdul Muktadir's father's house and gave her some hay to eat.

'The cow importers hit the nearby villages, searching for the cows that had dispersed and escaped. They also came to Abdul Muktadir's house and identified the long-limbed heifer that Mofiz had been entertaining as belonging to them. There was a conflict when Mofiz refused to return the heifer to them, but Syed Abdul Muktadir shaheb resolved it by paying off the cow-men with cash. The cow remained under Mofiz's care. Mofiz named it Jamila. He eschewed the intimacy with the bull at the District Animal Husbandry Officer's office and instead, with the assistance of a veterinarian, arranged for Jamila to be impregnated through the scientific, artificial method.

'Abdul Muktadir shaheb was concerned that if Mofiz remained in Kaliakoir for too long, he would lose control of his plot in Mansurabad, and so he instructed Mofiz to return to Dhaka. Mofiz went back to Dhaka with Jamila. In the tin-roof shack that had been constructed on the plot of land belonging to Abdul Muktadir, in due time, a calf was born to Jamila, and she began yielding milk twice a day, which amounted to five kilos. Selling that milk for sixty takas per kilo eased Mofiz's financial situation somewhat. However, his relationship with Jamila deteriorated because Mofiz would deprive the calf most cruelly and milk her as much as he could.

'One day, Mofiz was racked with fever. He fell onto his bed moaning. Jamila's son was glad as he watched Mofiz suffer. For the last few days, he had been repeating that when his horns came out, he was going to rip open Mofiz's belly. Jamila also thought Mofiz might as well die now. For then she would rip out her tether, free herself, and take her son away to wherever she wanted.

'But once Mofiz was bedridden and moaning with fever, Jamila began to starve. Her son was also starving, lowing, "Amma Amma!" After three days, tormented by hunger, one morning Jamila ripped her tether out and departed in search of grass, and thus she became enmeshed in danger. You know from media reports how she became a victim of the brutal actions of the law enforcement agency in the National Parliament area and what condition that left her in. The right to eat grass is a right that is natural and just, and thus it is a constitutional right. If I say it in English, I would phrase it thus: Natural rights must be constitutional rights. But neither the human nor the animal kind in Bangladesh have any understanding of the nature of rights. They know the constitution is a book, and the creatures of this society use that book only to create danger for others. Hence, let me discard the discussion on rights; let me talk about pity.

'Is there no more pity left? If Jamila had been shown the slightest pity, she would have been rescued from the pangs of hunger and the law enforcement officer would not have lost his life.

'Although manslaughter is a grave crime, if you examine the incident thoroughly, you will have to admit that Jamila did not kill anyone. When she was hit with a stick on her skull, she merely jerked her head; she had not intended to gore anyone with her horns. She did not have the space to consider that her horns might skewer a law enforcement officer and she should shake her head carefully. It is unsurprising that, upon being hit on the head with a stick, anyone would become befuddled and jerk their head.

'The death of a Parliament security detail while on duty was not something anyone had wanted to happen. However, those in the media who have written that if only Jamila had been a little more patient, this death could have been avoided, cannot be made to understand, not even if they are hit on their heads with iron bars, that when hit on the head with a baton, not only one's patience but all of one's judgement and wit might disappear forever. Fortunately, Jamila did not lose her life. Hence, it is now incumbent on the government to ensure that there is no lack in Jamila's medical treatment. It should be understood that Jamila was assaulted on her head, right in the middle. If one is hit on the head with a baton and one does not die, it is not unheard of for the brain to malfunction, although, so far, no such sign has been noted in Jamila. From the statement she provided after her arrest, it does not seem like her brain is malfunctioning. It seemed quite clear that her mental capacity to make the judgment that asking to eat grass is not a crime, and that she was not at fault in ripping out the guard's stomach, remains intact.

'Jamila's swift recovery and overall well-being should be something we all desire and hope for. And her unintended crime (manslaughter) should most necessarily be judged with forgiveness and grace.'

3

The surgeons at Pongu Hospital, which treated the disabled, pulled out two bullets from Jamila's posterior; the severed artery in her right leg was surgically stitched back together. But the law enforcement agency's formal statement declared that no bullets had been located in Jamila's body. Protests swept like a storm through the news media; it was alleged that evidence related to the incident was being concealed. An editorial essay in one of the dailies raised the question: If Jamila hadn't been shot, then how was she injured? How was her rump wounded so badly that it required eighteen stitches? How was the artery in her right leg damaged?

Of course, the law enforcement agencies paid no attention to these questions from the media; they released no more statements on Jamila. Several newspapers presented the allegation to the people, reporting that 'according to sources', 'according to information received', 'as told by a reliable source', as the physicians, nurses, attendants and cleaners at Pongu Hospital had been strictly warned by the law enforcement agencies against talking to journalists.

Questions about Jamila's status and latest location were asked on television talk shows and in newspaper columns. But the relevant government authorities were unresponsive. Several relentless reporters kept haunting the Tejgaon police station. They had discovered that after being released from Pongu Hospital, Jamila had been kept in the lockup at the station. But they weren't able to see her when they went there. The on-duty officer-in-charge as well as everyone else at the station kept their mouths shut; they were extremely annoyed by these repeated interrogations by the journalists. The reporters found out from people in the neighbourhood that Jamila had been tethered to a mango tree inside the police station compound, right next to the boundary wall. People had seen her eating mango leaves, banana peels and so on.

Jamila's owner, former chairman of the National Revenue Board, Syed Abdul Muktadir arrived in Dhaka from Kaliakoir and set out with the recently recovered Mofiz in search of Jamila. He introduced himself as Jamila's owner to Mohammad Alauddin, the officer-in-charge of Tejgaon police station. Dressed in a faded panjabi, his hair and beard dyed with henna, Abdul Muktadir appeared to be an average, simple person. OC Alauddin didn't pay him much attention.

Abdul Muktadir asked, 'Where is my Jamila?'

OC Alauddin turned the pages of the station logbook and, without looking at him, replied in a sombre, businesslike manner, 'She's been transferred to prison.'

Muktadir asked with a child's eagerness, 'When? What time?'

OC Alauddin responded without looking up from the logbook. 'That is none of your business. Go to the prison, you can see her there.'

Syed Abdul Muktadir set off in the direction of the Dhaka Central Prison. It took him an hour and forty-five minutes to get from Tejgaon to Lalbagh. He asked about the jailer and the deputy jailer of the Central Prison and found that both of them were busy elsewhere; they were absent from their workplace. He located a mid-ranking official and asked him in a tone of lament, 'Where is my Jamila?'

The prison official looked at Muktadir shaheb. His eyes and his face expressed immense annoyance, as if he were irritated with life itself. Muktadir shaheb repeated his question.

This time the prison official said in a scolding manner, 'Why are you asking me?'

Muktadir shaheb asked helplessly, 'Then who should I ask?'

'How do I know?'

'Who knows? Where, from whom, can I get news of Jamila?'

'News you get from the newspapers. We're not waiting around here with news.'

'They told me at the Tejgaon police station that she has been transferred to your prison. Won't I be able to see her even once?'

'No, you won't. Because she isn't here.'

'What do you mean not here? Did they lie at the police station?'

'I don't know. We also heard that she's been sent to prison. But we haven't received her here.'

'When was she sent?'

'Those who sent her would be able to tell you. You should go and ask them.'

Muktadir shaheb went back to the Tejgaon station. OC Alauddin wasn't there. Several constables sat there, chatting together. Muktadir shaheb asked them when Jamila had been sent to jail.

The constables exchanged glances. They said they knew nothing about it. It was late afternoon now; if Jamila had been sent to prison, it would have happened in the morning. When Muktadir shaheb asked to see the documentation for her transfer, they grew annoyed. One of them asked angrily, 'Who the hell do you think you are that you're asking to see the books at a police station?'

Muktadir shaheb naively explained that he was Jamila's owner. That the policemen hadn't asked him who he was, that instead they had said 'who the hell' to dismiss him and had barely restrained themselves from finishing that with the insult of 'which royal highness'—he didn't understand that at all. He pointed to Mofiz and said, 'Go on, ask him if I'm Jamila's owner or not.'

But the police didn't seem at all interested in verifying Jamila's ownership. They told Muktadir shaheb that they could make no comments regarding Jamila; they had been warned not to from above. Muktadir shaheb felt affronted now and, in his characteristic gentle manner, he made the threat that if he wasn't informed about her whereabouts and her condition, he was going to call a press conference.

But Muktadir shaheb's threat didn't seem to bring the police to their senses. Instead, one of them said, 'Buzz off then, go and do whatever. We don't know anything about Jamila. As far as we are concerned, you neither came to this police station, nor did you ask us anything.'

4

Syed Abdul Muktadir shaheb called a press conference at the National Press Club and described in detail all the harassment he had suffered at the hands of the police and the prison authorities, instead of their cooperation, when he tried to find out where Jamila was being held and how she was doing.

He noted that a member of the law enforcement agency being gored to death by Jamila's horns was a tragic event. 'Whatever the punishment for that is under the law, Jamila will welcome. I will have no objection either. Because I believe in the rule of law; I am deeply respectful towards the law. But before that, I have to know where she is and how she is. I cannot bear this mysterious manner in which the law enforcement agency is dealing with the question of her whereabouts. I am putting forth this humble request to the government to make Jamila's whereabouts public through my journalist brothers.'

A journalist asked, 'The law enforcement forces gave you no information on Jamila's whereabouts—what is your opinion on that? Why are they keeping this secret?'

Abdul Muktadir said, 'I can't really say. Like you, I also have questions about why this is being kept secret.'

Another journalist asked, 'Don't you think that something bad has happened to her in police custody and that is why there's all this secrecy?'

'I don't know,' Muktadir shaheb replied in a hesitant voice.

Yet another journalist asked, 'So, Muktadir shaheb, what are your comments on the statement from the ruling party that this entire thing is a conspiracy hatched by vested interests?'

'I don't know who might have hatched a conspiracy here.'

'To embarrass the government, to tarnish the image of the government abroad, and in particular, the blueprint to destroy the process of judging war crimes that the government has initiated—can this incident be part of that effort?'

'I don't know. All I want to know is where Jamila is now, how she is. Her three-month-old calf feeds only on milk; he's close to death without his mother. He just wants his mother back.'

A journalist from a national English daily said in a pointed tone, 'By the way, if the calf takes nothing but milk, then how has it survived all these days, almost a week actually?'

Muktadir shaheb was about to say something, but another reporter, from another English daily, which was in fierce competition with the first one, said in a loud voice, 'What is the meaning of these jokes?'

Immediately the journalist from the influential English daily protested, 'This is no joke. Muktadir shaheb is claiming that the calf feeds on nothing but its mother's milk. The mother hasn't been near it in a week. So how is this calf surviving? That is a very logical question.'

'But this is not a relevant question. Questions about Jamila's whereabouts have been raised here, and that is the most important question. She was taken from Pongu Hospital to Tejgaon station jail. That means governmental safe custody, for your kind information, my dear colleague.'

'Please don't try to teach me what governmental safe custody is. Why did you intervene in the middle of my question? This is very unfortoonet.'

'It's not unfortoonet, it's pronounced unfor-choo-net.'

'You, shut up. Don't teach me English—'

'Journalist brothers, my journalist brothers, please!' Abdul Muktadir shaheb pleaded with them in a tearful voice. His eyes had grown large; he placed his palms together in supplication and begged the reporters confronting each other to calm down, but his requests were in vain.

'You shut up and listen. Jamila disappeared while held in safe custody by the state; there can be no bigger human rights violation perpetrated by the government …'

'Oh, ho, ho, ho, ho. What words of knowledge, what wisdom!'

'Please, stop, now! This is a press conference, not a place for your quarrels.'

'Eh, useless! State safe custody! Four national leaders were killed while in prison in this country, and we're discussing this! End it, just end this press conference.'

'No, no! Jamila can't just disappear like a vanishing act. The state has to reveal her whereabouts. Because she was in the state's custody …'

'But the nation must also be informed how Jamila's calf has survived for a week without its mother's milk!'

'I'll tell you,' Mofiz spoke up. He was present at the Press Club to carry out errands for Muktadir shaheb. He had been standing in a corner of the conference room watching it all go down. He looked at the reporter who had asked the question and said, 'We have to buy three litres of Milk Vita daily for Jamila's son.'

5

Aside from the state-owned channel, every single satellite TV channel in the country broadcast Syed Abdul Muktadir's press conference. Several channels initiated live talk shows at midnight. One channel broadcast exclusive interviews with Muktadir shaheb and Mofiz; they showed footage of Jamila's starving, mourning calf: the dried up tear marks at the corners of its eyes, how Mofiz tried to feed it milk from a bottle but the calf turned away. Mofiz tried again and again to get the nipple into its mouth and failed. While this scene played, a sorrowful female voice could be heard in the background: 'How much longer does this innocent little child have to wait for its mother?'

The next day, all the national dailies published news of Syed Abdul Muktadir's press conference and his statements in great detail. Editorials, op-eds, news analyses and commentaries were written. Many readers called up the editorial offices and the news departments of the newspapers, as well as emailed them, to demand that the government disclose Jamila's whereabouts. Two human rights organisations, three environmental organisations, the National Lawyers' Association, the Supreme Court Bar Association, the United Women's Association, and the organisations of university teachers and students raised the same demand. Copies of a joint statement, signed by 101 intellectuals, reached the news departments of every newspaper and TV channel. Well-known intellectuals, professors, writers, poets, litterateurs, journalists, columnists, playwrights, filmmakers, actors, singers, dancers, painters, photographers, voice artists, magicians as well as the general public raised their voices demanding to know the whereabouts of Jamila.

In the afternoon, young men and women from an organisation, Young Citizens Endeavor, assembled in front of the national museum in Shahbagh with banners and festoons on which were emblazoned the words, 'Where is Jamila?' When a young professor from Dhaka University was giving a speech there, and a policeman suddenly snatched the microphone from him and instructed everyone to return to their homes, an argument broke out between the young people and the police. A rumour spread across campus that the police had attacked a revered professor. So, a protest rally approached the Shahbag intersection from the TSC area. The police obstructed the protest rally, which led to pushing and shoving between the police and the demonstrators. The pushing and shoving soon upgraded to pursuit and counter-pursuit. At one point, the police began wielding their batons and so the students and the other young protestors picked up rocks and bricks. When a rock broke a policeman's nose and he started to bleed, his fellow policemen began shooting at the sky. Three crows were flying overhead and one, shot dead, thudded onto the ground, and immediately fear spread everywhere in the Shahbag intersection, like splinters from bombs. When scared, bewildered people began running every which way. A bus ran over a pedestrian. The confused, fleeing people regained focus and attacked the killer bus. The protesting students joined them: bricks, sticks, iron bars, jerricans of petrol, matches. On the other side, the cracks and booms of the police firearms; and the screeching of millions of crows in the land and sky engulfed in tear gas.

The screeching of the crows continued throughout the night; the protesting crows flocked in the sky above the official residence of the home minister and screeched there. The crows screeched as they flocked together and circled above every single tree in the city, all the electric poles and wires in every single street, the cornices and rooftops of all the houses, the walls of various buildings and in the sky.

In their 9 p.m. news bulletins, the satellite channels reported: eleven members of the Dhaka Metropolitan Police had been pecked blind by crows. Seven among them were traffic policemen, one was stationed at the prime minister' office and the other three had been on sentry duty at the official residence of the home minister. They had lost one eye each while on duty due to surprise attacks from the crows.

Around 8 p.m., policemen on duty at the Nilkhet station fired their guns haphazardly at a flock of screaming crows in the Azimpur area. Three crows fell to the ground, shot, and the rest flew off towards the home minister's residence.

'There has been a slight deterioration in the law-and-order situation,' the home minister was heard saying on the 10 o'clock news. 'But this is nothing extraordinary, this can happen, it has happened in the past too,' the home minister continued in an unwavering voice. In a special interview granted to the state television channel, he said that a scheming group that was anti-liberation and anti-sovereignty had been trying to destabilise the country in the hopes of fishing in muddy waters. But the people of Bengal would not allow any conspiracy, any dreadful attempts they were going to make to be successful. The situation had already been brought under control; total peace and absolute safety had been ensured in Shahbagh and the surrounding neighbourhoods.

The announcement about the 11 o'clock human chain being organised the next day to protest the heinous attack on the youth demanding disclosure of Jamila's location, organised by the United Citizens Association, was broadcast on every TV channel and FM radio station except the state channel. And on the state television and radio channels, the announcement was made that from 8 a.m. to 2 p.m. the next day, the National Press Club and its surrounding neighbourhoods were under a curfew in accordance with Section 144.

The next day, from 7 a.m., Mohammad Ghulam Mustafa, a reputed non-violent, radical intellectual, vegetarian, unmarried, Gandhian, non-communal, Leftist writer and columnist, spread out bedding on the plinth of the Martyrs' Memorial and commenced a fast unto death. The television channels reported that he had sworn to continue his fast until the government made Jamila's location public. Five young men and three young women, members of the cultural organisation Dhaka Bratochari Shangha, surrounded Mohammad Ghulam Mustafa at the Martyrs' Memorial.

At eight thirty in the morning, a group of policemen approached Mohammad Ghulam Mustafa and requested him to leave the Martyrs' Memorial compound with his companions. Mohammad Ghulam Mustafa informed the police that since Section 144 had not been enacted for the Martyrs' Memorial area, this was where he would perform his fast. He opined that the police had no right to ask him to leave.

The officer leading the group of policemen spoke into his walkie-talkie. He was instructed by the police HQ: Clear out the Martyrs' Memorial right now, we don't want to hear any excuses. The officer slung his walkie-talkie in his waist pouch and gestured towards his colleagues. The four policemen moved forward as if they were commandos. When they attempted to haul Mohammad Ghulam Mustafa up by grabbing his arms and legs, they encountered strong resistance from the Bratochari men and women. There was much pushing and shoving, wrestling, hair-pulling and, at its peak, punching. The well-built Bratochari men wielded their hands, rendering the middle-aged, pot-bellied policemen flat on the ground, at which point, their officer pulled his gun out of the holster and fired two shots at the sky. At the sound of the shots, the Bratochari men and women looked at Mohammad Ghulam Mustafa, hoping for further instructions. Mohammad Ghulam Mustafa, the Gandhi follower, was about to say something, but when three other policemen grabbed his bony, lightweight body and ran down the steps of the Martyrs' Memorial, he bit down hard on the wrist of one of the policemen. The policeman yelled, 'Oh, Ma, I'm dead,' and when he yanked his wrist away, two of Mohammad Ghulam Mustafa's teeth fell onto the steps of the Martyrs' Memorial. One of the Bratochari young women picked up the teeth from the ground, wrapped them in a tissue, and placed them in her purse. Within seconds, Mohammad Ghulam Mustafa's gums and cheeks swelled up; his face distorted in such a way that when the officers of the state intelligence agency saw it on their television screens, they sensed impending doom.

Confrontations and clashes between youth and law enforcement agencies overtook different parts of the city. With incidents of offices, shops, departmental stores, hotels, restaurants and vehicles being vandalised, set ablaze or looted, anarchy descended all across the metropolis. All members of the metropolitan police force were deployed to regain control of the law-and-order situation; when this ended up only worsening the chaos, the BDR militia were deployed, and with the army under 'Be ready to move' orders, thirty-six hours of curfew was announced in the national media.

Within an hour, the streets of the metropolis emptied of all people and the silence of the grave descended.

Amidst that silence, at noon, the prime minister summoned the chief inspector of police, the director general of the Rapid Action Battalion, and the heads of the Detective Branch and the Criminal Investigations Branch to her office and issued her instructions: the people had to be informed within thirty-six hours about the whereabouts of Jamila.

But it was within eight hours, not thirty-six, that the home ministry's statement on Jamila was broadcast in news media: Following her medical treatment at Pongu Hospital, Jamila had been transferred to Tejgaon Police Station in the capital city. She had been tethered to a mango tree adjacent to the boundary wall of the station complex and provided with regular meals and hydration. On day three, in the deep of night, Jamila had ripped off her tether and disappeared from the station complex. The law enforcement agency had undertaken combing operations in the entire metropolitan area, but they had not been able to locate Jamila. The detective branch was conducting investigations to ascertain whether any scheming interests or individuals were holding her hostage in some secret location with the aim of tarnishing the image of the law enforcement agency and the government.

The next day, it was announced from the police headquarters that they had arrested Jamila from the Badda area. Fifteen minutes later, the Rapid Action Battalion aka RAB also claimed that they had arrested Jamila. According to them, the cow that the police had arrested was not Jamila.

There began a conflict between the two forces over this issue.

The Rapid Action Battalion aka RAB conducted a raid in Mansurabad and picked up Mofiz; after being held for twelve hours, he was taken to a cow and told, 'You're going to say in front of the media that this is your Jamila.'

The cow was chewing its cud and foaming around the mouth. It now looked at Mofiz and said, 'Bhai, my name is actually Rahima.'

The cow that the police had arrested blurted in front of the TV cameras, 'They said, if I didn't say my name was Jamila, they would slaughter me and eat me up.'

A senior police officer hit a TV camera with his baton and broke it. But he only broke one camera; the cow's statement was caught on tape on at least a dozen more. The television newsrooms all received a phone call: Not broadcasting the cow's statement would be beneficial for the nation, for democracy. In the interests of public order and national security, it is requested that you desist from broadcasting any footage of the cow or its statement.

As soon as that call was over, another arrived: irrefutable proof of what gigantic liars the police were had just been aired. You should broadcast the cow's statement with the actual footage and thus provide an outstanding example of responsible journalism and free flow of information.

The electronic and print media of the nation informed the people in almost the same voice that neither the police nor the RAB had succeeded in either arresting or rescuing the actual Jamila. The two cows arrested by the two forces from separate locations had no connection to Syed Abdul Muktadir or Mofiz. A few news outlets condemned the actions undertaken by these crucial state agencies to hoodwink the people.

There was no answer to where the real Jamila was and in what condition. The newspaper editorials opined: 'The police department cannot simply absolve themselves of responsibility by issuing a statement that Jamila had ripped out her tether and disappeared into the dark of night while in safe custody at the police station; rather this increases their responsibility even further.'

In addition to furthering the judicial process regarding Jamila, now there was the additional responsibility of locating Jamila and placing her in safe custody again. And in addition to all this, the issue of the weak security systems in police stations and the negligence displayed by members of the police force while on late night duty also came under the scanner.

Gradually, the critical tone of the news media began to soften. The ongoing intense screaming of the city's crow community also gradually quietened. A set of dentures were purchased with donations from a voluntary organisation and installed on Mohammad Ghulam Mostofa's gums. Silence descended on the intellectual community; and on the youth, exhaustion and dejection.

Except, in an online journal, blogger Dilbor Taus continued his efforts to keep the conscience of the people awake.

6

'The more I see and hear, the more apathy seems to be gaining ground. It is the actions of the major opposition party that is arousing the most vexation. In this moment of national crisis, the main opposition party has adopted the role of silent observer. History will never forgive them, never.

'An emergency meeting of the party's standing committee had indeed been convened. However, they were unable to reach a single decision. Instead, they vacillated over whether they should or should not take this opportunity to overthrow the government. They paid no heed to the fact that the nation was being decimated; they were wrapped up in their own schemes, in their desire to grab power.

'But even the courage to do that they could not muster …

'One leader stood up, looked at the chairperson and asked, "Are we prepared? I raise this question because during the small programmes we undertook, what happened was that we could not bear the burning sun and so we shortened the duration of our programmes and returned to our homes, to the cooling refuge of air conditioning. This proves just how eroded our will to sacrifice and suffer is. The police barely hit us once and we immediately shout and scream and wail and fall in the streets in a dead faint or pretending to faint. Then we are hauled into the prison vans by our arms and legs. And via electronic media, people watch these ludicrous scenes. They can see the condition our battles, our movement is in, or what an end our political promises and ethical resolve have reached. If the police take us into remand and even raise their voices, we shit our pants and are immediately at death's door. We stand in the courts and claim we are victims of bottle therapy and then proceed to describe that therapy in detail. Shameful! What a shameful thing! We stand in open court and say things like—a bottle was forced into my anus. We do not consider once what the people might think about a leader who has had bottles pushed into his anus.

'Another leader stood up and attacked the previous speaker. "Have you yourself been a victim of bottle therapy? Do you have any experience in the pain it causes? If you did, you wouldn't be able to say such a thing. It's the one who has suffered the pain that shouts."

'A cow was lost, crows died in police shootings, the police knocked out the teeth of a pacifist intellectual—the way these events aroused the people, their spontaneous protests, to the point where they forced the government to announce a curfew—compared to that, we, as the primary opposition party, were able to do nothing—this is breaking my heart.

'We did nothing; yet 1,300 of our leaders and activists have been arrested. Is that nothing? Have we kept ourselves informed about how the police are torturing them, whether they let them eat, whether they let them sleep?

'But how did the government have the nerve to make these mass arrests? They found the nerve to do this because of the disgraceful failure of our political promises and morale.

'Those who have been and continue to be the victims of torture will be properly valued at an appropriate time.

'When something occurs, the police conduct wholesale arrests of our leaders and workers, while they're also taking wholesale bribes. I won't even go into the issue of torture.

'We should not worry about all these expenditures. We will procure money again. Everyone must be patient.

'The duration of the Emergency Meeting of the main opposition party passed in such pointless discussion; they were unable to come to any decision about a specific plan of action. The truth of the matter was that they had not yet received the signal. They knew quite well that more time needed to pass before the signal would arrive. Hence, no matter how they proclaimed to rally the spirits of leaders and activists, they were unable to actually do anything. They knew very well that there was no real way to inspire the spirits of the leaders and activists when they had been out of power for three and a half years.

'Anyway, I shall waste no more time on the main opposition party. I shall now speak of our media, and attempt to show you the underside of those fine phrases such as untrammelled reportage, free flow of information, etc. Look, reader, the media flurry around Jamila has suddenly stopped. But they have not published the ultimate truth. Are you thinking that they weren't able to discover the truth? Then you're making a mistake. I am hoping that you shall not make such a mistake.

'Did the suspicion not arise in your mind that poor Jamila has become the victim of an extra-judicial killing? I assume it has. And this suspicion of yours is completely correct: Jamila has, without a doubt, become a victim of extra-judicial killing. I met an individual who is an eyewitness to this ruthless, dastardly murder. Before coming to me, he visited the head offices of five dailies and described, in detail, to the chief editors what he had seen. Similarly, he visited the senior officials of five satellite television channels and described his experience. But neither the newspapers nor the tv channels have published or broadcast his statement.

'Those amongst you who are interested in the nature of and trends in journalism, take note of this incident very carefully: how far can journalism go in this country—you will see just where, just how far, it can go before ending its journey. The eyewitness to Jamila's extra-judicial killing was an average member of the law enforcement agencies: a police constable. His name is Jagannath Saha. His father's name or his permanent address are not necessary. He told me that while Jamila was in safe custody, the employees of the law enforcement agencies slaughtered her, cooked her and ate her up, and sold her skin and divided the money amongst themselves. When they were about to slit her throat, their coworker Jagannath Saha had forbidden them. They did not listen to him. Jagannath Saha grabbed their hands and feet in supplication and wailed: Do not commit this sin!

'Reader, you must realise just how hard this Hindu man Jagannath Saha tried to rescue his sacred Mother Cow. But all his efforts, his pleading, and lastly, his invocation of the law—nothing succeeded in saving the Mother Cow. Just think about it: they simply slaughtered Jamila and ate her. I cannot quite decide whether terming this an extra-judicial killing is enough or appropriate.

'Now you will want to know, when Jagannath Saha conveyed this direct eyewitness account to the upper echelons of the news media, what did they say when rebuffing him? I, too, had asked Jagannath Saha this exact same question. He said that the bosses of the newspapers and the television channels told him, "We have heard your entire account. What a regrettable situation!" They lamented the situation by saying, "What is this country coming to day by day," and then said, "So, yes, we shall see what can be done."

'The reporter at one newspaper, on hearing Saha's account, pulled him aside and said, "You'll get into trouble—you already are: you don't have a job, and now your life will be at stake. You should immediately go to the embassy of that country and seek asylum."

'Subsequently, he himself accompanied Jagannath Saha to the embassy in question and, after presenting the entire account, requested them to grant him refuge. But the embassy bosses rejected Jagannath Saha without any explanation. Then the reporter took Jagannath Saha to the embassy of a European country, but the embassy people told them, "We can no longer deal with all this mess from your side. A few days ago, one of your journalists ran and took shelter here when he was pursued by your army, saying we had to grant him shelter on our soil, otherwise his life would be in danger. We gave him shelter at our embassy. Then we wanted to take him out and let him loose in the free air of our country. But how were we supposed to do that? We don't have the guts to take him to the airport from the embassy, in case something happens on the way. And now this case that you've brought here—we fear that this is even more crucial and complicated. We regret that we are unable to provide you with shelter in our embassy building. However, if, by some means, you are able to reach our country in one piece, then the law of our land will take on the responsibility of your safety."

'But Jagannath Saha could not make it to Europe. He had wanted to walk across the soil of his own country and flee to a safe distance. When he did, he was impeded by a barbed wire fence, and as he tried to overcome that barrier, he was fatally shot.

'I will say no more. I have already said more than enough. It is now time for me to prepare myself for bottle therapy.'

7

Cock-a-doodle-doo!

The rooster crowed from its cage on the rooftop next door. Jamila's calf moaned, 'Ha-amma!' Then he stretched out his neck, lowered his face, and exhaled so hard that all the dust around him blew away. There was a clank and then a sigh.

When Mofiz opened his eyes, he saw a pair of animal eyes right above him, just for a flash. Jamila's son's hornless head butted against his head, rattling his brain. He began to howl, 'Oh, maaaa, ammah!'

Akalu's Journey to the Land of Red Earth

1

In the villages of Roumari, when the last day of the month of Kartik stops in its tracks like a bullock cart with a broken wheel; when the *aaman* rice fields commence upon a terrible hostility, and that bastard rice crop swears not to ripen so easily because the field hands ought to be starved to death; when the dogs weep and whine in plaintive tones—that is when Akalu and others like him get the news that the rice paddies in the *khiyar* country, the region of red earth, have ripened. They head out immediately, rushing southwards in groups; there, they will find work harvesting rice, and there, they will be able to stuff themselves to their gills, three times a day, with tubs full of bright white rice.

When he reached Parbatipur, Akalu was ravenous. In general, he was always hungry, whether there was reason or not; but this hunger had reason. The road to Parbatipur had been very long. It had taken him two days to cross the vast sand banks on foot and then the Brahmaputra river on a scull, walking roads full of potholes, to reach the rail station at Kurigram and then, the junction at Parbatipur. Now Akalu's hunger knew no bounds. Darkness was descending on his eyes.

He shut his eyes and thought, 'Once I reach the khiyar, I'm going to eat so much, *so much* rice, my belly will explode.'

His thoughts drove his hunger to even more desperation. But he didn't want to dive into his only hoard of twelve takas, tucked into his waist. On the other hand, it felt like if he didn't toss something into his belly, his insides were going to digest themselves. Not that he had any objection to that—he wouldn't care at all whether his intestines remained fresh in his belly, or burned themselves to ashes, if only his stomach wasn't a raging inferno.

Therefore, Akalu spent a taka and bought a bun. But it was so small that he dispatched the entire thing to his belly in a single mouthful. It gave him the joy of having something in his mouth to chew but didn't quench the furnace burning in his belly. Instead, as if at the slightest of fuel, the fire raged higher.

He spent another taka. Even that didn't quell the lamentations of his belly. But Akalu decided he was not going to spend any more money here. He walked towards a rice hotel for some water. He thought to himself, It won't cost anything to drink a glass of water.

But along with the glass of water, he had to swallow a gallon of cursing. But curses weren't punches, so they didn't touch him. He bared his teeth in a grin and said to a hotel worker, 'Come, bhai, let me have another glass,' and poured himself a second glass of water from the plastic jug and, after chugging it down, with a distorted grin on his face, he wiped his mouth with the back of his right hand and exited the hotel. When he got to the station, he found none of his companions there; the train had left.

'I'm a fool!' he said to himself. Just like a fool, hand on hip, he stood on the edge of the platform.

Suddenly, someone called out, 'So … lost who?'

Akalu couldn't hear it clearly because of the crowd, but it seemed to him that someone had called him by name. He swivelled his neck to look back and saw a dreadlocked old man sitting on a length of red cotton fabric on the platform, looking right at him with a slight smile on his bearded face.

Akalu moved towards him. The old man said, 'Give me your right hand.'

Akalu was startled. 'Why?' Even though he could see the display of talismans and books interpreting dreams in front of the old man, he couldn't guess why the old man was asking for his hand.

'What do you mean why?' said the old man. 'Don't you want to know your fortune?'

Akalu understood what the dreadlocked man's business was. 'Will I have to pay?' he asked.

The old man smiled tenderly and said, 'Come here, give me your hand.'

'First tell me how much it'll cost?'

'Okay, just give me five takas.'

'No, I'm good. I don't need to know my fortune.'

'Come on, just give me three takas.'

'*Bahey*, I'm a poor man. I can maybe give you one taka.'

His voice dripping with sympathy, the old man said, 'Come, you can give me that.'

Akalu moved forward and sat on his haunches in front of the old man; he held out his right hand, holding his palm open. The old man pulled Akalu's hard, rough hand close. As he looked at the lines on his palm, the many wrinkles at the corners of his eyes began to ripple. With a trembling heart and eager eyes, Akalu stared at the old man's lined face with its beard and moustache.

'Hmm.' A muted, profound note emerged from the depths of the old man's throat.

Akalu asked in trepidation, 'What? What did you see?'

'Perils and misfortunes can be seen.'

'Eh?' Akalu yelped.

The old man looked him in the eye and said, 'Your body is not *napak*, unclean, is it?'

Akalu asked in a fearful tone, 'Why?'

'Do you use water after you piss?' The old man's voice was scolding.

Akalu forced out the lie. 'Yes, yes, I do, so what?'

The old man smiled like a generous but heartless angel and said, 'Lying is a sin.'

Akalu laughed like a little boy caught out in some mischief, and said, 'So what's written on my palm?'

'It's there: there are some perils and misfortunes.'

'What perils and misfortunes, *hujoor*?'

'Perils and misfortunes come to everyone's life at some time or another. But Allah also provides solutions.' As he spoke, the old man picked up a flat, square amulet from an aluminium box to his right. He clasped it in his right hand with veneration and, gazing at Akalu's face, he said, 'But your body is unclean now.'

Akalu couldn't figure out how to answer; hopelessly, he stared at the old man.

The old man waved his fist around, the amulet hidden inside, and said, 'In here is the sacred book of Allah. The entire holy Quran is contained within this amulet. Go, perform your ablutions and come back.'

'Do I have to pay separately for that?'

'You do. But I won't take too much from you. You're a good one, I can tell from your face.'

'How much?'

'For you, twenty takas.'

Akalu wailed, 'That's a disaster! You couldn't get twenty takas if you sold me off! Don't you all know that there's no work to be found anywhere in 'Oumari? We are starving to death here. If you all don't know that, what kind of fortune teller are you?'

The old man was unperturbed. The know-it-all smile on his face was undimmed. He told Akalu, 'Allah's words are a precious thing.'

'I get that. But tell me how it will benefit me to wear this talisman.'

The dreadlocked old man fluttered mystery in the corners of his eyes and said, 'What benefit do you want?'

'Give me an amulet so that I don't get hungry all the time.'

'You're mad. A person alive will always feel hungry. It's a dead man who feels no hunger.'

'Then I don't need that amulet.'

'*Arrey*, mad one, Allah has given us hunger, but He has also given us sustenance. That's not the issue. Life has perils and misfortunes.'

'What bigger misfortune can there be than hunger, bahey?'

Hearing himself being addressed as 'bahey' instead of 'hujoor,' the old man roared, 'What insolence!'

Akalu was dreadfully startled. The old man felt gratified. He stroked Akalu's head and said, 'Allah is the master of our sustenance. Why act so insolently with Him? Go, do your ablutions.'

Akalu said in a pleading voice, 'But, hujoor, I don't have twenty takas. All I have altogether is ten takas.'

The old man laughed and slapped him on the back. 'Go on, son, go do your ablutions.'

The mosque was right by the platform. A row of tube wells stood in front, where people were lined up, performing their ablutions. Akalu sat beside them, kneading his hands and feet as he washed them; he splashed water on his face several times and then he got up to hurry back to the old man. He bumped into a man who shouted, 'Son of a bitch, are you blind?' Akalu grinned and went on his way. When he reached, he saw that the old man was sitting there by himself, the same mysterious smile on his face. Akalu lowered himself on his haunches in front of him and held out his hand again. The old man suspended the silver square-shaped amulet by its thread and swung it, saying, 'Allah's holy book. The entire holy Quran. Be careful! Did you do your ablutions properly?'

Akalu nodded with a tremulous heart. The old man warned in a deep voice, 'Be careful!'

Akalu nodded again. The old man shut his eyes and muttered an *ayat* from Allah's book; then he opened his eyes and blew on the amulet three times. He gripped it in his fist and then held on to it, as if he couldn't bear to hand it over to Akalu, as if it was the most precious of possessions.

Akalu's right hand had already been spread out in front of the old man; now he started waving it around. Meaning, he was extremely eager to get the amulet. The old man placed it on Akalu's palm and closed his fingers over it. As if he wanted to say, 'Keep it hidden!'

Akalu held the amulet tightly in his fist; he kissed his fist and then, placing it in his *piraan* pocket very carefully, he touched the old man's feet in salaam. He said, 'What is the *fozilot* of this amulet, hujoor, what does it do?'

The old man said somberly, 'Perils and misfortunes will disappear.'

'And?'

'And what else do you want?'

'Hujoor, I just always want to eat rice.'

The old man pulled out a seeded banana from his sack. He peeled it himself, then muttered a prayer and blew on the banana three times. He held it out to Akalu and smiled tenderly.

Akalu accepted the banana with his right hand.

'Say *Bismillah*.'

Akalu pronounced *Bismillah* and bit into the banana. Countless seeds crackled loudly under his teeth.

'Eat it, chew it well and eat it!'

Akalu finished the banana in seconds. The old man laughed and said, 'What? Are you still hungry?'

'Even a hundred bananas like that won't fill my belly, hujoor. Give me something for my hunger!'

'You have Allah's sacred words with you. Allah will take care of everything. Now give me the *hadiya* for the amulet.'

'Hadiya?' Akalu almost wailed.

'Allah's sacred text, it doesn't come without an offering in return.'

'I only have ten takas, hujoor,' Akalu begged. 'I'm headed for the khiyar. There's no work to be found anywhere here, hujoor, I'm about to die from starvation!'

The old man said, solemnly, 'Bargaining over Allah's text? No, that's not good.'

Akalu grabbed the old man's feet and sobbed, 'Forgive me this time, hujoor!'

The old man slapped him on the back in an indulgent manner and said, 'What is of value, should not be accepted for free, you fool. Carry faith in your heart. Leave ten takas here; the banana is free—the fruit of Allah's tree.'

Now Akalu said, 'If you give one taka, you get back seventy?'

The old man nodded and said, 'Seventy thousand times more. You have to keep the faith in your heart.'

Akalu pulled out the last of his stash and placed the ten takas at the old man's feet. The old man looked at the money once, then placed his hand on Akalu's head and said, 'Allah will bring you good things. Keep the faith in your heart.'

2

Akalu sat dozing and swaying on the floor of the moving train, in the near darkness of an overcrowded car. The amulet that hung around his neck was alive, cool and quiet. As he nodded off, he saw rice paddies, spreading out into the horizon, as far as his eyes could see. In the sheaves of rice, grains had blossomed like white flowers. The aroma of rice permeated the field. The tip of Akalu's nose quivered and his nostrils flared.

Some other passengers were speaking in joyous voices, 'The paddy has ripened into rice, bahey! Now, just eat your fill. Eat as much as you can, bahey, keep eating. Even if you die from eating rice, that is some kind of peace!'

Akalu jumped into the rice field. It wasn't a field; it was a sea of rice. Like a shark, he began to gulp down clusters of rice grains as well as the sheaves.

'Eat, bahey, eat. Allah has given this to us; eat till doomsday and it still won't be finished.'

Akalu ate as he swam in the sea of rice. Not only with his mouth but with his entire body. White and aromatic, tonnes of rice entered his body through his skin.

But, alas, still his belly wasn't full, the fire wasn't quenched. Some people were saying, 'Allah, what deadly hunger have you given us! Will we now die from hunger?'

Akalu saw that all the rice in the field was gone; his belly was now swollen tight like a massive drum. He was lying flat on his back in the middle of a great field, with his belly risen up like a mountain. Villagers arrived in droves to drum on his belly, to sing and dance.

Then they hoisted Akalu onto their shoulders, as if carrying a corpse. They spoke amongst themselves, saying, 'He died, Akalu died from eating rice. Anyway, even that is some kind of peace.'

The men were carrying Akalu to the cremation ground. Had Akalu turned into a Hindu when he died? *Tauba, astag ferullah*, shame! Akalu stroked the living amulet that lay quietly on his chest with reverence. But the stubborn scene continued to exist in front of his eyes. There, the Hindu folks were burning their dead in the cremation ground.

'Where are you headed, bahey?'

'To the khiyar, bahey, to the land of the red earth. There's no work at all around here.'

'So who died then?'

'Nibaron. Nibaron starved to death.'

'*Bol Hari, Hari Bol!*'

The men were taking Akalu to the cremation ground on their shoulders. He lay there thinking, 'What sort of thing is this, bahey!'

Astonished, Akalu could only wonder. He had lost the strength to protest. He was now a corpse, and those who were carrying him to the cremation ground on their shoulders must be Hindus.

'So I really did die!'

The men chanted '*Bol Hari, Hari Bol!*' as they walked forward with his dead body. When they reached the riverside, they set the corpse on fire. Fire blazed all over Akalu. One from the group of mourners grabbed a wooden plank and slammed it down hard on Akalu's skull.

Akalu startled awake from his dozing. He saw that the man next to him was stroking his own forehead and saying to him, 'Are you hurt, bahey?'

Akalu laughed and said, 'Butting heads is a good game. But my head is like iron. Your forehead didn't crack open, did it?'

The man laughed this time. He smiled and asked, 'Where are you off to?'

'To the khiyar. There's no work to be found in this area; my ass is shrivelling up from starvation.'

'Hey, I'm headed for the khiyar too, bahey. Which village are you from?'

'Chitolmari. Which one is yours?'

'Shiyalmari. What's your name?'

'Akalu. What about you?'

'Abbas. So you're headed for the khiyar by yourself?'

'Don't even ask, bahey. Those bastards left me by myself and went ahead.'

Abbas said that unfortunately he too had been separated from his group, just like Akalu. They warmed up to each other as they chatted.

Abbas asked, 'Are you married?'

'I can barely feed myself, how will I marry!' Akalu laughed.

Before Akalu could ask, Abbas proffered, 'I married once. My wife died.'

'From starving?'

Abbas said, 'She had sores in her stomach. The doctor said it was called "ulcher". She died.'

Akalu said, in a consoling manner, 'If Allah keeps you alive, you'll find another wife.' Then he moved close to Abbas's ear and whispered, 'Do you have anything to eat?'

Abbas shook his head saying he had no food with him. He asked, 'You're hungry?'

Akalu said, 'Yes, I'm starving, bahey. It's been two days since I had rice. When I reached Parbatipur, I bought and ate two bun-breads, but damn, I barely felt anything in my belly. It needs about a couple hundred bun-breads. I think there's a giant inside my belly, bahey.'

Abbas smiled and said, 'Just get to the khiyar first. Then eat as much rice as you want—you'll eat so much, you'll lose your appetite for rice.'

Akalu asked eagerly if the farmers would give him as much rice as he could eat.

Abbas assured him as if he himself was one of the farmers. 'Of course! How much rice can you eat, bahey?'

Akalu told him he could eat a seer and a half's worth of rice at one go. Abbas laughed and jabbed at Akalu's shrivelled stomach. 'In that case, this belly of yours will go pop.'

Akalu chuckled. He asked Abbas that since the khiyar was such a large area, where exactly were they going in search of work? Abbas told him that he was going to the same place that he had gone to for aaman rice harvesting last year. The farmers there were good people. They weren't miserly; they cooked rice in gigantic pots in their households and they let their labourers eat their fill. Akalu, who was about twenty-five or twenty-six years old, who had never travelled to the khiyar to harvest rice, who had only heard stories about the harvest and the rice there, listened to Abbas speak of unending rice and the generosity of the farmers as he jiggled his feet.

3

As soon as Akalu and Abbas climbed off the train at dawn, several young men pushed and shoved them towards a corner of the platform. They saw that it wasn't just the two of them the young men were shoving. They were shoving and pushing many of the others who had just got off the train to one side. The young men's eyes were bloodshot; some carried big sticks, some canes. They shouted at them loudly, herding all of them towards a corner of the platform as if they were cows. They surrounded the group of men on all sides. Keeping a close eye on them so that none of them could slip through and escape.

'What's going on, bahey?' Akalu asked Abbas.

Abbas didn't have the chance to say anything. A young man grabbed the gamchcha tied around his waist and yanked. He said, 'Hey, you fucker, where do you think you're going?'

Abbas was taken aback and asked the young man, 'Why are you doing this? What do you want, bahey?'

'Sit here.' The young man yanked Akalu's gamchcha then and pushed him on the shoulder very hard, as if he was about to climb onto his back.

'What's the deal, bahey?'

'Sit, sit! Sit down, you fools! Nobody takes a single step.'

As if Akalu and the others were a herd of cows. They pushed and shoved against each other; some just sat down on the platform. One of the young men began a headcount as he smoked a cigarette. Another man came over to him and said, 'I need three.'

The young man told him, 'Ninety takas.'

The man yelled, 'What? Thirty takas a head?'

The young man said, 'That's right. Hand over ninety takas.'

The man started yelling even louder. 'What the hell are you doing? Is the country a free-for-all where you can do whatever you want?'

'Pay the money, take the men and leave quietly. Don't make trouble.'

'Thirty takas at ten taka a man. Not paying a penny more.'

The young man kicked the other man in the chest and said, 'You're the prince of which kingdom, eh? Get lost!'

Deflated from the assault, the other man said, 'Just the other day, I took men at ten takas each, bahey!'

Another man came over and said, 'I need seven men.'

'Two hundred and ten takas.'

The man was stunned at the boy's words. 'What did you say?'

A couple of police constables were lurking nearby and kept looking back at the crowd. The man shouted loud enough to make sure they heard: 'What is this torture? Is there no law and order in this country?'

The two police constables were now laughing. They did not come forward.

When Abbas stood up suddenly and stepped forward, a boy grabbed his hand. 'Hey, where are you off to?'

Abbas tried to wrest his hand away and said, 'Let me go, bahey!'

The boy cuffed Abbas on the head and said, 'Sit down, where do you think you're going?'

'What a load of trouble! Bahey, we're headed to Modhupur. We work there.'

'Pay us some money.'

'We are poor farmhands. It's the farmers who can pay,' Abbas said in a despondent manner.

'If you can't pay, you're not going anywhere,' the boy announced.

The pushing and shoving among the boys and the five men who had come to get their wages from the farmers turned into a fight. The boys began to whip everyone with their canes and sticks, and the men began to tussle with them. People converged at the station, rushing in from various directions; a loud commotion broke out. The two police constables stood at a distance, watching with amusement. Abbas took hold of Akalu's hand and said, 'Let's go, bahey!'

The two of them ran.

When they had crossed the town and reached the pucca road, Akalu asked Abbas, 'How far is this village of yours?'

'Ten miles.'

'We'll have to walk all the way there?' Akalu asked helplessly.

'Oh, yes,' Abbas said as he walked on, his head lowered.

'Why, isn't there a bus or something?'

'So what if there are buses? Won't you have to pay the fare?'

'Don't you have any money with you?'

'Do you?'

'I had ten takas, oh, bahey. A hujoor swindled me and took it. Gave me a talisman. Said all my misfortunes will disappear.'

'That's good news.' Abbas's voice held a rebuke.

'I'm a fool, aren't I?' Akalu disparaged himself.

Abbas didn't answer. Akalu understood why he had suddenly grown so dour. Abbas walked in long strides. He was quite tall, although bony. Akalu wasn't as tall as him; he matched his pace to Abbas's, like a younger brother.

When they had walked about ten miles and reached the extended backyard of Ibrahim Mondal's household, and Abbas shouted, 'Uncle, I'm back again,' it was 10 a.m.

Akalu didn't know how Abbas was doing. As for himself, if he could just lie down straight after eating his fill of rice, he would never wake up.

But the farm workers of Mondal's household had already eaten watered rice and gone off to the fields for the harvest. The rest of the household was also done with food for these hours. Preparations for lunch had just begun. So Akalu and Abbas didn't get any food other than some puffed rice with a sliver of palm sugar. But puffed rice wasn't something you could gorge on. There was a lot to be done with the teeth and tongue before you could send it to your belly. It didn't provide the satiation that rice did. Instead, the crisp sounds of chewing seemed a pointless exercise, because it never felt like the rice had actually reached the belly; it seemed to disappear straight from the mouth.

'Telling a lie and chewing on puffed rice are the same thing, bahey, there's no benefit to it,' Akalu said to Abbas as he chewed noisily on the crisp puffed rice.

A smile blossomed on Abbas's face.

4

A small field, as if a circular yard covered in gold. The field ended within eyeshot; it looked like the villages, covered thickly by trees, were hugging each other, encircling the field. From the western fields, the sound of rice being harvested rose from the three bighas of land owned by Ibrahim Mondal: together, the rice crops and the row of teeth on the serrated sickles created a mechanical whisper. An army of five had been harvesting rice since the morning; when Akalu and Abbas joined them, they numbered seven. Mondal's orders were that the seven finish harvesting all the rice from the three bighas in one day. There was no chance of cheating a little and indulging in chatter.

Eat as much rice as you can, but the job needs to be done right. Dillydallying, wafting the breeze over your skin to pass the days just wouldn't do.

Therefore, only rice being harvested in a mechanical whisper and only the heaving out of the seven tired men's laboured breaths could be heard.

Akalu's waist ached. His hands no longer wanted to work. His eyes felt stretched out, his legs cramped. And a fire burned in his belly.

'Since coming to the khiyar, I've not yet eaten a single plate of rice, o bahey!' Akalu muttered his sorrow out loud. But Abbas didn't hear him.

Akalu was wondering how long until it was lunchtime. He raised his eyes to the sky and saw that the sun had commenced its journey from the south to the southwest. Meaning that the afternoon was almost over.

Akalu jabbed Abbas, who was busy cutting the crop, with his elbow and said, 'What, bahey, do the khiyar people have no judgement?'

'Why? What happened?'

'Isn't it the afternoon? No bathing, no eating?'

'Be patient. How much can you eat?'

'When, bahey? When will they give us food?'

Abbas laughed. Akalu burned in annoyance. What kind of man was Abbas? Didn't he have hunger or thirst? And the other men, didn't they feel hunger? Thirst?

These questions arose in his mind, but he said nothing more. He vented his anger on the rice plants. The whisper of his sickle grew louder. The black backs of the labourers were shining with sweat. The whisper rode the wind, as did their breaths.

After a long while, Abbas elbowed Akalu in the ribs and said, 'Look over there, they're bringing rice for you. How much can you eat?'

Akalu turned around and saw that the young shepherd from the Mondal household was walking along the raised border of the field, a yoke with baskets suspended on either side balanced on his shoulder. What a beautiful scene it was; the young boy was dancing along the ridge, and from his shoulder pole swayed a *kolshi* pitcher and a tub. Akalu was counting the moments, counting the boy's steps. Beneath his tongue, on either side of his mouth, a salty fluid was gathering.

The shepherd boy reached and lowered his shoulder yoke on the ridge, stating like a grownup in a busy manner, 'Right, you all should eat now.'

Akalu rushed over and pushed aside the tub's lid. It was filled with bright white rice. A second upturned tub covered the kolshi. Akalu removed it to uncover a *ghonto* of kheshari and kalai legumes, very thick, like yogurt. Here and there floated bits and pieces of greens; green chillies and slices of onions could be spotted as well. But when he looked at the tub of rice again, Akalu's face fell.

'How many people is this rice for? Just this much for seven people?' he said. The other labourers began to laugh when they heard him. Because the tub of rice was not small.

Akalu scoffed, 'Bahey, will this rice fill even my belly? I thought the khiyar farmers weren't misers.'

The labourers were laughing. Abbas was laughing the hardest. As he laughed, he said in an indulgent tone, 'Mad, he's a mad one!'

Akalu said, 'Are all your bellies chicken bellies, bahey?'

Abbas chuckled and asked, 'And is your belly a *dabor*, for storing grain?'

'Not a bin, it's an ocean! My belly is an ocean for sure. I'm going to eat this rice all by myself. Bahey, tell them to bring rice for the rest of you.'

'Can you?'

'Can't I? You want to see?'

The labourers exclaimed together, 'Show us! We won't touch even a single grain. You eat it all by yourself. But if you can't finish it, you pay a fine.'

Akalu shouted, 'Challenge!'

The labourers shouted as well, 'Challenge!'

Akalu extracted the tub of rice from the yoke with both hands. He removed the smaller tub covering the mouth of the kolshi holding the legume ghonto, and although there were seven plates and a plastic glass, he tipped the waterpot and washed only his right hand. Then, without using plates or any other vessel, he placed the tub of rice in front of him and settled himself on the ground with legs splayed out. He upturned the entire vessel of kheshari ghonto onto the rice. And then he began to eat. Abbas and the other labourers surrounded him in a half circle. They had forgotten about their own hunger; on their faces were smiles of enjoyment.

Akalu was kneading fistfuls of rice with a little bit of the ghonto, shaping it into large balls and then popping them into his mouth. He moved his jaws once or twice, and then gulped it down.

And so it went. Akalu mixed the rice, made a ball, popped it into his mouth—didn't chew, just swallowed it down. This scene repeated itself again and again. Abbas and the others simply watched Akalu eating, him noisily gulping down the food. They glanced at his belly; they were surprised to see that the belly of the skin-and-bones Akalu wasn't swelling even the slightest.

Sweat beaded Akalu's forehead. Abbas and the others thought to themselves that now he would have to stop, because it just wasn't possible to eat food meant for seven people. But they could see no sign of him stopping. He continued to eat in the same way and his belly didn't swell up. Abbas and the others were astonished. They wondered if Akalu knew of some process to smuggle rice? Was he that legendary eater, the one who would visit various public feasts—such as *oroshes* held to commemorate holy men and *majlishes*—in various villages, and guzzle food, and everything he swallowed was somehow transported to the empty plates of his starving wife and children back home?

Half the tub was empty now. Abbas remembered that Akalu hadn't had even a sip of water in all this time. 'Hey, crazy one, have a few sips of water,' he said. Akalu didn't speak, only shook his head, dismissing Abbas's advice.

Now sweat was dripping from his forehead into the tub of rice. Sweat was furrowing lines along the back of his neck and shoulders. He didn't look up from the tub of rice; he had no time to spare.

The tub of rice grew empty. Akalu gathered the last of the rice into a handful. He took it into his palm and brought it to his mouth, opening up. But no, his hand, with the fistful of rice, descended. He put the rice back in the middle of the tub and exhaled heavily. When he expelled his breath, it felt as if there was no air entering his nostrils. He was suffocating. He raised his eyes and looked at Abbas.

As he stared at Akalu, it seemed to Abbas that Akalu's eyeballs were exploding. He said in a mocking tone, 'Well, what now? Your belly still isn't full?'

Akalu said nothing. The other labourers blurted out, 'Son of a bitch, what are we supposed to eat now?'

Akalu suddenly lay down, spreadeagled. But his breath seemed to stop at that. He propped himself up on his elbows, and splayed his legs, his arms holding up his upper body, and open-mouthed, he began to pant. But he felt no comfort. He tried to leverage himself up with his arms but couldn't manage to stand. He spread his arms out again and fell flat on his back. He gathered his hands over his belly and kept them there. As he gasped, trying to catch his breath, he said, 'Bahey, my belly's about to burst.'

Abbas and the others screamed in laughter.

Within minutes Akalu began rolling around on the ground. He writhed on the field of harvested rice and wept, 'I'm not going to make it, bahey, I'm dying!'

Akalu clasped the amulet to his chest with his right fist as he writhed on the ground and screamed in a choking voice, 'Oh, merciful Allah, forgive me! Please, forgive me!'

Abbas was laughing; the other farmers were looking at each other and laughing. The shepherd boy from the Mondal household clapped and danced.

The Meat Market

A week before Eid, my wife elbowed me awake at the crack of dawn and said, 'Go quickly.'

For a man who never managed to leave his bed before 9 a.m., this was sheer torture. But I couldn't protest. Like you, I too was afraid of my wife. No, I'm not afraid of being hit. Whatever else my wife did, she never hit me. I'm afraid of conflict. Protesting any of my wife's actions led to conflict. I, my brother, do not want conflict. I'm a very easy-going man.

Her continued jabbing ruined my slothfulness. But I had no idea what was going on, where I was supposed to go this early in the morning. I rubbed my eyes and asked, 'Where am I going?'

'You've already forgotten? Didn't I tell you last night? Go buy some meat. Eid's almost here. Meat's going to double in price any day now. Go on, get up!'

My bovine brother-in-law was fast asleep in the next room. She could have just sent him. But the loving heart of a sister couldn't bear to send out her brother, the virtuoso, so early in the morning in this bone-chilling winter. Therefore, I was the one who had to get up. As I slid my arms into my jacket sleeves, I asked, 'How much?'

'Ten kilograms.'

Who was going to eat ten kilograms of meat? No, my brother, I did not actually say this aloud. The question merely popped up in my mind. Let it pop up; how many men have the guts to spill all their questions to their wives?

As I counted my cash, my wife's advice flowed in a stream: 'Check the meat carefully before you buy it. Make sure they don't tamper with it. That's why you're being sent out this early. If they slaughter a sheep or a she-goat and try to doctor the *khashi* meat with that, you'll be right there to catch them in the act. Go on, hurry up.'

2

Even through the morning's haze, I could read the signage clearly: *East Rajabazaar Popular Meat Emporium. Excellent quality, pure khashi meat available here.*

Three other customers stood waiting in front of the shop. The black tar of the road was soaked dark red with blood. A khashi, a castrated goat, lay on the street with its throat slit open. Beside it, an employee of the shop was skinning a sheep with skilled hands. Beside him, two other butchers were slaughtering a bony, bearded she-goat, its dried-up udder resembling a raisin.

The three customers watched impassively. Their expressions were blank; there was no sense of urgency in them. They waited like obedient gentlemen. It didn't seem like the meat sellers were paying us any attention. They were absorbed in skinning the sheep and the she-goat. However, it was pertinent to wonder why the khashi splayed on the street hadn't already been skinned, its meat readied into cuts for sale. My common sense gave me the answer. They were going to separate the heads of the sheep and the she-goat, skin them and then take them out of sight. Then they would spike the khashi meat with the sheep and she-goat and sell it.

It was to make sure that we didn't fall victim to such a swindle that my wife had sent me here this early in the morning. In my head, I praised my wife for being so smart. At least they wouldn't be able to palm off their doctored meat to me.

The she-goat and the sheep were skinned in a flash. Then, just as quickly, they stripped the khashi of its skin. The other customers showed some signs of life. I shoved one of them aside and stepped ahead. I said, 'Ten kilograms of khashi for me.'

As he detached the khashi's front legs from its carcass, the shopkeeper said, 'You'll have to wait.'

The same technique was being applied to dismember the she-goat and the sheep. I waited. The other customers had arrived before me, so their orders began to be weighed first. Meat, bones and layers of fat were cut off from the carcasses of the khashi, the sheep and the she-goat, mixed together and piled onto the scales. The customers said nothing; they didn't protest. Their eyes and faces were expressionless, as if this was the norm.

I asked one of the other customers, 'What's this, bhai? What's happening here?'

The man looked at me and laughed in a way that made me feel like I was a fool, as if I had no experience at all in buying meat. The two other customers also glanced at me and laughed in the same way. The employees of the butcher shop continued their work of slicing and weighing the meat in a grave, busy manner.

I said to one of the staff, 'Give me ten kilos of khashi.'

'Getting it, sir, just wait a little.' He turned to his coworker and said, 'Hey, Soleiman, ten kilos for sir.'

Tall, gangly, angular-jawed, with bloodshot eyes and a cigarette dangling from his lips, Soleiman reached for the sheep. I shook my head in protest. 'Not sheep, not sheep. I wanted the khashi.'

'There's no mutton sold here, sir,' replied the first man as he served another customer.

I pointed at the carcass of the sheep and said, 'What's this then?'

'Khashi, it's all khashi.' Gangly Soleiman employed the knife on the limbs of the sheep as he spoke.

'I'm not taking this khashi of yours.' I pointed to the remnants of the actual khashi and said, 'Give me whatever's left from that one.'

'Not happening.' When the other customers heard the shopkeeper's dismissive response, they roared with laughter.

'Why? Why not?' I spoke quite harshly now.

The shopkeeper repeated in a sombre tone, 'Not happening.'

'Why not?' I shouted again.

'Go on, don't make any trouble here.'

'What do you mean, trouble? This is a rip-off! You're selling mutton as khashi meat right in front of my eyes ...'

'Don't shout. Just be quiet and go home.'

'Hey, mia, what do you mean, go home? What the hell is this, you just do whatever you want?'

'Yes, I do. Don't give me that heat. Go home.'

'What heat, you damn fraud!'

'Just go home while things are still okay. Otherwise, they'll take a bad turn.'

'Is that a threat? Are you threatening me?'

'Yeah, I am. Shut your trap right now and go home. Or else ...'

I'm not a brave man. I should have been terrified by the grim threats delivered in such a cold manner by the butchers. But who knows why, I wasn't the least bit frightened. Instead, I flew into a rage. Belligerent, I said, 'Or else what? What are you going to do to me?'

Gangly Soleiman raised his bloodshot eyes to mine as he honed one knife against another, and said, 'Slaughter you.'

I was livid. How dare a shopkeeper speak to a gentleman like this? Who did they think I was? I shouted, 'You sons of pigs, do you know who I am? Do you know what I can do to you? I'm going to destroy this scam of yours, and as for you—'

Before I could finish, the first butcher stood up straight, reached out with his right hand, and grabbed me by the throat. Newly arrived customers joined the earlier ones, and stood in a circle around us, preparing to watch the scene. I moaned and flapped my fingers, blustering. As my breath was cut off, my eyes spun, the eyeballs ready to pop.

The butcher dragged me by the throat and shoved me against the shop wall. Gangly Soleiman came forward with a long, shiny knife. The other butchers slammed me onto the ground, flat on my back, and held me down. I screamed as I flailed my legs. But the gentlemen waiting to buy meat merely watched like silent spectators. No one stepped forward to help me or restrain the butchers. They looked on with childlike curiosity, some with their hands resting on their hips, some with their weight resting on one leg, as if watching monkeys perform on the streets.

One of the butchers received a kick from my desperately thrashing legs and was knocked aside. Immediately two others rushed forward. They gripped my legs hard and, pulling them straight, climbed onto my knees and just stood there. Another man yanked my arms above my head and pinned them down with his knees. It became impossible for me to move at all. Gangly Soleiman grasped my unshaven, rough chin tightly with his left hand and yanked my head back. I pulled my head down closer to my chest with all my strength to try and protect my throat with my chin. But Soleiman's hands possessed demonic strength. He pushed my chin upwards so hard that my neckbones cracked loudly. Goggle-eyed, I saw Soleiman's bloodshot eyes turn into fireballs. Hot air issued from his nostrils, scorching my eyes and face. He bit down on his lower lip and lowered his hand that held the long, shiny knife.

3

Soleiman's long, shiny knife settled on my taut throat and began sawing forward, and then, after a moment's pause, sliding backwards, moving deeper every time it moved forward. My spirit was released completely from my body. Utterly unburdened, as if floating in air, I watched as Soleiman hunched over Aminul Islam (which had been my name in your world), the shiny, sharp blade sliding deeper as it moved forward and almost disappearing in the meat, fat, bones and cartilage of the neck as it slid back. Blood poured out in gouts from his throat, in a thick stream, while the blood coming out of the veins emerged in a spray with more force. After running the knife through a few more times in the same manner, Soleiman pulled back his hand and wiped off the blood that had splashed on his face with the flat of his palm. Aminul Islam's body thrashed and thumped on the black tar of the road until his flailing limbs gradually slackened.

Aminul Islam's slit throat gaped at the sky. His stilled eyes, wide, gazed to his right. The gentlemen who wished to buy meat surrounded him, looking on with their hands folded at their chests or their bellies, as if standing in prayer. They were waiting. They were very amenable gentlemen. They preferred not to embroil themselves in any trouble. They never poked their noses in the business of other people. They bought meat. They knew that beef was spiked with water-buffalo, or that the meat of she-goats and sheep were mixed in with khashi meat and sold as pure khashi. They were quite used to these things. They never went to the shops or the marketplace intending to buy water-buffalo meat or mutton. They knew one couldn't buy the meat of sheep, she-goat or water-buffalo in this city. Every night they saw herds of sheep, she-goats and water-buffalo on the city streets. But they knew that the meat of sheep wasn't sold in this city, the meat of she-goat wasn't sold in this city and the meat of water-buffalo wasn't sold in this city. They had no qualms about buying or eating mutton passed off as khashi.

Not only the meat trade, they weren't troubled or dissatisfied or in turmoil over any issue related to society or the world. They were citizens of the happiest nation on earth. Foreigners uncovered this fact by conducting public opinion surveys.

A little while ago, when I was still Aminul Islam, at the moment I was being slaughtered, I'd wondered in astonishment: had this country become an anarchy? (Perhaps one is only faced with this question when one is personally in danger of being slaughtered.) I was thinking, this attempt to slaughter a human being was taking place in broad daylight, in a public place, in front of so many people—how was this even possible? I couldn't imagine that it *was* possible. Even in my last moments I thought, these butchers are certainly enraged, but even if they injure me or whatever, they're not going to slit my throat. Slaughtering a human being just because you're angry—does that really happen?

But the whole thing was over before I could even comprehend what was happening. After my release from the prison of Aminul Islam's body, I saw that such things took place very easily in this country. In fact, things even more unthinkable occur. (Unthinkable for you. As you use words like unthinkable, unimaginable, impossible, unprecedented, gruesome, you can see for yourselves, day and night, night and day, how many different incidents are taking place all around you. You yourselves are making them happen.)

Gangly Soleiman positioned a wood chopping block under Aminul Islam's neck and hacked at it with a fairly heavy cleaver. With a thwack, he separated Aminul Islam's head from his body. He transferred the cleaver from his right hand to his left and grabbed a handful of Aminul Islam's hair. He stood up straight with Aminul Islam's head dangling from his hand. Aminul Islam's eyes stared towards the right like before.

Soleiman swung the head as he took it inside the shop. Two other men hoisted Aminul Islam's body and followed him. Inside, Soleiman placed Aminul Islam's head on the floor and thumped it with the handle of the cleaver. The cleaver hit with a *phat* sound, but Aminul Islam's brains didn't spill out so easily. It takes some effort to get at the brains of goats or cows; a human skull is no softer. Soleiman had to work at it. After a couple of more tries, he managed to crack the skull open on one side. It became easier. He pulled Aminul Islam's brain out with his fingers and, using his palms and fingers, positioned it nicely in an aluminium pot.

The two other butchers were a little bewildered due to their inexperience and pondered how to skin Aminul Islam. Human skin isn't as thick or furry as that of a cow, goat or sheep, so one couldn't just yank it off. The man Aminul Islam hadn't been at all plump. But when the butchers worked the knife on him, they observed that under his very thin skin there was just fat. If they tried to insert their fingers between the skin and the fat and tried to press it apart, the skin simply ripped.

Which actually helped. Someone came up with the idea that boiling water would make the process of skinning Aminul Islam's body much easier. By then, Ruchita Hotel and Restaurant, located across from the meat shop, had opened up for business. A bucketful of boiling water was brought over from there, and Aminul Islam's skin removed. After this, extremely skilled hands began the butchery process, separating the carcass into pieces. Within a short time, they extracted at least forty-five kilograms of sellable meat from Aminul Islam's sixty-five-kilogram body.

Aminul Islam's fatty meat was mixed in with the cuts of khashi, sheep and she-goat, and was put out for sale. The customers bought the meat in a peaceable manner before heading homewards. They knew that there was no such thing as pure khashi meat in the market: it was always adulterated with sheep and she-goat. So it didn't make that much difference if it was now also spiked with some human meat. Therefore, the meat market continued as usual. There was no disruption anywhere.

4

It was already 7 a.m., but there was no sign of Aminul Islam returning with the meat. Seething, his wife began to rant against her useless husband. When the clock hands crossed seven-thirty and were about to reach eight, Aminul Islam's wife Rubina Sultana jerked her younger brother awake from his happy dreams.

'See, what your Dulabhai's done? He went to get the meat ages ago but not a sign of him anywhere. He's just hanging out somewhere for sure. Just wait till he's back, I'll teach him how to have fun. Get up, come on! Go and bring back ten kilograms of khashi meat. Ah, will there be any pure khashi left this late! We'll have to eat meat doctored with sheep and goat, and that's what we'll have to feed our guests. What, why aren't you getting up? Can't you hear me?'

'Sure, I'll bring ten kilograms, but what if Dulabhai too brings back ten kilograms? Where will you then store so much meat?'

'I'll store it on your head! Does your Dulabhai even remember that I sent him out to get the meat? He has probably completely forgotten all about it and is just standing somewhere, chatting away. He's going to come back with that cash still in his pocket and then bite his tongue and say, oh, I forgot! Then I'll teach him a lesson in forgetting. Now come on, get up!'

'Why are you assuming that Dulabhai is hanging out somewhere? There might have been an accident. Who knows if muggers got him!'

'Don't blather. It's a three-minute walk from here; are muggers going to come right into our neighbourhood? And you think I don't know your Dulabhai?'

If, within that three-minute walk, right in the neighbourhood, muggers had caught Aminul Islam, taken his money and stabbed him in the gut, it really wouldn't have been surprising. Because in reality something much worse had happened. But no such apprehension arose in Rubina Sultana's mind. The people in this country no longer lived in anxiety. They saw the man next door being murdered in the middle of the street in the middle of the day; like foxes snatching a chicken, young men grabbed a young woman on her way home from her job at a garment factory, and they gang-raped her in the sliver of space between two houses right on the street; because the paan-seller paid ten takas less than the extortionists demanded, his shop, with the seller inside it, was doused in petrol and burnt to ashes. But everyone thought calamity would visit other people: I'm safe; nothing can happen to me.

Rubina Sultana was also in possession of a normal sense of safety. Until she received confirmation that her husband was in the clutches of muggers, she would think that such a disaster might befall someone else but not her husband. Her husband had merely forgotten to buy the meat and was holed up somewhere, unworried, drinking tea and talking up a storm.

5

My brother-in-law came home with ten kilos of khashi meat. It included meat from my thigh, my arm and my ribs, some fat, and some tender bones from my chest area. Although the meat was meant for Eid, he asked his sister to cook a portion for lunch today. The sister was always very loving towards her brother. It had never happened that he had asked for a particular dish and she hadn't cooked it for him. So, with a lot of care and a lot of spices, she cooked the meat.

Brother and sister sat down to lunch together in the afternoon. She lovingly served pieces to her brother, and then placed a few on her own plate.

I shouted, 'Rubina, don't eat! Rubel, don't eat!'

But my shouting was probably inaudible. I had left behind the world of sound.

My wife bit down on one of my ribs with pleasure and praised her brother. 'You've bought some wonderful meat, Rubel. From now on, you're in charge of buying meat. Your Dulabhai is just useless.'

Pony Masud

An Account of the Tangled Stories and Gossip about him as Narrated by the People of Roop Nagar

1

The people of Roop Nagar believe that daybreak dreams come true. In which case, Pony Masud's death during a 'crossfire' with the Rapid Action Battalion aka RAB was inevitable, because right after the hour for the fazr prayers, as she lay in the house of her son's stepfather Brickly Mukhles, Pony Masud's mother Laili Begum dreamt that her son's chest was riddled with bullets; hot air was pulsing out of the holes in his lungs, and she could hear the call of, 'Ma! Ma!' coming from that air.

When the Dhaka newspapers reached Roop Nagar that morning, people saw the headline printed out in big, red letters: *Top Terror Pony Majid Arrested by RAB*.

Laili Begum began weeping with hawk-like shrieks and then added a sad, prolonged tune. The people of Roop Nagar told each other, 'Laili Begum is doing the *binaki*, the lamentation.'

When it was discovered that the terrorist who had been arrested was called Pony Majid, not Pony Masud, Laili Begum's grieving lessened somewhat. But soon she was wailing loudly again because it was her belief that the newspaper people had misprinted Pony Masud as Pony Majid.

The people of Roop Nagar weren't sure whether there was a terrorist in Dhaka called Pony Majid because it was now quite impossible to count the number of such miscreants operating in Bangladesh.

So they were unable to console Laili Begum by telling her that the man who had been arrested under the name of Pony Majid wasn't her son Pony Masud. And Laili Begum's sobbing continued. As she continued 'doing the *binaki*,' she went to the house of Pony Masud's actual father, Majed-the-Principal. She didn't find him home because the principal was busy with something important at the college: a hundred and seventy-five students had sat for the B.A. exams from his college and not a single one had passed, so now his college was about to be dropped from the list of colleges that received the governmental MPO or monthly pay order. 'What to do, what can be done,' etc. were topics that the college committee members were now discussing in a meeting.

'My son's been killed, and his father's attending meetings! I'll show him meetings!' Muttering, Laili Begum took a rickshaw van and headed for Atapara College, which was eight miles away. But on her way there, she was stopped by Brickly Mukhles.

Brickly Mukhles, lover man, waylaid his woman Laili Begum because he was afraid that the news of the death of the child she had carried in her womb was bringing her and the actual father of that child back together again. 'I'll bring back news of your son,' he told her. He pulled her by the hand, got her into a rickshaw, and took her home.

When she reached home, Laili Begum flung herself on the bed. Her wailing gradually turned into whimpers.

Laili Begum's daybreak dream would come true; Pony Masud's actual father Majed-the-Principal would have to travel to Dhaka to take possession of his dead body; Laili Begum would instruct her second husband, Pony Masud's stepfather Brickly Mukhles, to accompany Majed-the-Principal to Dhaka; and if Laili Begum issued an order, not even Brickly Mukhles' father would dare to ignore it; and so, after many years, the people of Roop Nagar were able to see Laili Begum's former and current husband together, side by side—and amidst all the gossip and imaginings, it was said that on that very morning, a mysterious old beggar had shown up in Roop Nagar.

He had walked along the street past Majed-the-Principal's house, muttering, 'There's news, oh, is there news!' The old man, with his moustache and beard as white as jute, and his deep black robe, had said, 'There's news, oh, is there news!' and then disappeared, and even after he disappeared, his voice rang out in the wind, 'There's news, oh, is there news!'

The mysterious old man had stepped foot in Roop Nagar again after many years and pronounced in an infallible voice, 'There's news, oh, is there news!' and right away the Dhaka newspapers rushed in with the news that a person, whose name the journalists had mistakenly recorded as Pony Majid, who couldn't possibly be anyone other than Pony Masud from Roop Nagar, had been captured by RAB, the law enforcement force that Allah Himself had sent along.

Thus, the people of Roop Nagar were reminded of days past; they became engrossed in wild stories and gossip about Pony Masud.

2

That morning, Masud had gone to his stepfather Brickly Mokhles' house with the intention of seeing his mother. Brickly Mokhles wasn't home. What could have transpired if he had been home and met Masud was a matter of varied conjecture. At any rate, Masud hadn't gone to see his stepfather, he had gone to see his mother. So it was irrelevant whether Brickly Mokhles had been home at that moment or not; but the people of Roop Nagar loved to pull in the tangential, the non-relevant, into any topic under discussion. Pony Masud had gone to Brickly Mokhles' house: this was big news in the town of Roop Nagar. But before asking why he had gone there, the people of Roop Nagar wanted to know whether Brickly Mokhles was home at the time, and whether the two of them had come face to face with each other. If they had, what would have happened then was something that every Roop Nagar resident could imagine for themselves. For some, perhaps, it was even beyond their imagination.

Anyway, Brickly Mokhles wasn't home right then, but Masud's mother was, as usual; on seeing her son, the woman had apparently not even asked how he was doing, but said in an urgent manner, 'Drop off ten thousand takas.'

From that, some people surmised that this was the first time Masud had gone to meet his mother since she had moved in with Brickly Mokhles, but that wasn't the case. Actually, Masud's contact with his mother was unbroken throughout; not only that, he would quite often give his mother money.

Some people said that it wasn't as if Masud gave his mother money because he really wanted to; the mother often asked the son for money, and if his dear mother wanted some, the only son could never leave his mother's presence without forking over some cash.

Many people said that because the mother's maw was always wide open to eat, the son had to make money through extortionist practices, but others did not support this reasoning. They said that Masud himself had wanted to get rich quick, and because the young man realised that extortion was the easiest way to obtain wealth in Bangladesh, that was the method he chose. How Masud had discovered the easiest and shortest path to wealth at such a tender age was what astonished the people of Roop Nagar. Of course, they knew that not everyone could embark on the shortcut path to gaining wealth just because they wanted to—Masud had both the quality and the courage to do so, and also the opportunity played right into his hands, and therefore, it was impossible for him to become anything other than what he became.

But, of course, on this issue, Masud's mother had to have some influence as well. The people of Roop Nagar said many derogatory things about Masud's mother, the runaway wife of Majed-the-Principal, but when they witnessed Masud's attachment to that very same woman, they couldn't help but praise the boy. That day when his mother asked for 'about ten thousand takas', Masud had about eight thousand in his pocket. He felt very small; to his mother, he said, 'Patience,' and then he left Brickly Mokhles' house and got on his horse, roared its engine, and rushed to Murari's seat of business, and there he saw Murari Prasad sitting in between two huge bolsters and dozing. It was then that Masud had demanded ten thousand takas from Murari Prasad. Many people thought that Murari had hemmed and hawed at first, because '... there isn't another *maura*, a Marwari businessman, you know, not in all of Roop Nagar as big a tightwad as that one.' But it was impossible to slip out of Masud's grasp, and finally Murari Prasad wrote out a cheque for ten thousand takas and signed it with a trembling hand and held it out to Masud, and Masud plucked the cheque from him and then kicked him right in the face, and therefore, Murari Prasad, that young man of thirty-six, who weighed eighty-two kilograms and his flabby body (fed on ghee and butter), trader of iron rods and cement, emitted a dull moan from his mouth and he 'upside somersaulted', meaning he fell flat on the ground from his seat, and Masud 'slid into the chamber' of the manager of the Roop Nagar branch of Sonali Bank. The manager told him that the amount mentioned on the cheque would be deposited to Mohammad Masudur Rahman's account a day later, but Masud solemnly informed the manager that he wanted that money straightaway. As soon as the manager, in fearful politeness, uttered, 'But that isn't poss ...', meaning that Masud didn't even give him the chance to pronounce the word 'possible' in full, Masud slapped him on the cheek. The sound of the slap in the crowded bank alerted the bank employees and they rushed over and then Masud '... pulled out his live-wire pistol from his pocket'. Several bank employees began to rush around when they saw the gun, crawling under tables and chairs like little boys, and a few of them grabbed each other trying to hide their heads and faces under each other's armpits, against shoulders, in their arms, and others began 'shouting-spouting' for no good reason and yelled, 'Robbers! Robbers!' and therefore, the knees of the single security guard with the double-barrelled gun on duty at the bank's scissor gates began to knock against each other.

Later on, people joked that the reason the bank employees created that ruckus was less because they themselves had been afraid, but more to scare the 'scurty guard'. That day, if he had wanted to, Masud could easily have helped himself to all the cash in the bank, and then gone back to his stepfather Brickly Mokhles' house unhindered and poured out sacks of money at his mother's feet, and breathed in deeply, filling his chest; but instead of doing that, he strode out of the building amidst all the 'shouting-spouting' or fearful ruckus of the bank employees, and then climbed onto the seat of his Yamaha 124 motorcycle, which leant on its kickstand in front of the bank (which the people of Roop Nagar never called a motorcycle, they called it Masud's pony). Masud started the engine and then kept revving the accelerator with his right hand, as if he were tweaking a horse's ear, and so the horse kept rumbling like a stubborn beast and emitted white smoke (according to the description from the uncouth wags of Roop Nagar, 'Masud's pony was farting') and that constant curl of smoky farts gave rise to cloud clusters. Thus, he expelled his rage through the anus of his horse for much longer than was necessary, and then, shaking the air and the sky of the town, he sped off like an arrow, but nobody could say for sure in which direction.

The news immediately reached the police station which was five hundred yards away from the building in which Sonali Bank's Roop Nagar branch was located, but the police did not step foot at the incident location as soon as they heard about it; they came slow and steady, after they had indulged their bellies with the midday rice-curry and puffs of tobacco. They listened to the account and commented that robbing a bank was indeed a serious criminal offence; however, Masud had not carried out any such crime, and therefore, there was no need for the police to busy themselves over this. And anyway, in their language, because he had 'done a scene-create', therefore, with blinking eyes and pursed lips, they enquired of the bank manager whether he was interested in filing a case or a general diary regarding this issue. Sonali Bank's Roop Nagar branch manager, who had a wife lusciously ripe at thirty-six years of age, a sixteen- year-old daughter, and a precious son of twelve in his household, shook his head, right to left, hard, in response to the police's jokey question. According to the descriptions of the people of Roop Nagar, his headshaking was worth watching because it was as if Masud was still standing right in front of him with his gun and the police officer was smiling with his eyes while testing his nerves.

A little while later, the ruling party Member of Parliament Mr Abu Karim himself showed up at the scene; he expressed indulgence about Pony Masud by referring to him as 'that wild lad' and rained disapproval on the bank manager regarding why the wild lad's whim had not been humoured. The leader shouted within earshot of everyone present that Masud had not gone there to rob anyone, he had gone there to cash a cheque, which was not at all a criminal act; it was, in fact, the bank manager himself who was in the wrong by not giving Masud's urgent requirement the appropriate level of importance.

The people of Roop Nagar said that Masud had been quite capable that day of grabbing every single bank note in Sonali Bank's Roop Nagar branch and laying it at the feet of his dear mother and that would have been natural for him. Of course, it wasn't as if just because he was quite capable of going into any bank at any given moment and taking as much money as he wanted and leaving without any obstruction, he was doing this every day; instead, the truth was that when he went to the bank for something as basic as cashing a cheque and encountered such resistance from the manager, it would have been quite normal for him to react with something as daring as firing a shot, or assaulting the manager more severely, or cleaning out the cashiers' drawers or something like that. But why he hadn't reacted like that on that day was something for which the people of Roop Nagar could not find an explanation. To them, the mystery of most of Masud's (the one whom they called Pony Masud) actions was unclear. For instance, they never could find a good answer to the question of why, when his mother Laili Begum abandoned her husband Majed-the-Principal's household, as if it was a desert, and ran away holding the hand of Mokhles Ali, aka Brickly Mokhles, who was the former owner of a brick kiln, Masud didn't shoot off Brickly Mokhles' testicles.

3

Most people in this area referred to Roop Nagar as 'oop Nagar. The adjective 'roop', indicating beauty, they pronounced as 'oop' but not as a slight; if the most basic form of a city or a *shohor* was a suburb or an *ooposhohor*, then calling Roop Nagar, city of beauty, 'oop Nagar' could never detract from the beauty of this locality. In fact, the folks on whose tongues the sharpness of Roop Nagar's 'roo' was lost in the pronunciation of 'oo', were the farmers and peasants from the nearby villages. Their forefathers called the rajah 'ajah' and the queen, 'ani-ma' instead of rani-ma. They call the hero of legend Roopban 'oopban', and the division of Rongpur, to which they belonged, 'ongpur', and following the same rule, the word for politics, *rajniti*, became 'ajniti' in their pronunciation, although they were more used to deploying the English term for it: 'poltics'. Most of the time, 'poltics' was not related to the state; instead, they used this word to indicate the deceitful, conspiratorial actions and mindsets of people. Among folks who were educated or who were studying, the letter 'r' was something to be intensely aware of. Blurting out 'oop Nagar' due to carelessness was a matter of terrible shame. Those who underwent such a downfall aroused suspicions in the minds of their audience regarding their refinement. Not all inhabitants of Roop Nagar were gentlemen; just like everywhere else, there too the lower classes were large in number. Even these people sometimes became excessively cautious regarding pronouncing the letter 'r'; it was not a rare occurrence that some of them would call the Eid festival 'Reid', to try and ascend to the genteel class.

The people of Roop Nagar town did not talk like the villagers around them. In terms of verb usage, they had left the village and moved closer to the city, but they had failed to obtain the conviction of the city dwellers. For instance, the villagers, when they use the verbs *korochhi*, *dhorochhi*, *marochhi*, they mean *korchhi*, *dhorchhi*, *marchhi*—doing, catching, hitting. The genteel folks of Roop Nagar town had most probably attempted something similar, but for what reason these verbs took the form of *korichhi*, *dhorichhi*, *marichhi* on their tongues was hard to ascertain after such a long time. Perhaps they were shy about pronouncing it *korchhi* because it felt too cultivated. But saying *korochhi* was, in their judgement, too rustic; thus, they adopted a middle ground and began pronouncing it *korichhi*, and felt satisfied by considering themselves refined and such pronunciation as ascension from unsophistication. These verbs no longer create any discomfort or wariness in them, as does the usage of the letter 'r'.

Roop Nagar was a subdistrict about two decades ago; it had become a district due to the magnanimity of (former president) H.M. Ershad. Ershad was a guy from Rangpur; Rangpur wasn't far from Roop Nagar; it was about a hundred miles to the south. Roop Nagar was a small town; about four or five miles on the east-west side and about four miles on the north-south segment—the people of Roop Nagar had not measured it out with a measuring tape. There was only one big road, the main road. A couple of buses or five-tonne trucks could make it side by side along the road. The road ran from east to west or maybe west to east. It's better to say west to east because there wasn't that much land belonging to Bangladesh towards the west; there would be an obstruction in about ten miles. People call it India. There was no barbed-wire fence at the border; there were rumours that one was about to be built, but it hadn't happened yet. If it had, it would be a nuisance—it would become difficult to bring in salt, sugar, saris, weed, Phensedyl, heroin, and even smuggling bell metal-brass-gold would be a bother.

The town had grown depending on that single main road; the houses all looked towards that pathway. The structures on either side of the road were shops, banks, clinics, beauty parlours (only for women, but there were rumours that some magistrates went there to get their hair cut) and other commercial facilities. The residences were a little inwards. Narrow streets, like alleyways, twisted and turned through those neighbourhoods. There were even a few bazaars and marketplaces in those inner locales. Those were each a *potti*, a zone—the potato zone, the fish zone, the fabric zone, etc. There was one where husked and unhusked rice was traded. It used to be called Dhanahati, the rice market, but now the people of Roop Nagar called it Dhanmondi, after the nice neighbourhood in the capital.

A few streets, relatively smaller than the main road, went off to the left or the right. For instance, one went northwards, from the turning by Panchu's Hotel past Hili-Birampur to Dinajpur. This one was called Hili Road; from the land port of Hili, weed and Phensedyl rode in on trucks alongside rice and onions, the currency traders took sacks full of cash into India. Hili Road was a particular favourite of DCs, SPs and the members of the police and BDR forces. This road was important in Pony Masud's story. Pony Masud's actual father Majed-the-Principal's house as well as his stepfather Brickly Mokhles' house were both in a neighbourhood right next to this road. Right next to the road was also a hospital, the hospital where, during Masud's time of crisis, his actual father and stepfather were seen together or side by side. It was on this road that, allegedly, Pony Masud kicked a blind beggar in the ass and was cursed.

Another road went southwards from the turning by the Bata shoe store—towards Jamalganj, Akkelpur, Shantahar. This road was called Jamalganj Road and was located at the southern end of the town; a weekly marketplace used to be set up beside this road. Pony Masud was extremely active there, because the yield from the open-air marketplace had always been considerable. The marketplace was also famous for assault and murder; before the arrival of Pony Masud when other gangs were active there, there was chaos among the extortionists. Rival extortionists would cut off each other's arms and legs. The people of Roop Nagar were afraid of them because they used knives and cleavers from the marketplace butchers. Pony Masud arrived and established order in the extortion processes.

There was a degree college operating in Roop Nagar. The college had been established through soliciting donations way back in the Pakistan period, when, it is said, students were still focused on their studies. The boys from that college took up arms during the Liberation War. They liberated the country, but after that they lost their zest for education. The year after liberation, what was pretty much a cheating factory was set up in that college, and that factory never really closed shop. At one point, a veritable festival of cheating began taking place during the intermediate and degree exams; microphones were attached to tree branches to announce the answers to the exam questions to the students, and the fathers, brothers, uncles, brothers-in-law of the examinees climbed ladders to supply them with cheat-sheets. They say that the young men of Roop Nagar felt tenderness towards this college, so they organised rallies and gatherings to have it proclaimed a government college. When President Ziaur Rahman, the one who wore black sunglasses, visited Roop Nagar for the first time, the college boys lay down on the road in front of his car. Their demand was to turn the college into a government institution. Until he did, the president would not be allowed to leave Roop Nagar. Ziaur Rahman acceded to their demand and proclaimed that it would be made a government college, and before the year was over, a new signboard was strung up in front of the college building that said 'Roop Nagar Governmental College'. Since then, the young men of Roop Nagar had been unable to forget that particular president. When, a few years later, news came that Ziaur Rahman's traitorous soldiers had shot him dead at the Chittagong Circuit House, the students of Roop Nagar had wept. It wasn't just the students; most of Roop Nagar's residents felt deep sorrow at Ziaur Rahman's death, because they had fallen in love with the sunglass-wearing 'ishmart' president. Because he had stood shoulder to shoulder with them, digging a canal with his own hands wearing a T-shirt and tennis shoes. Because he had shaken their hands. And after his death, they had seen on the television screen an old suitcase that held his frayed shirts. The people of Roop Nagar had come to love sheaves of wheat, the electoral symbol of his party, dearly. Of course, they also loved H.M. Ershad. They'd been happy when President Ershad came and confiscated the sub-district administrator's jeep and forced him to commute to work in a rickshaw. The wife and children of the sub-district administrator were parading about in the jeep, using up petrol bought with the people's money; Ershad put a stop to that misdeed. Ershad's soldiers bludgeoned the bribe-taking policeman Inspector Sattar and sent him to jail; they chopped off the long hair of the town's thugs and shaved their heads. When Ershad proclaimed a jihad against corruption, the people of Roop Nagar were overjoyed and said to each other, 'Now, there's a real man. This is how it's done. Everyone's going to be straightened out now.' But gradually they grew disappointed and upset with Ershad as well. At one point, they'd begun to curse him as *atkura*, sterile, and then finally one day they came out onto the streets in groups and, together, called for his throne to be set on fire. But since Ershad himself or even his throne was not within their reach, they attacked the residence of the Member of Parliament belonging to his party, and set fire to the party's Roop Nagar district office.

There was also a government-owned women's college in Roop Nagar. This too had been non-governmental in the beginning. Ershad converted it into a governmental school. When he had performed this good deed, the people of Roop Nagar had praised him. But now they call Ershad a 'bastard' and lambast his character. They remember that the day he came to announce that the women's college was now a government school, he had pulled a pretty student almost onto his lap. At that moment, that scene had not seemed untoward to them, because they were innocent people, and Ershad's womanising had not become infamous yet. But on the day that Ershad's throne was set on fire, the people of Roop Nagar remembered that scene from many years ago and they understood in their hearts that he had not had the pretty student sit on his lap out of simple affection, rather it was to satisfy his lust. Hence, when they heard that the dethroned Ershad was fleeing to Dhaka airport with his life in his hands, attempting to leave the country, they began to shout, calling on themselves, 'Let's head to Dhaka, let's get the damned *atkura* and crush his balls.'

The train tracks sliced through Roop Nagar's heart; many people travelled from Rangpur to Roop Nagar on the train, smoking bidis from Haragacch; many crossed Roop Nagar and travelled farther south. Many even crossed Shantahar, reached Natore, bought and ate *kanchagolla* sweets as they travelled through Ishwardi on to Khulna. After that, it's possible to decouple the train's engine from the head and attach it to the ass, and turn the ass into the head, and then in the same manner rumble its way towards Rajshahi and even to Amnura.

But there was no reason to travel to such terribly distant places to hear the saga of Pony Masud. Stories and gossip about him exist mostly in Roop Nagar. However, the stories and gossip that the people of Roop Nagar share about him are almost impossible to present in a neat and tidy manner because all their stories are tangled up and knotted. They describe later events early, and earlier events later, they go off on tangents, skip from one topic to another, and then they lose track of all these topics and suddenly go back to their original topic, and then start telling the same story again in a new manner.

While they talk about Pony Masud, they begin to talk about his father, and while they're talking about Majed-the-Principal, they even start telling stories about *his* father, and while they gossip about Majed's father Sajed Mandal's rice trade, they pull in a thread about his in-laws, and while they jabber about the medical exploits of the LMF doctor Kafiluddin, who went around on his pony wearing a pith hat, they start describing his daughter, and while they're talking about his daughter Laili Begum, it is inevitable that Majed-the-Principal and Brickly Mokhles crop up, and then suddenly they discard everyone else and again immerse themselves in talking about Pony Masud—and this is how they tangle all the stories up.

4

Hammers, mallets, axes and shovels—all these tools, which had not been invented for the purpose of killing people, were deployed by Pony Masud to pulverise the bones of living humans. He never used these tools in any other way. His use of knives, daggers, pistols, rifles wasn't noteworthy; such weapons were mundane to him. But the people of Roop Nagar remember that Pony Masud had killed people even without weapons.

One day, they read about a Bihari man in the newspapers, a man who had fought during the War of Liberation against the Pakistani Army, and therefore, suddenly, they were reminded of Rahim Bihari.

One day, Pony Masud was speeding along the road in front of Rahim Bihari's house on his horse (his Yamaha 125), when his horse's wheel went over a piece of brick. It juddered quite badly, and that sudden juddering seemed to slam inside Masud's chest. He screamed the seventy-year-old Rahim Bihari's name right there on the street. He yelled 'you damn old *razakar*, collaborator, fucking Bihari, why is there such a jungle in front of your house? Can't you keep the streets clean? Get over here, bring a broom,' etc.

Pony Masud stopped his motorcycle and was swearing at Rahim Bihari, calling him an old collaborator, son of a *hanadar*, and the old man was bent at the waist, leaning forward as he swept the road in front of him. A few people from the neighborhood suspended their work or their non-work and gathered there; they stood in a circle watching the scene, in the same way that the children of Roop Nagar watched the monkey trainer and his tricks at the train station. The eager eyes of the neighborhood women were also in evidence at the windows of the houses nearby.

The people of Roop Nagar loved exaggeration; here, any incident was quickly imbued with the elements of folktales or myth. Thus, the description of Rahim Bihari's humiliation on that day became a little like this: the old man was sweeping the street in a crouch and tears were dripping from his eyes; Rahim Bihari's tears did what large drops of rain do when they splash onto the ground displacing dirt. Pony Masud had been 'puffing on a cig while astride his pony' and was watching the old man with the air of a great know-it-all. As it had been left undefined just how much of the road Rahim Bihari was required to sweep to complete his penance, a kind of uncertainty reigned among the audience, and they whispered among themselves: was Pony Masud going to make Rahim Bihari sweep the streets of the entire municipality? But at some point, when Pony Masud roared, 'Halt!' like an army man, Rahim Bihari dropped the broom and ran as fast as he could into his house; then, for the next fifteen days—although some say twenty-one, and some say a month—nobody in the neighborhood caught even a glimpse of Rahim Bihari's face anywhere outside.

The people of Roop Nagar do not call Rahim Bihari a razakar or a hanadar collaborator. His ancestors had come from Bihar during the British era; they had been railway employees. They never returned to Bihar; they stayed on in Roop Nagar, made their homes there, fathered children and became permanent residents of the town. In 1971, when the raging Bengali horde attacked and looted Biharipara, the Bihari neighbourhood, Rahim Bihari's house did not fall victim to that attack because his house wasn't in the Bihari neighbourhood.

Rahim Bihari, at least, had never acted as a collaborator openly, but neither had he taken part in the struggle to liberate Bangladesh. After liberation, nobody had heard him say anything like he wanted to take his family and leave for Pakistan. Neither was there any talk about his retaining any communication or connection with his ancestral land of Bihar.

Such an inoffensive old man, who couldn't possibly be blamed for having hay or clods of earth or pieces of broken brick on the street in front of his house, to call him son of the hanadar, old collaborator and worse, and to force him to sweep the streets was a heartbreaking thing. Even if the insensitive people of Roop Nagar couldn't quite understand that day, Rahim Bihari and his family realised the significance of those curses quite clearly. In their assessment, if Pony Masud had called Rahim Bihari a dog, a cat, or his favourite curse word, *chudir bhai*, brother of a fucker, then it would have been clear that the hot-tempered young man had lost it suddenly without reason. But the significance of calling him the son of the hanadar and an old collaborator was that it was August 1996, when, after a prolonged twenty-one years, the people's mandate had returned the political party, the Bangladesh Awami League, to the throne of power. Later, even the common folks of Roop Nagar discovered that it was soon after that incident that Pony Masud had transformed from a soldier of the martyred Zia to a Mujib Shena, a warrior for the founding father Sheikh Mujib.

A month after that, one afternoon, the people of Roop Nagar saw that Rahim Bihari was being transported to the hospital in a rickshaw-van. His five sons were walking behind the van; there were no words in their mouths, they were walking with their heads lowered, staring at the ground. When they saw that, the people of Roop Nagar knew with certainty that old Rahim Bihari's time was up, he was only going to the hospital to be pronounced dead. Then they thought of Pony Masud, because after the crucial incident of being made to sweep the streets, that was the first time that Rahim Bihari had been seen in public; they decided that the incident from that other day was the cause of death for Rahim Bihari; in fact, some even drew the spiritual conclusion that Rahim Bihari had really died that day while sweeping the road.

He lay flat on his back in the rickshaw-van on the way to the hospital, his thin body covered with a quilt, his face uncovered. Rahim Bihari lay flat in the rickshaw-van on his way to the hospital, staring sightlessly at the sky, but his eyes were impassive; there was no tenderness for the earthly world in his gaze, nor any concern for his five unemployed sons, and actually, as the people of Roop Nagar say, by then Rahim Bihari had already entered the afterlife.

Later on, people heard that before his death, Rahim Bihari had wanted to eat hilsa fish, but at the time there had been a nationwide scarcity of hilsa. The day his eldest son finally brought home a hilsa he had purchased for four hundred and fifty takas, Rahim Bihari's pissing and shitting and eating had all stopped. Hilsas arrived at the Roop Nagar marketplace from quite a distance because there wasn't a single river in the region where hilsa could be found. But hilsa was a fish very dear to the people of Roop Nagar. There were frequent arguments and fights among customers in the marketplace over hilsa. Pony Masud's father, Majed-the-Principal, was renowned for shouting at the fish market. The people of Roop Nagar recounted those stories quite often, and sometimes while they were telling those stories, they became nostalgic about fish and began to reminisce about the wealth and diversity of the fish in the rice paddies around Roop Nagar during the months of Sraban to Kartik.

But as they spoke of fields brimming with the rains of the months of Sraban and Bhadra, they would suddenly begin to speak of the barren fields of Magh and Phalgun, the fields that they called the *pathar*. In between the villages surrounding Roop Nagar lay perfectly level fields. After the *aman* rice was harvested in Aghran and Poush, the fields lay empty and vast. Boys grazed cattle there and played *furti-panti*, and they gobbled up all the potatoes that some householders used to plant after the harvest. The shepherds would gather the potatoes, light a fire with straw and grill the potatoes; they hopped around with the hot, charred potatoes in their palms and, blowing on them to cool them down, they sang songs of happiness. They sang and ate the charred potatoes, and played furti-panti. After the potatoes came wheat, but wheat hadn't become a popular crop yet; fields full of hoary wheat were still rare, and anyway, the shepherds had nothing to do in the wheat fields; they went off to the *boot-kalai* fields. They uprooted the boot-kalai plants and dipped them into the cold water of the lake and chewed on the boot-kalai like peanuts and sang. Then, from some unknown region, the indigenous Bunas came to graze their pigs, and the herd of pigs drank from the lake, and the shepherds watched them, thinking that the Buna people were making the water *napak*, unclean, and so they flogged the pigs with the bamboo *pantis* they used to herd their cows. The inoffensive Bunas would plead with them, 'Oh, brother, don't beat!' and mouthing sounds like *hoooey hooou-ish*, they quickly herded their hogs away.

The people of Roop Nagar speak of the damage pesticides caused in the rice fields and their hand in the destruction of fish varieties, and suddenly they begin to analyse their food habits. The people of Roop Nagar eat rice and fish. People are still able to procure rice, but most of them are no longer able to get fish, because rivers and canals are rare around Roop Nagar, and the dried riverbed of the Tulsiganga, the only river in the region, is where parval is farmed now, and also because of pesticide usage, although the rice paddies yielded high yields of high-yield rice, they no longer sustained fish, so fish was scarce. Fish, these days, were food for the rich; most people ate potatoes with their rice: potatoes mashed, potatoes stewed, potatoes cut in shoestrings and curried, potatoes cooked with parval-eggplant-bitter melon—whatever vegetable was available seasonally—in a sauce to eat with rice.

But such food was not a cause of pride for them; parval-bitter melon-eggplant was food for the peddlers, or so said the well-to-do householders in the villages surrounding Roop

Nagar. Regular consumption of rice and *nirala*, meaning fish and meat, was a marker of pride and class. Even a short while ago, the rich folks of Roop Nagar didn't eat greens or vegetables; although now they did a little, due to the instigation of the Diabetic Association, the health pages in the newspapers and the NGOs. Nevertheless, despite knowing that taro greens, taro stems and arum roots were extremely beneficial foods, the people of this region still used taro to scold each other. You son of a taro-eating trader, eat taro, you'll get taro, you *hatkura* and other such taro-related phrases and idioms of varied meaning and nuance were used frequently. The old-money rich of Roop Nagar did, in recent times, go to the marketplace and buy taro for health reasons, but they tried to hide them when ferrying them back home; if their grocery bags did not succeed in concealing, and if an acquaintance looked at the verdant taro greens peeking out of their bag with too close a gaze, the taro-carrying person's face turned red in mortification. If the looking-neighbour was of a plain-spoken funny nature, they wasted no time in having a little fun by embarrassing the old-money gentleman. They would bare their teeth and say, 'So these days you've even started eating taro!' It should be noted that people who could stomach such stinging jokes were very rare in Roop Nagar. Therefore, if, on witnessing some aristocratic gentleman proud of his lineage looking embarrassed at carrying taro greens, some ill-spoken humourist provoked him by commenting, 'So you've begun eating taro these days!' a great discord was born. Or, if the gentleman under attack was of a non-confrontational nature, then, without understanding the joke, he would supply a serious response: 'Taro is a good source of iron.' Which opened the door to repeated attacks, and thus the next dart flew in his direction: 'Has all the iron in Murari's rod-cement store been sold off?' And this time it would be difficult for even the non-confrontational gentleman to tolerate the scene; he would quicken his steps homewards, and encountering acquaintances on the way, he bad-mouthed the ill-spoken humourist by saying that the man took bribes, or he was a cheat.

The word 'cheater' sometimes brought memories of Brickly Mokhles to mind as the people of Roop Nagar called Brickly Mokhles 'Cheater Mokhles' as well, because being friends with Majed-the-Principal and then luring his wife away wasn't what a good person did—it was how cheaters behaved.

5

The principal of Atapara Non-governmental Degree College, Majedur Rahman aka Majed-the-Principal aka Pony Masud's father, would repeat within earshot of his students, 'You seen movies? You seen rough and tough villains in movies? My son is a real live villain, get it?'

There was an explanation prevalent about why he felt the need to scare his meek students like this: Atapara College was renowned throughout the nation as a location for cheating. Students came from far-off places like Dhaka, Chittagong, Cox's Bazar to avail themselves of the opportunity to cheat during exams. They paid Majed-the-Principal a lot of money to obtain these cheating privileges, and if security during exams was tightened, they grew upset at the principal; there had been a few incidents where he had been besieged.

The connection became clear when, while discussing the difference between different eras, the people of Roop Nagar determined that Pony Masud's era was Koli Yuga, the age of darkness. Of course, objections arose because to the inhabitants of each era, their own time appeared to be the age of darkness. Even in 1972, the people of Roop Nagar were overheard saying, 'What time do we live in when these boys stick daggers into their exam hall desks so they can cheat, and they wolf-whistle at girls.'

A handful of people, who once used to be top thugs, whose time had passed and they were now among the fallen, were overheard saying with regret, 'We too could have shone.' They believed that they could have grown to be such uber-terrors that today's Pony Masud would have shat his pants upon hearing their names.

'But our problem was that we didn't get the support of our parents, the kind that the Pony Masuds these days have.'

There were more than enough people in Roop Nagar to console the retired goons who voiced such regrets. They chuckled and said, 'Come on, don't moan. Say your prayers and beg Allah so that in the next life you get parents like Pony Masud's.'

Having said that, the people of Roop Nagar never said anything about Principal Majid playing any kind of active role in his son becoming Pony Masud. Everyone believed that the role of his mother, Laili Begum, was the most crucial. There were many stories floating around about Laili Begum's special ministrations that aimed to make her son brave from the very beginning. For instance, when little Masud came home crying from the playground because he was bullied by bigger boys and complained to his mother, she wrapped her sari tight around her waist, like a soldier's belt, and showed up at the playground like an Amazon, towing her son behind her and demanding that he show her which boy had bullied him. Her son raised his tiny finger and pointed at the bully and she ordered her son, 'Go on, useless boy, give it to him good!'

The people of Roop Nagar said that it was those lessons from his mother that led Pony Masud, before he was even eighteen, to shove the almost-fifty, dauntless-at-one-time labour leader Farid on his chest and threaten to kick him out of town.

Those who had the chance that afternoon to watch this scene unfold in Salamot's Honda Garage, under the koroi tree and across from Mina Confectionary on Sugar Mill Road, witnessed many other hair-raising incidents that Pony Masud carried out later on. But that particular incident was unparalleled, and they were unable to forget it for the rest of their lives.

Farid was a leader of the Sugar Mill Workers' Union. Although he was no longer in his heyday, everyone remembered the authority with which he had once engaged in labour politics, led scuffles and brawls, stopped the mill's machinery at will and restarted them when he pleased. His tongue-lashing had once made even the general manager of the mill flee the office and run home to hide in his wife's lap. And it was that Farid whose chest the newbie Masud shoved while yelling, 'Who the hell are you?'

The people of Roop Nagar said it would have been one thing if Farid had done anything wrong, but he wasn't at fault at all. He had gone to Salamot's garage to get his motorcycle repaired before Masud; Salamot had even begun to work on Farid's vehicle, when Masud blew in from somewhere and told Salamot, 'Hey, check this, what's happened to my ride?'

Salamot raised his head from Farid's vehicle and looked at Masud, upon which all Farid said was that he was in a rush. But that was all it took—Masud jumped up in a fury, smacked Farid on the chest and roared, 'Who the hell are you?'

That Masud had addressed the intrepid labour leader Fariduddin as *tui*, the overly familiar pronoun, was enough to render Farid speechless. He was bereft of even the ability to be surprised, and the others who witnessed the episode, including Salamot, were befuddled. Within a split second they accepted that this was no longer Farid's day—it was Pony Masud's time. Still, they were afraid of the possibility that Masud would slap Farid on the cheek and that would give rise to a scandal that would mortify even the audience.

He didn't land a slap, of course, but the way he shoved Farid again and again on the chest, and repeated, 'Go on, son of a bitch, don't let me see you in this town again, pack up and get lost,' forcing Farid to back away—that in itself mortified people. The scene had stunned everyone because at that point, they still had not come to expect such behaviour from Masud; his clout had not yet reached such a peak.

The observant among the people of Roop Nagar later opined that that particular afternoon was a milestone in the creation of Pony Masud's reputation. That was the day on which Pony Masud was acknowledged as the top thug in town. But it is difficult to determine this moment based on the tangled-up tales told by the people of Roop Nagar, because according to many of them, the first incident of Masud wielding a gun in broad daylight, which was a hundred times more sensational than him smacking labour leader Farid in the chest, had actually happened even earlier.

That morning, around eleven, Masud was sitting in Panchu's hotel with his cronies, drinking tea and smoking. He looked out of the window, spotted a man, jumped up from his chair, went out into the street, and barred the man's way. The man, when he didn't recognise Masud and found his path impeded in such a brazen manner, wrinkled his forehead.

Masud reminded him that about three years ago, he had found Masud smoking a cigarette and had grabbed the cigarette from the lips of the under-age (in his opinion) boy, telling him, 'The principal's son and you're so ill-mannered?' and then he had gently prodded him on the cheek.

The man, who had been a bit of a thug back then, but later on had abandoned all that and gone off to Khulna or maybe Jessore for business, remembered the incident and gazed at Masud with an avuncular smile; Masud returned his smile and right in the middle of the street, in the bright sunshine of eleven in the morning, pulled out a gun and, grinding his teeth together, threatened, 'You son of a pig, I'm going to pull your smile out through your ass,' and with his right hand, he pointed the gun at the man's chest and said that he was going to count from one to ten and the man, whose name was Solaiman, who, because he had at some point in time sat for the BA exams as a private student from Atapara College, considered himself a student of Majed-the-Principal, and thought of Masud as a sort of nephew, which is why he had corrected him gently that day—that man could survive if he ran for his life fast enough, otherwise he was going to be shot so hard that his 'ass was going to get a hole'.

Masud proclaimed this ultimatum and right away began the countdown in a loud voice, 'One … two … three …'

Everything suddenly went silent at the intersection of Panchu's hotel. In the same way that the sky is baleful just before a storm, the wind quieted, everyone's breathing stopped; in fear and surprise, they kept watching the scene open-mouthed. Solaiman was perplexed and stared at Masud for a few moments; he too was not breathing, his mouth slightly open. Masud held his arm straight out and rocked the muzzle of his gun gently as he continued to count in a loud voice, '… three, four, five …'. As soon as the word 'five' emerged from his lips, Uncle Solaiman slapped his own ass twice and then ran like the wind.

The people of Roop Nagar say that on that day, they experienced tumult like never before; they had, before that, seen many thugs and political goons, they had heard that they all carried guns in their pockets, but that one could aim a gun at someone, in the heart of town, in broad daylight, in front of hundreds of people, they had never, in their lifetimes, heard of any thug in their town as daring as that.

Of course, it was said that nowadays even the schoolboys of this town carried loaded pistols in their pockets, but that was perhaps more an adornment, a tool to instill fear. Naughty boys pulled out their guns to scare their teachers, but they weren't that naughty yet that they would actually fire off shots.

The people of Roop Nagar noticed that the use of firearms wasn't that common in this town. There was, of course, some usage of guns and ammo immediately after the Liberation War, but for whatever reason, that practice soon disappeared. The brutal boys of later days didn't fire guns anymore; people say that bullets cost money, and at times it was hard to procure them, and guns were loud and would splash the news throughout the town. So they preferred to use daggers, knives, ramdaos and Chinese axes in silence.

Prior to that, their weapons of choice were hockey sticks, iron rods and bicycle chains. In the old days, it was mostly bamboo sticks that were used in the fights that took place in Roop Nagar College. Laltu-the-Thug was the first one to introduce bicycle chains. During his reign, bicycle chains became quite fashionable as weapons. Then later, when Kung Fu and Karate became prevalent, an instrument called nunchaku was spotted in the hands of the boys, which was made by connecting a pair of smooth and hard wooden batons with an iron chain. There was a time when the town's ironsmiths were kept busy fashioning nunchakus; but people didn't view those as badly as daggers or knives or bicycle chains. People said Karate was a martial art; it wasn't considered a bad thing to learn it because every year, on Independence Day and Victory Day, Karate displays were held during the parades at the stadium in front of the district administrator, the local member of parliament and other governmental and non-governmental authorities.

Those who had witnessed Pony Masud pointing his gun at Solaiman's chest that morning had thought that he was going to shoot Solaiman in the back or in the ass, but many people believed that he wouldn't have shot him for real, he'd just wanted to scare Solaiman a little. Others claimed that Masud had wanted to scare not only Solaiman but terrorise the rest of the townspeople as well. In truth, on that day he had wanted to try and let everyone know—and he did let everyone know—that Pony Masud had arrived. As a result, that day or maybe the next, nobody could say for sure, Masud was summoned to the court of Hafiz Mondal, the General Secretary for the ruling party.

Some say, that very afternoon, Hafiz Mondal had spotted Masud on the street and waved his hand at him, saying, 'Come over to my den.'

Masud, allegedly, had shouted back at Mondal, 'Why are you calling me "tui"?'

When he heard Masud, Mondal had laughed indulgently, walked towards him, slapped him gently on the shoulder and, using the more formal *tumi*, said, 'Come over, brother, come.'

Hafiz Mondal, who was old enough to be Pony Masud's father, who was the General Secretary for the ruling party, and who, although he had not been granted the party nomination during the last election, nevertheless possessed an infinite amount of clout and power, who, because the current president was old, was the de facto main leader locally, usually addressed

Majed-the-Principal as 'brother', and so when he called Pony Masud 'brother' instead of 'nephew', the townspeople were immediately assured of Pony Masud's value and respect to Hafiz Mondal.

The next evening, in response to Hafiz Mondal's invitation, Masud showed up at his den. Mondal entertained him in his customary manner and told him that Roop Nagar had been waiting all this time for the emergence of Pony Masud, that this town needed him desperately. People said that Mondal told him that he would build Masud into such a big deal that the mothers of this town would put their children to sleep to the warning of 'Pony Masud's coming', and that the shutters of all the shops in the town would slam shut at the words 'Pony Masud's raving'.

The handgun incident that lasted just moments, which spread Pony Masud's fame throughout the town, and which raised his profile among the most influential of the ruling party leaders—well, that handgun was also the story of Masud's inheritance. When Masud's deceased maternal grandfather, the LMF Doctor Kafiluddin of Abhay Nagar, wore a pith hat and rode his pony visiting patients from village to village, he would keep a German pistol tucked into the waistband of his loose pantaloons. Word is that he even used that pistol once; he shot a man straight in the chest. The man he had killed was, allegedly, a dacoit, and so he faced no punishment. People say that just because you have a gun in hand doesn't mean you can shoot someone in the chest, and therefore Masud's maternal grandfather must have been a very brave man. They also say that the source of Pony Masud's imperious courage was his mother's side of the family, not his father's lineage; because his father Majed-the-Principal was a coward; he feared Brickly Mokhles, who, despite being his friend had seduced his wife and taken her away, like the devil. And it was said that Masud's paternal grandfather had also been a man who was timid by nature. Masud had no similarities with his father in physique either; he looked like his maternal uncles and grandfather. Masud's father was as dark as a water buffalo, but Masud's complexion was as fair as his mother's with a golden hint of raw turmeric. His father's neck was so short that it looked like his head had been set directly on his torso, but Masud's neck was long and narrow, almost like a woman's. The father's body was like a fat pig, but the son's was merely a structure of bones. The father was short, the son quite tall. The father's face, without a jawline, without a chin, was almost like a ball, in the middle of which the nose jutted out like a betelnut; the son's face was long, his jaw pronounced and insolent; from his forehead to his chin seemed to be half an arm's length, in the middle of which his nose jutted out like a Chinese axe. The father's eyes were tiny, like an elephant's; the son's eyes weren't merely eyes, they were limpid pools—such beauty was only seen in the wide eyes of cows. Laili Begum told people that her only son had been born like her pony-riding doctor father, who was as handsome as the Prophet Yusuf; his ancestors had arrived in Bengal from Persia, the land of the rose.

6

The people of Roop Nagar found great pleasure in chewing the cud over various stories again and again, such as how Pony Masud's father, Majed-the-Principal, completed his MA with a third class by taking the exams as a private student, how a private college was opened in Atapara where no students wanted to be admitted, how gradually that same college gained national reputation as a locale for cheating. Majed-the-Principal's milk-and-rose skinned little wife, whose name was Laili Begum, because of whom the neighbours called her husband Majnu behind his back after the legend of Laili and Majnu, had not wanted to carry a child so that she could hold on to her buxom luscious youthful beauty for eternity, but people doubted Majed-the-Principal's masculinity, whispered and gossiped about him and christened him with the moniker *atkura*, right until the day that they noticed Laili Begum's belly was swelling and their servant was picking *helencha* greens from the pond adjacent to their house and Laili Begum was eating tamarind and vomiting day in day out, hard enough to startle the flock of neighbourhood crows.

She became pregnant after they had been married for over ten years, and then the false suspicions about Majed-the-Principal being unmanly disappeared, and once the neighbours witnessed the bovine appearance of the pink-skinned young woman named Laili Begum, their attraction to her also disappeared. Hence, Masud's birth didn't create much of a stir in town. At least a dozen more babies were born in Roop Nagar that same year, and nobody could have known beforehand that the child that had just leapt out of Laili Begum's womb would best everyone else of his generation to one day become the one and only Pony Masud.

The town where Majed-the-Principal lived as the helmsman of an entire educational institution used to have respect, admiration and appreciation for teachers. Even primary school teachers had the respect of people; that college teachers were admired went without saying. But there was something in the manner, the actions of Majed-the-Principal that made it hard for people to think that the man was part of the respected community of teachers. He got into disputes with vendors at the fish market, he borrowed money from friends but considered himself debt-free, he didn't observe any religious rites or say his prayers, in fact, he wouldn't even step foot in the mosque on Jumma prayer days, and it was said that before his son had hit it rich, he loaned money to the goldsmiths of Kundu Para at high interest rates, which meant that he was a usurer.

All of these were latter-day discussions; before Majed's son Masud became the town's top terror and came to be known as Pony Masud, neither Majed's nature nor his character were topics worth discussing. Majed became worthy of discussion only after the rise of Pony Masud, as his real, authentic father.

When Masud was a little boy, nobody paid attention to him because he was no prodigy. But once he became Pony Masud, many legends grew around him. For instance, once he demanded a pony. As Laili Begum's beloved only son, he succeeded in wangling a pony out of his father, and thus, at ten, Masud acquired a little notoriety if not in the entire town, at least in their neighbourhood.

People recall occasionally seeing an ice cream vendor on horseback on the streets of Roop Nagar. He would show up suddenly on the school grounds and bang the lid of his wooden box while he sat astride his horse, so the *fottash fottash* resounded throughout the school playing fields, and the noise echoed along the walls of the schoolhouse, and in between that sound and the echoes, the bony, leaf-thin ice cream vendor from the Bihari community would rasp out, i-c-e-c-r-e-a-m! His horse was skinny just like him, as if it weren't a live horse but a skeleton. But it was seeing that horse that provoked little Masud's demand for one. By then, horses were a rare breed in that region, and other than that single horse, there were none to be seen anywhere in town. But Masud was, after all, Laili Begum's only son—what choice did Majed-the-Principal have but to fulfill his desires?

Later on, people discovered that Masud's connection to horses had ancient roots. Once upon a time, his grandfather, meaning Majed-the-Principal's long-dead father, rode a horse to faraway marketplaces in Dhap, Moslemganj, Punot, Molamgari and other places to trade in rice. Back then, boys would recite a poem whenever they saw the horse:

Hey, horsey, what's beneath your hooves?
Pegs,
And one and a half lame legs.

Masud's maternal grandfather, Laili Begum's doctor father who had an LMF degree, who had passed away a long while ago, had also owned a pony. He used to don a pith helmet like the English sahibs and ride his pony through the villages to visit his patients.

Which meant that it was discovered that Pony Masud's connection to horses was inherited from both sides of his family. Therefore, at a very young age, fate determined that Masud should own a horse. And so, Majed-the-Principal desperately searched everywhere: where did horse-trading take place, or at which marketplaces were horses sold alongside cows and bullocks; such research continued for quite a long while. But nobody was able to give him news of a horse market, or a cow-bullock marketplace that had a mix of horses. With no alternative in sight, he finally approached the Bihari ice cream seller, in case he was able to give him news of some horse market, but the fellow couldn't give him any such information; instead, he proposed to unload his own horse on Masud's father. But ten-year-old Masud, whose dream was to ride a spirited winged horse like the film stars Wasim or Jashim to conduct robberies, looked at the skeletal horse belonging to the leaf-thin ice cream seller and spat at it, because not only was it practically a skeleton, there was no saddle on its back, there were no stirrups to place his feet in. The horse couldn't gallop, and it walked with wobbly steps as if it were a dying donkey, as if it would fall down at any moment and fail to stand up again even if whipped a hundred times. But the owner said that the horse was a true Arabian, and that it was in such a condition because he was unable to feed it properly. If properly fed, the horse would regain its vigour within a few days and gallop as fast as a winged horse. The sly ice cream vendor was a seller for sure; people still talk about how he had maneuvered two and a half thousand takas out of Majed-the-Principal.

But the horse didn't survive in Majed-the-Principal's house; one day it fell flat on the ground foaming at the mouth and couldn't get up again. The day the news of the horse's death was announced was the day that the Bihari ice cream seller stopped coming around anymore, and three new ice cream factories were established in Roop Nagar; there began an epidemic of tonsillitis, colds and sore throats among the town's children.

It wasn't when Masud became the owner of a real live horse that his friends began to call him Pony Masud; it was when he became the owner of a dead horse that he was given that moniker. When the people of Roop Nagar recognised the advent of Pony Masud's era, it wasn't as if the playing field had been empty, it never was. And Masud had not emerged thinking that he would be scoring goals on an empty field. People say that Pony Masud knew quite well that he would have to face off with Ghostly Pintu.

Ghostly Pintu owned the playing field at that time; his patron or godfather Abu Karim was a lawmaker who had run under the electoral symbol of the rice sheaf and was elected by a massive margin. The problem was that although Karim himself was an MP, his party had not managed to get elected; and therefore, Ghostly Pintu was merely the star cadre of an opposition MP, and people say that therein lay the seeds of his fall. They feared that Pony Masud would finish off Ghostly Pintu, because Masud was a weapon that belonged to the ruling party, and in their opinion, there was no thug as big as the government in this golden Bengal.

When the party that Ghostly Pintu's godfather belonged to had just lost power, there wasn't much they could do other than carrying out *hartaals* or strikes; news was oozing in from other parts of the country that the naughty opposition party was calling for strikes and they were creating severe distress among the common people trying to enforce the strikes and therefore, the ruling party invented a strategy to circumvent the opposition's actions which made it impossible for the picketers to hold successful strikes. But in Roop Nagar, Ghostly Pintu's dominance ensured that even when the ruling party thugs had the direct cooperation of the government servants in uniform flaunting batons-rifles-tear gas, they still couldn't stick it out in the streets with their anti-strike rallies. Ghostly Pintu, to whose name people had added that adjective because his complexion was as dark as a ghost's, whose eyes were always burning like a furnace due to Phensedyl and weed, who tucked a gun into his waistband and wielded swords in each hand, was so much more skillful than master butchers at severing the limbs of his enemies that when people spotted him in the streets during strikes with his naked swords, they cried for their mothers and fled to their homes and locked their doors, and the governmental 'peace rally' did an about turn and headed for a different alleyway.

The people of Roop Nagar knew even before Pony Masud's emergence that the praise and esteem that the opposition party's Roop Nagar branch and its leader Abu Karim enjoyed because of Ghostly Pintu would not last long. They were merely waiting in accordance with the law of politics; with the emergence of Pony Masud, they were immediately reassured of the accuracy of those laws.

Therefore, they continued to wait for the day when Ghostly Pintu would be slaughtered by Pony Masud. But before that, the leaders of the ruling party's Roop Nagar branch tested Masud's mettle; the responsibility of completely disrupting the opposition leader's programme during her Roop Nagar visit fell on his shoulders. With floral garlands in hand, the opposition MP and other leaders and party workers gazed along the leader's path of arrival, waiting avidly at the juncture where the town began, where they had built pleasing archways. The long hours seemed to go on forever and forever and forever. Finally, at some point, the cell phone rang in the MP's pocket; about ten miles away from the town, a dozen trucks were waiting on the highway like insolent boys. Ghostly Pintu and his pals roared their way there on their Hondas, but how were the precious boyos supposed to move forward? Pony Masud and his gang were circling just a few yards ahead. Bombs exploded on the streets; Pony Masud chased Ghostly Pintu on his Yamaha horse. People say that that was the first time Ghostly Pintu was scared; he abandoned everyone else and retreated on his Honda, and apparently his Honda wailed as it sped off while Pony Masud followed him popping his gun. The farmers and farmhands who were watching as they worked the fields on either side of the road described a scene as exciting as a movie; they testified that they had even heard five or maybe seven rounds of bullets being fired, but not a single one reached its target. From this episode, the people of Roop Nagar determined that Pony Masud was not a good shot.

That afternoon Ghostly Pintu announced that Pony Masud's time had run out, now he had to start his journey towards the afterlife. Apparently, Ghostly Pintu went as far as the entrance to Brickly Mokhles' house to deliver his threat to Pony Masud's mother. Then people began to smell blood in the air; but they couldn't be certain whose blood they smelled, for whom the bell was tolling, and whose time was up—Pony Masud's or Ghostly Pintu's. Of course, the realists were certain that the grave was being dug for Pintu because the governmental wind was blowing against him, and who didn't know that in this golden Bengal, the mightiest hurricanes were born of governmental winds.

The people of Roop Nagar waited for an afternoon when the darkness of early evening descended before the watch hand reached the evening hours, and the shops all shut down, the faithful exited the mosque after the Magreb prayers and whispered on their way home where they latched their doors, the streets and alleys of the town emptied out, the air grew heavy and motionless, the leaves did not flutter, pond water stopped rippling, and even the birds in the trees that lined the bank of the pond postponed their evening chirring and observed silence.

After a night of breathlessness, the sun rose; in the morning light, the people of Roop Nagar saw not one but two corpses by the side of the road, in the narrow passage between two houses; the shoulder of one was hacked asunder, run through the belly and the back, while the other's ribs were damaged all over.

Later on, it was discovered that on the previous afternoon, Pony Masud's pals had spotted Ghostly Pintu in blue jeans and a white shirt; after the azaan sounded for the Isha prayers, when they saw Ghostly Pintu and his pals walking towards the rail station along Bodor Master Road, they quietly followed them with guns in their pockets and *kirich* and Chinese axes in their hands and saw that there were two of them wearing white shirts. When they reached the last turning of the road, and Pony Masud and his pals jumped Ghostly Pintu and his pals, there was no resistance from the victims. They were stunned into rushing this way and that way, trying to flee. The ones in dark-coloured clothing disappeared within moments; in the darkness, only two white shirts ran in the same direction; the white ones couldn't find an escape and, bewildered, they tried to enter the dark passage between two houses. And because the passage was so narrow, in their desperate attempt to survive, they began shoving each other to be the first to enter, when the *kiriches* and Chinese axes came after them.

The townspeople saw that Ghostly Pintu's time had run out; Roop Nagar was no longer where he could lay down his head. He disappeared. Ghostly Pintu departed, leaving Roop Nagar empty, impoverished. Then the people of Roop Nagar recalled that Ghostly Pintu wasn't a child of this town; they remembered that his father, the gentleman who had arrived here to work at the sugar mill, was an inoffensive, good-natured person. Why a thug like Ghostly Pintu was born in the home of such a good man was something the people of Roop Nagar could not figure out.

Those who became friends with a brutal terrorist like Ghostly Pintu, smoked weed and chugged Phensedyl with him, killed people, carried out all kinds of misdoings; they were not good boys. Still, the townspeople felt sad for the two dead boys; in their minds, they saw all their past wild behaviours with a gaze beautiful with forgiveness, and they prayed for their souls incarnate, and placed their consoling hands on the shoulders of the fathers bewildered by grief. The opposition party organised a memorial; there, the dead boys were transformed into martyrs, their fathers received some verbal consolation as well as the instigation to file murder cases.

The fathers who had lost their sons went to the police station, a deposition naming Pony Masud as the main accused was written out, and henceforth the police defined the very fresh case with the adjective 'dead' while smiling in disappointment because they wouldn't be able to pocket a single dime from the accused; instead, scheming to con the aggrieved fathers, they said that the accused would be arrested if they agreed to spend two lakh takas. The fathers who had just lost their sons were not ready to take on too much loss, so they returned home from the police station, slapping their foreheads in frustration, and sat on their prayer mats with their hands raised in supplication to the court of Allah the Great. And on Hafiz Mondal's terrace, a feast was held because Ghostly Pintu had fled Roop Nagar clutching his life in his hands.

7

Brickly Mokhles was at first a razakar, a collaborator, and then he became a freedom fighter. When he was a razakar, he broke the law of Pakistan and looted many households, regardless of whether they belonged to Hindus or Muslims. Then, when the town's administration fell apart because the freedom fighters were intimidating them, he went to the *mahakuma* administrator's residence and advised him that since the banks of Roop Nagar were going to be looted, they should be brought under their possession. The people of Roop Nagar say that the SDO and Brickly Mokhles took sacks full of cash with them and rode bullock carts to India. In India, Brickly Mokhles signed up with the freedom fighters, but he didn't come back to Bangladesh to fight; he spent his days watching movies in Balurghat, Siliguri and Calcutta. He came back when the country was liberated and established a brick kiln, and that is why the people of Roop Nagar named him Brickly Mokhles.

Later on, because Brickly Mokhles lured Majed-the-Principal's formally married wife away and became Pony Masud's stepfather, and because everyone still remembered the history of bank embezzlement that was part of his curriculum vitae, the people of Roop Nagar went back to recounting the 'attempt to bank robbery' that was later carried out by Brickly Mokhles' stepson, and as they recounted Masud's story, they speculated on his mother and his mother's lover, i.e. the love affair of Laili Begum and Brickly Mokhles, and the inexplicability of Pony Masud's perspective on that affair, and sometimes it happened that as they talked about Brickly Mokhles, Jabbar Ali Mia's name popped up, the only explanation for that being that one day, in front of Jabbar Ali Mia's shop, stepfather Brickly Mokhles met stepson Pony Masud face to face. Apparently Brickly Mokhles hurriedly pretended to have some urgent errand and fled, and Jabbar Ali pursed his lips in a smirk. Pony Masud spotted his smile and immediately challenged Jabbar Ali. 'Why did you laugh?'

People say that the former communist rebel and still unmarried Jabbar Ali Mia wasn't one to be scared of Pony Masud, that 'shrimp that was two days old' (although many held a differing view on this); he was a man who had practised political activism with the rebel doctor Abdul Kader Chowdhury who was originally from Panchbibi, and Jabbar Ali Mia had suffered and returned from political exile in the Andaman Islands. Apparently, he didn't pay the slightest attention to Pony Masud and began discussing the political situation of the country with the esteemed gentlemen sitting on stools in front of his store.

Among the gentlemen were college professors, lawyers, doctors and even a couple of former cultural activists. Therefore, clearly nothing else had happened there, because no one can recall what Masud said after that or when he left that place.

When they noticed that Pony Masud was no longer there, Jabbar Ali began reciting the saga of how Majed-the-Principal had cheated his way through the BA exams, and with that thread, he went back to 1972, when a great festival of exam hall cheating had kicked off in the country, a festival that continued for the next twenty-two years. Jabbar Ali blamed the war; he said that war was never a good thing, because it was a storm, it upended everything, it ate up people's judgement of right and wrong, it gave birth to examples that didn't even occur in the imagination of people before a war.

Jabbar Ali was a communist, but he loved Sheikh Mujib much more than he loved Mani Sinha. On the morning of 15 August 1975, when he heard the arrogant voice of Major Dalim announcing the assassination of Sheikh Mujib, he had wailed, 'This is disaster!' Of course, on that day, the people of Roop Nagar had not expressed any sympathy for Jabbar Ali's distress. In fact, some of them actually said that without the assassination there was no way forward, and many others also said that they had known all along that this was going to happen. Jabbar Ali had asked them, 'Then do you know this too, what is going to happen to Bangladesh?' Nobody answered his question, but Jabbar Ali himself told them, 'Bangladesh will become fodder for vultures. All the vultures here and abroad will come to peck and tear and eat Bangladesh and finish it off.

One day, you'll see, there won't even be a fucking entry called Bangladesh on the map.'

But the esteemed personalities who used to hang out at Jabbar Ali Mia's library did not consider him an oracle. Nor were they pessimistic like him; after Sheikh Mujib's assassination, they began to dream of Bangladesh again. The emergence of Ziaur Rahman lit the flame of hope in their minds, and they tried to illuminate even Jabbar Ali's despairing mind with that light. They spoke of a multi-party democracy while residing within the tight bounds of martial law. But Jabbar Ali Mia laughed in mockery when he heard their words and only said, 'Just wait, just wait.'

In May 1981, the esteemed gentlemen of Roop Nagar comprehended what it was that Jabbar Ali had told them to wait for. When Ziaur Rahman's traitorous soldiers riddled his body with bullets, the people of Roop Nagar looked at each other in befuddlement and said, 'What just happened?' Jabbar Ali Mia said, in the same old manner, 'Just wait, just wait.' As the people of Roop Nagar waited, H.M. Ershad arrived, and still Jabbar Ali's voice repeated the same mantra, 'Just wait.'

Jabbar Ali looked like Jyoti Basu, former Chief Minister of the Indian state of West Bengal. He wore a *fatua* like him, a loose shirt the people of Roop Nagar defined as a panjabi with a shirt collar. People knew that Jabbar Ali was a communist, which meant he was a rabid atheist, but he went to the mosque to say his prayers to pull the wool over people's eyes. Of course, Jabbar Ali himself claimed that he was a better Muslim than many of the Imams employed at the town mosques, and had no dearth of knowledge of the Quran or the Hadiths.

Although the parties were barely noticeable anymore, for a long time he had been close to the members of the NAP-CPB in town. A plastic table fan was always whirring away on a corner of the table in his shop; it was 'Made in Soviet Union', it didn't have a frame, and the three ghee-coloured blades of the fan had, like Jabbar Ali's acne-ridden face, turned blackish over the last fifteen or twenty years. Everyone knew that when Comrade Belal Uddin had worked as Professor Muzaffar Ahmed's sole agent in Roop Nagar, he had, that one time, gotten the chance to tour Moscow. When he returned, he brought back that table fan for Comrade Jabbar Ali Mia, as a gift from socialism.

The people of Roop Nagar say in a gossipy tone that Comrade Belal's trade had been to send students to the Soviet Union. When the wayward son of Shariful the Lawyer had finished his studies in weed and charas and had just started on heroin, then, to rescue him from the clutches of addiction, the lawyer handed Comrade Belal a cheque for a lakh takas and said, 'Send my son off to Moscow then.'

Comrade Belal, the NAP leader, didn't get much of a share from the student scholarships; the CPB men would take most of the cut. But that year, fortune had favoured Comrade Belal in this one thing: after many trips to and from Dhaka, he finally managed to procure a scholarship for Shariful the Lawyer's wayward son. But not for Moscow; he was able to send the son to Tashkent. In the socialist republic of Uzbekistan, weed or heroin was hard to come by, but vodka was in ample supply. Therefore, Shariful the Lawyer's unfortunate son drank bottle after bottle of vodka instead of taking weed or heroin, and thus, he destroyed his liver and eventually died. Ever since his dead body came back from Tashkent, the people of Roop Nagar had been bad mouthing Comrade Belal quite unfairly. 'That atkura Belal never got married anyway, what does he need so much money for, eh?'

The people of Roop Nagar didn't necessarily have a bad impression of communists, it was just Comrade Belal that they disliked; why, nobody could say for sure. Belal didn't broadcast himself as being a 'comrade', but the people of Roop Nagar had seen that, just like the CPB men, he too spoke of communism, and if it rained in Moscow, he held an umbrella open in the drought of Roop Nagar. And if he wasn't a communist, then how did he get to visit Moscow and how did he manage to procure a scholarship for Shariful the Lawyer's son and earn a lakh taka? By then the people of Roop Nagar had forgotten about the electoral symbol of the 'cottage'—the owner of this symbol had bestowed the responsibility of establishing both communism and religious faith side by side on Belal. By then NAP, the National Awami Party, no longer existed, but those who knew a little bit of political history joked whenever NAP was mentioned that the party had wrapped itself in a blanket and gone to take a nap.

Even when nobody except CPB and its affiliate the Farm Labourers' Association were active in the struggle to establish Communism, Jabbar Ali's shop remained the main space for political prattling. People felt a little nostalgic and talked about how the shop beside the post office, under the rain tree, that had a signboard proclaiming, 'Messrs. Jabbar Ali Mia: Elite Newspaper Agent', where, when there wasn't enough space, esteemed personalities of town, leaders and workers of the political and cultural world would stand around all day, was truly a hub of intellectual entertainment and pursuits. People remember that across from Jabbar Ali's shop, on the other side of the street, was Bhulu Thakur's sweetmeat shop, which was connected to Jabbar Ali's shop via an invisible bridge. When there was no more space on Jabbar Ali's pair of stools, the chatterboxes consumed tea and shingaras on the other side, at Bhulu Thakur's shop, as they jabbered about politics and culture. Day and night there continued a steady coming and going of saucers and cups of tea and shingaras from one side to the other.

Jabbar Ali was quite quick-tempered back then, but he didn't yet have diabetes. Actually, people say, Jabbar Ali was just full of himself because he was the local newspaper agent; he never called his shop a shop, he called it a library. There were other libraries, meaning bookstores, in Roop Nagar at the time, but Jabbar Ali was dismissive of the other ones because the learned and esteemed among the townspeople did not congregate in those stores to practise their intellectualism. Jabbar Ali said that there existed only one vibrant hub for intellectual pursuits in town and that was his library. But the chatterboxes, especially the young ones, mocked his pride about this. The key provocateur for the group was Bhulu, the owner of the sweetshop across the road, who was probably half the age of Jabbar Ali. Bhulu was always picking on Jabbar Ali, he couldn't digest his food properly if he didn't taunt Jabbar Ali.

Once Bhulu spread the rumour that Jabbar Ali smoked weed and that's why his eyes were bloodshot sometimes. Bhulu used to get the mischievous ones among the college boys to go after Jabbar Ali; a boy would perhaps approach Jabbar Ali and ask him directly, 'Comrade, why are your eyes red?' Jabbar Ali wouldn't respond because his five senses were on alert and he would figure out that Bhulu had cooked up another prank to provoke him.

One day, at Bhulu's instigation, a guileless young man went up to Jabbar Ali and asked him point blank, 'So you've started to smoke weed at this age?' Jabbar Ali didn't say anything to the young man, instead he glared across the street and started yelling in Bhulu's direction. 'You son of a *malaun*, I shall wreak havoc on your entire family.'

Bhulu immediately became very industrious and shouted back, 'Guru, I'm sending some tea over right now.'

Jabbar Ali shouted even louder, 'You malaun's spawn, I piss in your tea!"

But when the steaming hot cup of tea was presented in front of him, he sipped it in silence.

The people of Roop Nagar remember that once the shutters of the library were drawn for several days because Jabbar Ali was sick. Around that time, an itinerant madman showed up. He slept in front of Jabbar Ali's shop at night and disappeared during the daytime. One afternoon, when he spotted a lungi owned by the madman spread out on a tree branch, Bhulu spread the rumour that Jabbar Ali had gone mad, hung up his lungi on the branch of a tree, and was roaming the streets naked.

When Jabbar Ali recovered from his illness and reopened his shop, people looked at his appearance and pursed their lips in laughter. Then, at Bhulu's instigation, a young man went up to him and said, 'Comrade, I heard you've gone mad? You took off your lungi and hung it on a tree and have been roaming the streets naked?'

Jabbar Ali hurled his Made-in-Soviet-Union table fan at the boy's head and simultaneously shouted, 'You son of a malaun, I shall wreak havoc on your entire family.'

The saucers of shingara and tea had been rushed over from the other side, but this time Jabbar Ali was so angry that two of Bhulu's saucers ended up smashed on the street, a cup handle got broken and a shingara was eaten by a dog, and the parched earth absorbed a cup of tea.

One day a man from the village was riding his bike on his way to town; he had an empty bottle tied to his handlebars to buy kerosene. The bottle banged against the bike and shattered, and the poor man came and stood in front of Bhulu's shop. When he saw Bhulu, he told him about his misfortune with the broken bottle and pleaded, 'Son, can you give me an empty bottle?'

Bhulu Thakur pointed to the shop across the street and advised the man, 'Go over to that store, they sell bottles there.'

The simple villager went and stood in front of Jabbar Ali's desk. Jabbar Ali was engrossed in a book by Aroj Ali Matubbar, the self-taught farmer-philosopher, and he didn't have the time to pay any attention to the man. The man had mewled, 'Son, do you sell empty bottles and such here?'

Eyewitnesses say that at first Jabbar Ali didn't quite understand what the man was asking. His reaction came a little later; suddenly he looked up from his book and looked the man in the eye, then he wrinkled his brow and asked, 'Say what?'

The guileless villager didn't understand the tenor of Jabbar Ali's question, and he repeated in his simple manner, 'Do you sell bottles and such in your store?'

Jabbar Ali roared, 'Says who?'

The man raised his finger to point to Bhulu Thakur's store, where Bhulu stood with several other young men, eagerly looking towards Jabbar Ali and smirking. Jabbar Ali paid them no attention and scolded the villager as, 'Ignorant Bengali', and said, 'You idiot, there are no bottles sold here, it is books that are sold, books!' And he turned his bloodshot eyes to the other side of the street and began shouting, 'You malaun spawn, just let the riots start up again. I'll take your blood.'

Then Bhulu Thakur himself (the people of Roop Nagar realised only later on that Bhulu was scared because the riots were mentioned) ran over to Jabbar Ali with a cup of tea on a saucer and a shingara in another. Jabbar Ali had then thrown the saucer with the shingara onto the ground but pulled the cup of tea to himself and begun to drink it.

8

Once when Bhulu Thakur had gone to Rahim Undershirt Store, he got into a fight with the owner of the store, Abdur Rahim. The alleged reason for the fight was that Rahim had bared his teeth and asked Bhulu, 'How many houses have you bought in India from selling those sweets?' Nobody remembers Bhulu's response anymore because this had happened many years ago. Pony Masud was still only Masud back then; he was probably still nursing at his mother's breast. But the people of Roop Nagar bring Abdur Rahim over to the era of Pony Masud.

The incident that they reminisce about is connected to Salamot's Honda Garage and they are reminded of the incident when the once-fearsome labour leader Farid was horribly humiliated by Pony Masud in that garage. That day Masud's horse broke down badly far from town. It burped in the middle of the road several times, stopped, and just wouldn't start up again. People say that Masud lost his temper so badly that he threw the motorcycle he had purchased for over a lakh takas by the side of the road and began kicking it every which way. The pain that he felt when he kicked the metal body of the machine with his feet made of flesh, enraged him even further and he pulled a cigarette lighter from his pocket and attempted to set it on fire. No information is available on why he didn't carry out this action, or who had stopped him. Hence, people said that this story was just made up. Perhaps Pony Masud himself floated this particular rumour. But others said that Masud wasn't much of a talker, so it didn't seem likely that he was in the habit of making up stories about himself. They said that that story had been fabricated by his friends.

But the latter part of this story is eminently credible: Pony Masud was standing beside his dead horse, perhaps wondering what he should do. A rickshaw-van was going past him with six passengers. Pony Masud forced the passengers to climb off the rickshaw-van by saying, 'Hey, you fuckers, off!' and made them load up his nonfunctioning motorcycle on the van, and then he climbed on himself and instructed the driver to head for Salamot's garage, and fast. The displaced passengers, since they had been forced to get off in the middle of the road, far from their destination, and because they would have to shell out more money to get to their destination, refused to pay the van driver the fare. Pony Masud then kicked them each on their asses in order to establish justice, but justice was not established, because the passengers ran away when their asses were kicked and so the van-driver was deprived of their fare money.

When they reached Salamot's garage and the van driver unloaded Masud's dead horse and held out his hand for the fare, Pony Masud slapped his left cheek with his right hand. The slap rang out loudly and the van driver began to sob. Salamot came forward and reproached the simple, rural van-driver as an idiot, and without explaining the noteworthiness of Pony Masud's identity, he said, 'Do you know who you just asked for money, do you know?' Then the simple, rural young man looked at Pony Masud's face with infinite surprise. Pony Masud paid no attention to him and ordered Salamot to get his motorcycle running in ten minutes. Salamot tinkered around a little and said, 'You've run this machine to the ground, driving it any way you want to. It's going to take time.'

Pony Masud said, 'Don't have time.'

Then Salamot had said in a mildly annoyed tone, 'It doesn't help to say you don't have time, it's not like I know magic.'

Pony Masud raised his hand in a slap and said, 'Remember who you're talking to! Keep your eyes lowered, you fucker. Work. I'll be back in half an hour. Make sure it's ready.'

Thus, placing Salamot in a hard test, Pony Masud strode off towards the railway crossing. When he was near the crossing, he saw the owner of Rahim Undershirt Store, Abdur Rahim, riding towards him in a leisurely manner on a shiny new Hero Honda. Pony Masud stopped him with a raised hand. Abdur Rahim displayed his teeth and asked him in a bubbly voice, 'Masud, are you well?'

Pony Masud paid no attention to his question, which was intended to butter him up, and asked, 'You bought this ride; how much was it?'

Abdur Rahim, who had nine years of schooling, said in English, 'Sebinty fibe thousand. How does it look?'

Pony Masud didn't praise the motorcycle but said, 'Tax?'

Rahim pulled out a hundred-taka bill from his pocket and held it out to Masud. 'Here, have some tea.'

Masud pushed Rahim's hand, with the money, away with his right hand and said, 'Get off.'

Abdur Rahim's eyes blazed, grew bigger, and he blurted out, 'What do you mean?'

Pony Masud told him again to get off his motorcycle, but according to how people described it, this time Pony Masud didn't sound like a thug because, like a reasonable person, he explained his need. 'My ride broke down suddenly. I have to get to Hili urgently. You'll get your ride back in the afternoon.'

People say that when he heard such a reasonable request from Pony Masud, Abdur Rahim voluntarily stepped off his motorcycle, and Masud climbed on it right away, but then suddenly Abdur Rahim, for some reason, expressed some doubt. 'Truly?'

The observant among the people of Roop Nagar later analysed it thus: with that last question, Rahim himself arranged for a pounding of his anus. Pony Masud had initially thought of returning his motorcycle that very afternoon, because initially he hadn't thought of expropriating an expensive thing belonging to someone else. It was when Abdur Rahim questioned aloud whether Pony Masud would truly return his motorcycle that afternoon, that the notion pierced Masud's brain—that was the moment he got the idea. So, Abdur Rahim never got his motorcycle back.

That afternoon, Abdur Rahim went looking for Masud at the house of his actual father, Majed-the-Principal, but he didn't find Masud there, instead he found Majed. The father had apparently heard the story about his son borrowing Abdur Rahim's motorcycle and chuckled without making any comment. And apparently, when he saw that chuckle, Abdur Rahim thought that he already knew about this incident, that father and son had conspired together to make it happen. Later on, Abdur Rahim told people that he realised from Majed-the-Principal's behaviour right away that his beloved motorcycle had been seized from him forever. But people do not believe Abdur Rahim. They say that Abdur Rahim must have gone to Majed-the-Principal's house with the hope of getting his motorcycle back, and that hope was what kept him waiting there for hours into the evening, because if he had understood right then and there that he wasn't getting his bike back, then he wouldn't have left his shop and wasted three whole hours just waiting there, because he was so dedicated to his shop that he wouldn't leave even when his wife was in labour.

Two days after that, or maybe two weeks (or it could even be two months), it was medicine-seller Mottalib Hossain's misfortune that he ran into Pony Masud while on his way to deposit two lakh takas in Janata Bank, when according to one eyewitness, Masud swiped the bag of money from him and just walked away in front of everyone; people watched Mottalib

Hossain stand unmoving in the middle of the sun-scorched street like a corpse hit by lightning from a cloudless sky.

Mottalib Hossain didn't go to the police station, he went to Pony Masud's father. He clasped the man's hand, weeping and pleading, saying that his son could keep one lakh taka and return one lakh to him, or else he would be out on the streets. Majed-the-Principal had then said to Mottalib Hossain, 'What can you do, son! You've just got bad luck, nothing to do about that!'

A few days later, masons showed up at Majed-the-Principal's house and, smoking bidis, chewing betel leaf and chatting about Pony Masud's heroism, they rolled up their sleeves and busied themselves in transforming Majed-the-Principal's one-storied house into two stories. People said that Pony Masud didn't necessarily need to grab Mottalib Hossain's money to build another story on Majed-the-Principal's house. Because by then he had already made a lot of money.

Then the incident of Masud grabbing three lakh takas in cash from a *hundi* trader, who transferred money on credit for people, resurfaces. People talk about the bus which had 'Dhaka to Hili via Roop Nagar' painted on its windscreen, which a hundi trader had caught in Bogra, and who had three lakh in cash resting in a gunny sack by his feet. They say that Pony Masud wasn't merely a thug, he must have had some supernatural powers. Otherwise, how could he have known that Agarwal the hundi trader was taking three lakh takas in a sack to Hili? It was afternoon, and high up in the sky the sun burned. It is incomprehensible as to why the people of Roop Nagar disregard other issues and keep mentioning details like mid-afternoon, broad daylight, etc. Because for Pony Masud, broad daylight was no different than the dead of night. If he decided to break someone's neck, broad daylight didn't have the power to impede him; he didn't need the darkness of the dead night. He could, in the brightness of day, slide a six-inch blade into the fat belly of a Marwari hundi trader right up to the hilt, and all the people would watch the scene with their mouths hanging open, and the police SI would show up later upon receiving the news and say, 'Damn straight, brother Masud, these malaun spawns will eat and eat in Bangladesh, but they'll benefit only India. These bastards have no end to their wealth, but look at how the bastards live in tin houses; they don't even build proper housing, as if they're living in tents. To them, Bangladesh is a marketplace: do business here and make money and then send it to India, and whatever you want to build, houses, mansions, do it in India, not in Bangladesh.'

It wasn't just the police that held this view of Hindus and Marwaris; the majority of people of Roop Nagar believed that Hindus and Marwaris didn't consider Bangladesh their native land, that they did not love this country. Day and night, asleep or awake, they dreamt of India. They brought in weed and Phensedyl to fuck the asses of the youth here, and they took bell metal-brass-gold back to India; they wanted to transform India into a land of gold while making all arrangements for transforming Bangladesh into a cremation ground.

As they talked about Hindus and Marwaris, the people of Roop Nagar who had strong memories recalled that the town had once belonged mostly to the Hindus. The red houses on either side of the main street, the remnants of which were still there, were not owned by any Muslims. They recalled Jogendra Lal Nandi, because of whom they thought the name of Roop Nagar, the beautiful city, was apt; because that wealthy son of the local zamindar wasn't merely wealthy, he was an actor even more skilled than Chhabi Biswas, but because he didn't really care for fame, he curtailed his rapacity to become famous throughout the land by going to Calcutta and proving his prowess there, and he gloried in loving the tiny town of Roop Nagar. The festivities that would commence each year after the *Nabanna*, the new harvest!

The people then recalled a man known as Ajit the Doctor, the young son of a zamindar who, alongside healing Muslim subjects, was also deeply focused on attaining excellence in football. At this point, the people of Roop Nagar, especially people like Jabbar Ali Mia, said that they had sinned. Because Muslim boys humiliated Ajit the Doctor on the football field, the bastard country called Pakistan was born, and millions of Bengalis gave their blood to break up that country. The sons of the Muslim subjects who Ajit the Doctor had transformed into skilled footballers grew angry after 1965. They said that the sin wasn't just on one side; the question of why the fishmongers at the marketplace wouldn't let Muslims even touch the biggest rohu and carp, and why only the Brahmins had a monopoly on purchasing the big fish, came up. It was then that the Hindu Babus realised that those days were gone. Nevertheless, according to the people of Roop Nagar, the riots of 1946 happened, as did the Partition of 1947, yet the harmony of Roop Nagar remained unmarred. The curtains did not fall on the theater stage of the Jogendra Lal Nandis. During 1960-65, the era of intense anti-Rabindranath sentiment, Rabindranath Tagore's play *Blood Oleander* was staged in Roop Nagar; they said 'what can we tell you about 1971, *bahey*! Those Punjabi soldiers shot their bullets, *fotash-fotash*—where were we supposed to run off to? There was no way other than fleeing to India. Mongol Bari, Pagla Dewan, Hili—whichever way we could take, we had no choice but to take our lives in our hands and slide into India.'

At this point, the people of Roop Nagar spoke of Sheikh Mujib; the man's name was magic back then. It was that magic which had led to fierce battle; this fight wasn't just a fight, the people of Roop Nagar had never seen such a war in all of their fourteen generations. But it was possible that the people of Roop Nagar did not truly enjoy stories of war; their descriptions of the Liberation War were not that long. They noticed suddenly that the enchantment engendered by the magic of Sheikh Mujib's name had disappeared. The people of Roop Nagar said that Sheikh shaheb had given them nothing, his men had gotten richer by stealing the blankets supplied as relief goods while people across the country starved to death. They remembered that when a cake weighing fifty-four pounds was being cut in Dhaka to commemorate Sheikh shaheb's birthday, the villagers living near Roop Nagar were dying while trying to quell their hunger with hog-potatoes, though hog-potatoes were not human food—they were only digestible in a hog's belly.

It is possible that a kind of regret or disappointment about the Liberation War existed in the minds of the people of Roop Nagar. It was mostly the bitter memories from those days that they combed through. They recalled, for no particular reason, that the freedom fighter Habibur Rahman had become a magistrate after the war, and when his old friends lobbied him and offered biryani, he would say, 'Habib doesn't eat biryani, it's money he eats, money!'

They also discussed the money-hunger of Aftab, the general secretary of Awami League. When the well-known collaborator Abdul Halim had taken a drubbing from the freedom fighters and sought shelter at the house of Maqbul Haji, when Maqbul Haji's young brother Lutfor had engaged in battle with Aftab's group with his double-barreled gun to protect Abdul Halim, then, in the middle of the glorious Liberation War, they bargained over how much Aftab would need to be paid to desist from his attempts to kill the collaborator Abdul Halim. Back then, in 1971, the deal was struck for twenty thousand takas; the Awami League leader and freedom fighter Aftab had granted the razakar Abdul Halim the opportunity to flee to safe shelter in exchange for twenty thousand takas.

9

There came a time in Pony Masud's life when he seemed to have gone mad. The people of Roop Nagar could not describe the cruelty of his actions in detail, possibly because it made them sick. All they could say was that Pony Masud slit open this man's throat and then washed his face and his hands with water from the tube-well in the district school playground, and then pulled out a cigarette from his pocket and smoked it. Or they could say that Pony Masud pulverised the arms and legs of that boy with a hammer. Or they could say that Pony Masud threw that other man on the ground, flat on his back, and jumped up and down on his chest. After killing sixteen people and maiming forty with such methods, a time came when he could find pleasure in nothing, and he started drinking too much alcohol. By then he no longer had any more rivals in Roop Nagar and he no longer found joy in killing people; and hence, apparently, his days and nights had become dreadfully monotonous and dreary. People say that Pony Masud grew drowsy.

But that was merely a temporary condition. It didn't take long for it to pass; one day, he shook himself awake and for pretty much no reason at all, he thrashed the district administrator's driver, ripping his uniform so badly that the man was almost naked. The victim's crime was that he had delayed moving his car to the side when Pony Masud had attempted to overtake him. The district administrator wasn't in the car at that moment; and there was some slight difference of opinion regarding whether his presence would have made any difference in how Pony Masud flexed his muscles. It was said that the district administrator's driver, who was a young man from the Garo tribe, had told his employer that if he didn't sort out this unfair abuse by Pony Masud, he would no longer work for him. Later on, the district administrator summoned Pony Masud via Hafiz Mondal to the DC office, but Pony Masud had ignored his summons. The district administrator, according to the townspeople, didn't 'push it' and hence the incident was resolved.

A few days later, the townspeople noticed a new chauffeur driving the district administrator's car and they were split in their opinions: one side claimed that the Garo driver, when he witnessed his boss's cowardice, kicked the job in the face and left; the other side claimed that he abandoned the job because he was scared of Pony Masud and fled the town with his life in his hand.

But Ruhul Sir couldn't afford to abandon this town with his daughter because he owned a house here. The day that Pony Masud called the teen daughter of his high school English teacher 'hot stuff', which prompted the strict district school teacher Ruhul Amin to roar out the colonial era curse of 'rascal', that day, right there, when the townspeople saw Pony Masud threaten his former teacher with, 'Just go straight home, sir, or there's going to be trouble', they realised that the days when it was still possible to live in this town with one's daughter and wife maintaining some amount of dignity was over.

But it is difficult to determine precisely when this incident occurred, because the people of Roop Nagar tell the stories that happened later first and tell the stories that happen first later. After killing sixteen people and maiming forty, it was no big deal for Pony Masud to call a young girl (even if she was the daughter of a respected teacher) 'hot stuff.' But pinpointing the time of the occurrence was of no use to the people of Roop Nagar. They recalled that Ruhul Amin, the strict English teacher of the district school, had also been the teacher of the once-fearsome Laltu-the-Thug. The number of boys on whose backs he had broken canes was beyond count. Even a mighty goon like Laltu-the-Thug had never had the guts to puff a cigarette in front of him. To call the daughter of that teacher 'hot stuff', and that too in front of him, and when the teacher protested, to order him to go straight home, threatening that otherwise things would turn bad, was an unprecedented 'terrifically serious' act. After that incident, worried whether it would be possible for any decent family with wives-mothers-daughters to survive in Roop Nagar with their dignity intact, the people of Roop Nagar began to tell the story of the rape of a young girl from the Santal tribe.

Some said that the young girl had been raped under the leadership of Pony Masud. Others said that Pony himself wasn't involved in the incident; it was some of his friends, whose tastes ran lower than his, who partook of excessive amounts of Phensedyl and weed, who did this bad thing. They abducted a young girl from the Santal locality, which was separated from the northside of town by a few acres of sugarcane, and brought her to a nearby school building, where they threw her onto the ground and gang-raped her.

But there was some doubt, because an eyewitness to a part of the incident, the young girl's paternal grandmother, had only named Pony Masud. The people of Roop Nagar figured that the old woman had uttered his name because Pony Masud was famous for such incidents and she hadn't known anyone else's name. It could also be true that the old Santal woman only knew Pony Masud's name and had never actually seen him with her own eyes before. It was also said that Masud or his friends hadn't picked the girl up from her home, that on the evening of the incident, she had been on her way home with her elderly grandmother and, just as foxes snatch a hen, they grabbed the girl and took her away. Dholabari Primary School was right beside the road, and some say that they pulled together a few benches into a makeshift cot in one of the classrooms, while others say it was right on the dry, hard floor of the classroom that she was thrown flat on her back, and with Pony Masud, or perhaps without him, his friends had raped the girl again and again. When the girl's heart was lodged in her throat, the Santal men surrounded the Dholabari Primary School, roaring and carrying their bows and arrows. But it's clear that they did not surround the schoolhouse properly because the rapists climbed through the broken windows in the back and easily fled into the darkness of the night.

The people of Roop Nagar had thought that Santals wouldn't let such a grave offence go; surely they would besiege Majed-the-Principal's house, bows and arrows in hand. But they saw that nothing like that was happening; then they said that these Santals were no longer like the Santals of the olden days, or perhaps they had never been that fearsome anyway. Some said that the Santal men and boys who had rushed towards Dholabari School that evening ululating weren't carrying bows or arrows.

Then their discussion began to go off in irrelevant directions. Actually, they wanted to talk about the bows and arrows they had seen in childhood and experience a little romance from that loss. But they were thoroughly lacking in the practice of maintaining continuity in their stories. The Santals had forgotten the use of bows and arrows a long time ago—they mentioned this and then immediately began to describe the tidy, neat, well-kept front yards of Santal households and said that they knew how to prepare a delicious masoor dal. Many Santals had become Christian, there were almost no non-Christian Santals left anymore. And after noting these details with regret, they enquired among themselves whether the Santals had been Hindu before converting to Christianity, because of course they'd never been Muslim, and they remembered that they used to perform weird poojas and rituals. As they speculated on why, before 'those pig-eating Christians' showed up to turn the Santals next door into Christians, they couldn't have been turned into Muslims, and whether this negligence in spreading the word of Islam was a major sin on the part of the Muslims, the people of Roop Nagar discovered that they had never sought to discover whether all those who lived in the Santal Patti were Santals, or whether there were people of the Orao or Buna tribes there as well, or whether there actually was any difference in how they lived their daily lives.

At any rate, those black-skinned, bony, short men and women, especially the women, now worked in the fields for the farmers in the neighbouring villages. The Santal women, with their babies bound to their backs, could be spotted sowing or reaping rice in the middle of the fields, bent at the waist. The people of Roop Nagar praised the endurance of the Santal women; they were astonished when they saw that the Santal women would chew a couple of fistfuls of flattened rice, down it with a couple of gulps of water, bind their babies to their backs, and descend into the farmers' fields to sow rice seedlings, and once they hunched down, they didn't look up or straighten their spines even once until they finished sowing the entire field. The people of Roop Nagar asked in surprise, what do the Santal men do? It's only the women who are seen working in the fields—what kind of work do the men do for their livelihoods? But they didn't search for an answer to this question and instead began to tell stories about bows and arrows. Apparently, the Santal men used to hunt hawks and vultures and even crows with their bows, and hunting meant eating—apparently, there was no creature in Allah's creation that they wouldn't eat. The people of Roop Nagar took this opportunity to return to the nostalgia-suffused days of their own childhoods, and therefore, the incident of the Santal girl being raped disappeared under their memories.

When they still lived in the villages, before their fathers and grandfathers came to Roop Nagar town to build their homes, back in those days, in the wintry evenings of Poush and Magh, the men and children of the Santal and Buna tribes would attack the rat burrows in the recently harvested empty fields, and they would pull out the fattened-from-gorging-on-rice rats using fantastic skills and then they would whoop loudly and chase those fleeing rats across the empty fields, and with astonishing dexterity, grab the tails of the fleeing rats and slam them on the ground, and the rats would go thwack; and then they would hang the dead rats from their waist-wraps by their long tails and rush back to seek even more burrows. With dead rats garlanding their waists, they whooped their way across the fields, in search of more rats. Then they would gather straw and kindling and build a fire and roast the rats and eat them.

'Yuck, those filthy animals!' The people of Roop Nagar distorted their faces and spoke with disgust about the tastes of the Santal people, and then suddenly they mentioned that the day after Pony Masud called Ruhul Sir's daughter, who was a student of class nine, 'hot stuff', she was seen wearing a borkha. The people of Roop Nagar felt a crisis about living in that town with their daughters and wives and dignity and suddenly they shifted to analysing Pony Masud's sexual proclivities and they discovered that, compared to his power and his ferocity, his record of carrying out rapes was, as of yet, insignificant; perhaps they were attempting to reassure themselves with this discovery. Some said in a mocking tone, Pony Masud's rape record wasn't low so far because he lacked the urge; they faux-praised him and said, 'Oh, that Herculean body just can't hack it, you know.' However, this opinion was not accepted by all. The general consensus was that the topmost thugs were not necessarily the topmost lechers. They mentioned Lame Khokhon, who had once or twice pulled the scarves off schoolgirls but hadn't had a reputation for rape. They also recalled Laltu-the-Thug; at one point, his depredations had led to where the young girls and women of Roop Nagar had almost stopped attending their schools or colleges, but it wasn't because lust had turned him into a crazed bull lusting in heat; in truth, he was looking for a girlfriend, but no girl had grown enamoured of his heroism and held out her hand to him. Laltu-the-Thug had even, allegedly, stood at the intersection and shouted within earshot of the girls on their way to school, 'Why does nobody love me?'

Ruhul Sir's young daughter began attending school imprisoned in a borkha top to toe. Who knows whether they were copying her, but the townspeople saw that among the crowd of girls wearing the uniforms of blue dress-white scarf-white loose pants-white sneakers, one by one, the number of incongruous black-clad phantoms grew. Of course, borkhas began to receive love in Roop Nagar even before that, it was difficult to say whether this was a strategy to avoid notice of the thugs because most of the women who went about caged in their borkhas weren't young, rather they were past their prime; even if they weren't wearing borkhas, the bad men wouldn't really set their eyes on them. Many of these women had once upon a time worn gauzy chiffon saris and sleeveless blouses. They had, once upon a time, worn their saris below the navel and visited flower shows, Baishakhi festivals, victory day celebrations, prize distribution ceremonies and cultural programmes at their children's schools, and now children spotted borkha-clad figures in the streets or departmental stores and shouted, 'Ghosts! Ghosts!' in fear. These borkhas truly were fearsome; there was no way to even see the eyes of those wearing the borkhas as their eyes were covered with a piece of netting. They didn't leave their houses without borkhas, and when inside their homes, they strictly maintained the purdah even in front of their husbands, sons or grandsons. Their blouse sleeves extended to their wrists, and their necklines were high, like turtleneck sweaters.

The people of Roop Nagar praised the women's modesty, but they also had amusing comments about the drawbacks of the borkha system. They said that the number of borkhas had increased in Roop Nagar although adultery had not decreased; that nobody could say that the swapping of hearts between these women and men had ebbed just because more of the women were wearing borkhas. And in the context of men and women mingling illicitly in secret, borkhas were a very convenient cover.

It wasn't just women who wore the borkha, apparently in Roop Nagar, men also used borkhas when needed. Brickly Mokhles himself was a burning example of this practice: if the thing called borkha had never been invented, then it would never have been possible for Brickly Mokhles to seduce Majed-the-Principal's wife. Although the people of Roop Nagar had been unable to discover how Laili Begum's dalliance with Brickly Mokhles had begun, they had heard that Brickly

Mokhles was able to show up at Majed-the-Principal's house in person due to the virtues of the borkha. Sometimes it even happened that Majed-the-Principal was home, he was sitting in the veranda, grading papers or doing some other chore, and Brickly Mokhles would slide right into Majed-the-Principal's bedroom. The vulgar among the people of Roop Nagar said that it was the borkha's marvel that had allowed Brickly Mokhles to fuck Majed-the-Principal right in the ass.

10

The people of Roop Nagar couldn't agree on which direction Pony Masud took that day when he roared off on his Yamaha 125 horse right in front of the wide eyes of the officers, other employees and customers of the Roop Nagar branch of Sonali Bank, and the passersby on the streets. At first everyone saw him speeding off eastwards, but there was disagreement about whether he went farther east after crossing the railway shack or whether he turned left onto Hili Road. Most people claimed that he didn't go farther east, and instead had made a left turn. One or two people, who claimed to be eyewitnesses, said that Masud crossed the rail shack and turned left near Pachu's hotel and sped along Hili Road. The problem was that Pony Masud's father Majed-the-Principal and stepfather Brickly Mokhles both had houses at different points along that road. Nobody was sure about which of his fathers' homes Masud had entered. Many said that he had gone to his stepfather's house again because his mother was waiting for the money there. But others said that Pony Masud didn't return to that house that day, because at that point all he had in his pocket was still that same eight and a half thousand takas because he had flung the cheque from Murari Prasad Dutta on the desk of the manager of Sonali Bank

Roop Nagar Branch instead of depositing it. They believed that Masud was not a guy who would show up to visit his mother without the amount she had specified.

Despite the fact that the woman had a bad character, Pony Masud loved his mother dearly; this one piece of praise was what the people of Roop Nagar repeated about him. They said that it was an unthinkable situation for Pony Masud that his mother had asked him for money and he couldn't immediately give it to her; and therefore, in that moment, he felt discombobulated. It wasn't like he didn't have money in the bank—in fact, people believed that he had millions of takas saved in the bank—but the thought that he had been unable to hand his mother a mere ten thousand takas the moment she asked for it set his brain on fire. Thus, the Masud who had the nerve to walk into the den of any businessman and walk out with thousands of takas in cash, couldn't even think properly when he couldn't get the cash from Murari, and instead of hitting up another trader's establishment, he grew crazed with extreme rage.

The devotees of filial devotion reported that the inability to give a mere ten thousand takas as soon as the number came out of his mother's mouth made Masud lose all practical sense, and therefore, even when he had a cheque for ten thousand takas in his hand, he kicked the inoffensive Murari Prasad in the face and broke his fleshy nose, slapped the bank manager, pulled his gun out in broad daylight inside the bank and did a 'scene create'. But in the moment, it didn't occur to him that there were at least twenty more businessmen like Murari Prasad in town, and he could easily descend on the lair of any of them and leave with not just ten, but twenty, even fifty thousand in cash and give it to his mother, without creating a scene.

People believed that an inexorable ill omen was working behind all of this. That morning, in the alley in front of their house, Masud had kicked an old beggar in the ass and the beggar he had just assaulted muttered, 'You have misfortune written for you today.' Soon after, the old man had vanished, never to be seen again. Suddenly, the people of Roop Nagar were reminded of Khokon-the-Cripple; this memory arose quite suddenly, because nobody could even remember when, it must have been ages ago, Khokon-the-Cripple had died and slipped below ground.

But Khokon's face and the gradual evolution of his appearance floated in front of their eyes: the shirt with the collar like a dog's tongue clung to Khokon's body as if he was wearing nothing at all, and Khokon's buttocks and thighs clad in bell bottoms with ankles that were forty inches wide were famous. His full head of jet-black hair grew down to the base of his neck—he was a hippie, and the young men of Roop Nagar called him 'Hippppie'. He used to walk around with a dagger in his pocket, drink and yank off the scarves that the college girls wore, and the boys of the town, on seeing a movie villain roam around, simultaneously felt fear and elation.

The fruit orchard behind Khokon's family house was known to everyone as Jania's orchard, but nobody knew who Jania was, or how long ago he was from. Jania's orchard had many different kinds of fruit trees, and among them were a famous pair of lychee trees. Khokon's maternal grandfather's house was in Dinajpur and apparently his father, right after he got married, brought back saplings of the famed pomegranate-lychees from the land of his father-in-law and planted them in the orchard. The pomegranate-lychees of Dinajpur, or so the people of Roop Nagar said, were far tastier than Rajshahi lychees; in fact, the finest kind of lychees grew in Dinajpur, not in Rajshahi. Among the Dinajpur lychees, the finest breed was the pomegranate-lychee, which had tiny pits, and thus were enticingly meaty.

So Khokon's father, before Khokon was even born, planted a pair of saplings in his own garden brought over from Dinajpur with the far-reaching dream of enjoying the small-pitted, fleshy pomegranate-lychees not only at his in-laws', but also in his own home across the generations. But when the trees fruited, Khokon's father was astonished to see that the lychee pits were quite large. After he plucked a ripe lychee from the tree and ate it, people overheard him say with the pit in his palm and his brows creased, 'Damn, are these lychee pits or goats' balls?' Still, no other tree in Roop Nagar bore such luscious lychees; in fact, there were no other lychee trees in the town at all. Khokon adored lychees and he used to guard those trees from when he was a little boy. When they spoke of Khokon's infatuation with lychees, people said Khokon had a thing for lychees.

That was the year after the war; the schools had only just begun to teach the national anthem 'My golden Bengal'. One day, several shirtless, barefoot, naughty little boys went to the Jania orchard to steal lychees. Suddenly, Khokon appeared out of nowhere; he hadn't become a thug yet, but that kind of spunk he had been born with. There was a bamboo grove beside the lychee trees; he broke off an unripened bamboo cane, and when he whacked the bare backs of those boys a few times apparently, they wailed, 'Oh, ma, oh, ma, oh golden Bengal, I'm dying,' and fled the scene. The people of Roop Nagar laughed uproariously at that and then admitted that once upon a time they used to listen to 'My golden Bengal' on the radio quite often and sang it throughout the day.

Although the Liberation War took place when both of Khokon's legs were still undamaged, he had neither gone off to fight nor had he joined the razakar collaborator force. Khokon hadn't gone off to war, but it was with regard to him that the people of Roop Nagar spoke of the Liberation War; the stories that everyone knew were the ones that they told this way and that, again and again. Khokon had no connection to the war, but whenever the subject of the Liberation War came up, they said that Khokon's moustache had already sprouted by then and many boys his age had gone to war, so surely why he didn't go was a question. Had he joined the collaborators, there would have been a justification/explanation. Why, despite being such a spunky, vigorous young man, Khokon had remained aloof during that fierce time, or where he had been during that period of nine months or how he had spent his days, gave rise to much conjecture. Many people said that Khokon had no interest in politics, but others immediately protested that during that time, many other people who went off to war had had absolutely no connection to politics. Therefore, according to them, participating in the Liberation War was an act utterly disconnected from interest or disinterest in politics. The people of Roop Nagar recalled that two renowned thugs of the time, Nader and Qader, had also gone to war, and a mere three days before liberation arrived, they had been martyred during direct combat with the Pakistani forces at the Hili border, and so they passed judgement that although Nader and Qader had been thugs, they had also been patriots, which they had proved by laying their lives down for the country. Of course, a few people expressed doubt that if they hadn't been martyred, and if they had returned to a liberated country, they would not have obeyed the orders of the leader Sheikh Mujib and surrendered their weapons like good boys; instead, they would have used those weapons to commit burglaries. Because, they said, many of the good boys had returned from war looking like thugs; their hair and beards evoked fear, and many of them remained within the dazed addiction to bullets that they had fallen into while training for war.

The people of Roop Nagar recalled that at the beginning of the war, there was looting that happened in the Bihari neighbourhood; regular people who were enraged wanted to kill the Biharis, and they *had* killed them, and bad-natured men had looted their homes. In early April, three corpses floated face down in Salam Bihari's pond; the corpses were women, because the dead bodies of men do not float face down. The people of Roop Nagar, those who had seen the corpses or heard stories about other people seeing the corpses, described the episode with the confidence of eyewitnesses: people were so angry that the boys from the Students' Union and Chhatra League had to stand guard in the Bihari neighbourhood all night to protect the innocent Biharis from them.

It seemed that while they stood watch over the Bihari neighbourhood, the war ended. They told these stories as if the nation's liberation and the Awami League people pilfering the wheat and the blankets that had been supplied as relief goods had all happened in the blink of an eye. The Students' Union boys recovered many sacks of the relief-wheat from the house a minor Awami League leader, Mafiz the Wheat Thief, and they piled the sacks in front of the railway shack and made Mafiz stand atop that heap with a garland of shoes around his neck. And thus they repaired the vision of the just-concluded Liberation War. And then, the Rakkhi Bahini, elite militia, rushed over from the CO Colony and began shooting off, *phot phot phot*, and the Students' Union boys had to flee Roop Nagar, just as they had once escaped the Pakistani forces.

Then the people of Roop Nagar, without any warning, began to praise Field Marshal Ayyub Khan. They said that the Pakistani period had been better than the present, that back then thieves didn't speak out with their voices loud; people carried out bribery and corruption in secrecy; nobody could get rich by illegal means and show off—they found no respect in society, nor did they have any clout. 'Son of a gun,' they praised Ayyub Khan and reported that his police force were true friends to the people and that the police force of liberated Bangladesh were all in cahoots with thieves and robbers. The people of Roop Nagar spoke of SDOs and magistrates from Ayyub Khan's era with respect, and they swore that the current DCs and SPs were all dick pubes, because these administrators, according to the people of Roop Nagar, licked the asses of the weed and Phensedyl smugglers.

Khokon-the-Cripple had not fought during the War of Liberation either as a razakar or as a freedom fighter, but during the early days of his youth after the war, he had become a thug, a hippie. He hadn't been able to pass the test even though he sat for the exams with a dagger stuck on his seat at the exam hall, but he was an ace at assault. The people of Roop Nagar, who had been boys back then but were now adults, tried to trace the source of such brazen shows of power. Khokon was not politically minded, he belonged to no political party or godfather (someone interrupted this account to correct an error and confidently claimed that the term 'godfather' wasn't even in vogue then), and nobody could even remember Khokon carrying a dagger instead of a pistol, in which case, as they explored the question of the roots of Khokon's displays, they discovered that times changed. They came to the conclusion that back then, the patronage of a political party wasn't essential to becoming a thug, but in the present, it wasn't possible to even become a small-time thug unless one stood under the umbrella of a political party. Khokon was scared of the police and didn't smoke in front of the esteemed gentlemen of the city. Someone said that Khokon was socially isolated and hated, and he himself had been aware of this. Burglars don't brag that they've become burglars; they perpetrate their burglaries in the dark of night, never identifying themselves as burglars in the light of day. Khokon's father would sorrowfully say that his son had gone bad and Khokon used to get drunk and wail that he was a boy gone bad. But now Masud stuck his chest out and proclaimed in public that he was Pony Masud, and even the DC would offer him a chair and pamper him in a thousand ways.

While discussing Pony Masud's good relationship with the District Administrator of Roop Nagar, the topic of police came up. The people of Roop Nagar repeated stories about the 'falling on each other's neck with love' between Pony Masud and the police in a snide manner. Although they themselves said that the word 'love' about Pony Masud's relationship with the police wasn't really accurate, because other than one superintendent of police, Pony Masud didn't give a hoot about any other policemen. Instead, they described various scenes that were the very opposite in nature:

Sub-Inspector Malek had held open a pack of 555 cigarettes and offered it to Pony Masud, and Pony Masud waved it away scornfully, saying, 'Masud's brand is Benson & Hedges.' And then SI Malek said, 'Oh, I completely forgot,' and shouted at the shopkeeper nearby, 'Hey, bring over a pack of Bensons!'

The people of Roop Nagar also talked about a newly arrived and quickly departed police superintendent, who had a beautiful young daughter, and the daughter went to college in the governmental jeep, and she had caught Pony Masud's eye. But she was, after all, the daughter of the SP, as the people of Roop Nagar say, and why should the SP's daughter tolerate being ogled by a nasty thug? She complained to daddy, and then SI Malek had shown up to see Pony Masud. 'Masud Bhai, please, don't get into any clashes with the new boss. He's got a terrible temper.' Pony Masud had, allegedly, chuckled and said, 'Your sir will be weeping soon.'

'Don't say such disastrous things, brother. If sir issues the order, we're left with no choice.'

Pony Masud took the SI's feeble warning as a serious threat issued in a gentle tone, and in return, he issued a challenge that 'all the swine' from Roop Nagar police station should join forces and try to pull out a single strand of pubic hair from the base of his male organ.

One day the superintendent invited Pony Masud to tea. Pony Masud sat with his legs crossed, smoking a cigarette in the presence of this man who was his father's age, and said, 'Get a transfer and leave.'

People said that the SP had been so astonished on hearing that straight to his face, 'not even an "ah" came out through his lips' for several minutes.

Then the DC (who luckily did not have a young daughter) advised the superintendent that, in the interests of peace and self-respect, it would be best for him to get a transfer elsewhere. Of course, the backstory that people heard was that the new superintendent had gotten into an unresolvable conflict with the DC over their shares of the smuggling and the loan-business at the Hili border, and that Pony Masud had taken the DC's side.

11

Because of Laili Begum's dream at daybreak, and the appearance of a mysterious old traveller that very morning, and then his disappearance right after proclaiming, 'There's news, *khobor achhey*', and then the newspapers reporting the arrest of Pony Majid or Pony Masud, the people of Roop

Nagar remembered Khokon-the-Cripple because within their minds moved a magical image very much like the old beggar who Pony Masud kicked in the ass and was cursed by, and to them the curses of such an old man seemed to hold profound significance. It was an elderly traveller, who had been called a beggar, but who wasn't really a beggar, and why did he come back to this town again and again and why was it that other than a fortunate few, nobody else ever saw him?

Khokon-the-Cripple had been walking along the railway tracks one evening, drunk, and for no good reason, he had kicked the blind, old man in the back, and the eye sockets of the blind traveller—where instead of eyes there were two holes—had lit up like balls of fire, and his unfailing curse had echoed across the sky and the earth, 'a bamboo will make its way, you devil!'

Some people said that the old man had prophesied in very clear words that a bamboo was going to go up Khokon's anus; but when, seven years later, Khokon-the-Cripple died because the tip of a bamboo stabbed him in the guts. disembowelling him, many people concluded that the old man had not specified whether the bamboo would enter his anus or rip his belly apart. All the old man had said was 'a bamboo will make its way', and had ended with the word 'devil', which echoed for a long time across Baro Ghati, the pond by the train tracks.

But there was a seven year wait until the bamboo; before that, Khokon had to pass through several levels of the blind traveller's curse. After that accursed evening, nobody saw the blind traveller around anymore, and therefore he received the honour of being a *darbesh*, a holy man, and one afternoon, Khokon stumbled at exactly that same spot on the tracks and the big toe of his right foot began gushing blood and then the wound became septic.

A little later, people saw Khokon walking by with a pair of newly bought crutches wedged in his armpits; the bottom part of his right pants leg hung loose, swaying, and the cuffs narrowed by then, and his shirt collar was a little narrower and looked less like a dog's tongue.

Even when Khokon walked by with his crutches, he scared boys by the fire in his eyes, and girls fled when they happened to come face to face with him. Someone described it thus: 'One day Khokon was going by, and his pant leg was just hanging below his amputated leg, and I ran over and grabbed the bit that was hanging loose, but Khokon didn't say anything, he just lowered his face and smiled at me. But then the boys started shouting and that made Khokon lose his temper, and so when he raised his right crutch to bring it down on my back, I just ran like the wind.'

Then he began reminiscing about playing *golla chhut*, and golla chhut soon turned into football, and football took no time to transform itself into cricket, and by then the crutches had disappeared from Khokon's armpits, and he was in a colourful rickshaw with a loudspeaker balanced on its front handlebars, and Khokon was in the seat with both of his legs now missing from knees down, and he rasped into the mouthpiece that was wrapped in a handkerchief, 'Running now, running now, a grand showing at Chitra Cinema, on their silver screen, the King of All Heroes Razzaq and the Beauty Queen Shabana in the movie titled …'

Khokon became a movie canvasser, and his eyes grew redder, his mouth foamed and his breath was malodorous because he drank rotten liquor, and he smoked Haragachh bidis, and as he announced the movies, he grew angrier and angrier, and he began to curse the neighbourhood folks through his microphone, and unable to tolerate his unspeakable swearing, many people, on many days, came by to just deliver a slap to the back of his neck, but Khokon was unable to get out of the rickshaw, and he pulled out a knife from under his ass, one that was as long as a sword but blunt and black, and he brandished it, but alas (as the people of Roop Nagar still regret), all of it took place while he was stuck in the rickshaw because Khokon no longer had the capacity to move even a hair's breadth off that seat. The rickshaw driver, who was paid to be his day-long companion by the theatre owner, lifted him out of the rickshaw in the evening and deposited him by his doorway; without that help, Khokon wasn't capable of climbing down from the rickshaw by himself, let alone attacking anyone.

One evening, while Khokon sat in that rickshaw canvassing for the movies, the angel of death Azrael seized him. He arrived from the opposite direction, riding a bullock cart. The description of Azrael's arrival via bullock cart seemed a little enigmatic, which annoyed someone, and so he, in his own words, attempted to describe it in more material terms: a bullock cart laden with tal-bamboos was travelling on its way, evening had descended, the power was out along the road so it was quite dark everywhere, which is why Khokon's rickshaw driver hadn't spotted the honed tips of the bamboos sticking out quite a bit from the cart, and Khokon himself was drowsing after imbibing *pochani*, the local liquor, and so a sharpened bamboo entered Khokon's belly as he sat in the rickshaw and hoisted him into space. He began 'shouting, shouting, and shaking, shaking', which drew the attention of the rickshaw driver who looked back and saw that Khokon's legless mangled body was writhing on the tip of the bamboo and he was lowing like a cow. When the rickshaw driver caught him and lowered him to the ground, he realised that Khokon's intestines had knotted themselves around the bamboo tip in a fairly complicated manner. He couldn't manage to untangle Khokon's intestines no matter how hard he tried, and in the meantime, the bullock cart kept moving forward.

The blind traveller's curse finally led to Khokon-the-Cripple's death. But the people of Roop Nagar knew that even without curses, thugs and such, folks could come to rather tragic ends. In the context of tragic ends, suddenly Laltu's name surfaced, about whom some people said that his ending wasn't so tragic really, because he was still alive and was still involved in politics. But Laltu still pissed blood, and despite being married for ten years, he had failed to father a single child.

Just like the daredevil doings of these thugs were entertaining stories, the times when they were in hot water were also juicy stories. Thus, at this point, Laltu Mastaan, or Laltu-the-Thug, came up in conversation. He was designated a pioneer in the field of political thuggery, because President Ziaur Rahman himself had 'given him a *han-shake*' and placed him in charge of overseeing multi-party democracy at Roop Nagar College, and in Roop Nagar, Laltu was the first to demonstrate that it was possible for a student to squabble face to face with the college principal, and it was even possible for a student to yank out the wires of the principal's office telephone right in front of him and pretty much place him under house arrest.

The people of Roop Nagar said that the male students of the college got into fights with each other even before the advent of Laltu-the-Thug, but back then, the stricter and more imposing among the teachers would step forward and pull the rioting students to one side by their ears and resolve the fighting. But when Laltu-the-Thug started off serious political violence in the college, the strict and imposing professors lost the nerve to resolve those disputes. In the history of thuggery in Roop Nagar, Laltu was a milestone of sorts: before him, the thugs in the town walked in front of the esteemed elite with their heads lowered, they raised their hands to their foreheads in salaam, and they almost never smoked in front of them. Laltu-the-Thug was the first to accomplish a revolution: he was the one who had the guts for the first time ever to walk along the streets while dragging on a cigarette right in front of elders the age of his father. It was also in the era of Laltu-the-Thug when the practice of using college students as hired goons began; it started during the elections of the sugar mill workers union.

The people of Roop Nagar continued to tell Laltu-the-Thug's stories, whose pestering was pretty much preventing school- and college-going girls from going outside, and then the people leapt to that evening, when a sudden calamity befell Laltu-the-Thug. A description of the environs of the sugar mill surfaced, an area where stealing even green coconuts was dangerous, because the security guards of the sugar mill's general manager were on duty the entire night, wielding batons.

That night, late in the evening, the general manager, the DC and the big contractors, doctors and lawyers in town had settled down to a gambling session; people said that they were drinking Indian rum and chomping on chicken drumsticks, which Laltu-the-Thug couldn't quite stomach. He stood at the entrance of the rest house where they were, and called the district administrator, the general manager of the sugar mill and other prominent luminaries 'sons of pigs' and repeatedly threatened to do bad things with their mothers, until the night guards employed by the GM grabbed him, threw him flat on his back to the ground and climbed onto his chest. The DC called the police station and summoned the constabulary, who arrived and gave Laltu a good thrashing, then tied his arms and legs and took him to the station house where they again beat him within an inch of his life and hung him from the beams for the rest of the night.

For about a month after that, Laltu-the-Thug was nowhere to be seen. When he resurfaced, everybody in town knew that he was pissing blood, and his thuggery, in their words, had gone right out of his ass. If Laltu-the-Thug could end up like that despite being a political henchman, that meant that the godfather system must not have emerged yet, or else how could men of such negligible power like a mere district administrator and the GM of a sugar mill bring about such a situation for a big-name thug like him?

12

The day Pony Masud (by then Hafiz Mondal had begun to give him a share of the money pilfered from construction tenders in town; some people say he had been forced to do so) almost buried an assistant engineer of the LGED division alive in a pile of sand and cement at the site of an under-construction bridge in Tikka Para, was the day that the common people of Roop Nagar felt themselves under attack. Because this engineer wasn't a thug, had no connection to politics and was known for his integrity and courtesy. The people of Roop Nagar realised that even the lives of innocent, non-confrontational gentlemen weren't safe around Pony Masud. Pony Masud and his friends tormented shopkeepers, acted as if the hotels and restaurants were owned by their fathers, snatched cash from passersby, and for incomprehensible reasons, assaulted inoffensive common people. The rumour spread through town that Hafiz Mondal's spies were everywhere; those who spoke ill of him and his general Pony Masud behind their backs would have their tongues cut out, their mouths sewn shut, their heads shaved, have buttermilk poured all over them, and then they would be paraded nude around town.

Then came a time when the people of Roop Nagar noted that the blaze in Pony Masud's eyes had gone out.

They said, 'We just couldn't figure out what was going on. Why did the crazed dog suddenly go quiet? And then we realised, oh yeah, the elections are here, so now Mondal will be out and about begging for votes. So he calmed down his mad dog.'

Hafiz Mondal then bought Pony Masud a microbus and told him to organise his old crew back together again, because the elections were nigh and this time, he would certainly be granted the party's nomination, because the old chairman had grown senile.

'But you've suddenly taken this guise of a good person—where are you going to go with that, little boy?' People took jabs at Pony Masud in his absence. 'You think you'll get a pass just because you're disguising yourself as a good man? Look over there, all your fathers are coming for you.' And thus the people of Roop Nagar praised the Caretaker Government; within a week of taking charge of the country, the Caretaker Government arrested and took Pony Masud and his pals away. 'Roop Nagar *districk* jail; now sit in there and eat red rice to your full.' They said these things about Pony Masud and laughed bitterly.

'We voted for the sheaf of rice symbol,' said someone. 'That bastard Mondal needed to be taught a lesson, and also to make sure that Majed-the-Principal's bastard rots in jail for the rest of his life. That's why we voted for the sheaf of rice.'

Then began the stories about the event held at Majed-the-Principal's Atapara College for the newly elected Member of

Parliament Abu Karim. Pony Masud was released from jail, and the newly elected Parliamentarian Abu Karim, a soldier following the ideology of martyred Zia (this time his party was forming the government), threw a garland of flowers around his neck at the prison entrance. Pony Masud, once again, was transformed into a soldier of martyred Zia from previously being a soldier for Sheikh Mujib, and he went and set fire to Hafiz Mondal's terrace.

Mujib-soldiers like Hafiz Mondal—it was to teach people like him a lesson that the people of Roop Nagar had voted for the sheaf of rice—were punished severely; many of them had to flee their own homes. Then, in the same way that the people of Roop Nagar used to curse out Hafiz Mondal, they began to curse Abu Karim as well. Alongside which, they also cursed Pony Masud's dead grandparents, and they pulled in Brickly Mokhles and Laili Begum, and they discussed imaginary narratives of their sexual behaviour and joked about them in deplorable language.

They described an exchange between Pony Masud and a journalist from Dhaka. Someone said, 'Pony Masud told that journo, I'll cut your head off and send it to your mother, and I'll leave the rest of your body at the entrance to the home minister's house.' They talked about the rape of the Santal girl again, which had happened before the Dhaka journalist had shown up, and while talking about the Santal girl's rape, they dissected Laili Begum's character, and then they recalled the story about the grandmother of the raped girl, an eighty-year-old woman, getting her head shaved because she was going about the city crying and seeking justice and named Pony Masud, for which she was scalped and her skull was exposed. They spoke about the terrifying silence and the indifferent behaviour of the police after the death of the old woman, and while talking about that, they also pulled out the memory of Khokon-the-Cripple; they argued and disagreed about the curse of the mysterious old traveller, and suddenly they began to curse the deceased parents of Parliamentarian Abu Karim with obscene words; in this manner, they told later stories first, and earlier stories later, and created a tangle.

The morning when Pony Masud kicked the old beggar and the old man uttered a warning for Pony Masud, was the day on which all their imaginings and conjectures centred themselves. That day, which was several years ago, Pony Masud went to get money from Murari Prasad, and Murari, instead of cash, had given him a cheque, whereupon Pony Masud grew furious and kicked him in the face and then took the cheque to Sonali Bank, and there he did a 'scene create' by slapping the bank manager hard on the cheek and then pulling out his gun.

If that was all that had happened on that day, then the old beggar's curse would have gone to waste, because kicking Murari in the face and slapping the bank manager on the cheek weren't hardships for Masud, rather these were acts to enjoy. However, on that very day, in the afternoon, in a place beside Parulia village on Hili Road, the militia force Bangladesh Rifles (BDR) visited violence upon Pony Masud. The people of Roop Nagar had absolutely no doubt that the violence had descended from the skies because of the old beggar's curse. The description of Pony Masud being thrashed to his bones by the BDR became the head-to-toe review of Pony Masud's era, and the stories describing Masud's childhood and how he grew into Pony Masud floated like disconnected images.

13

The amused view with which at one time the common people of Roop Nagar watched the squabbles and clashes among Pony Masud, Ghostly Pintu and their armed companions, like an audience in a stadium, when they watched them compete in bloodletting and bluster from afar, which they had thought were isolated from the common lives of the common people, which they had considered the internal doings of young men who were bad and cruel to each other—that indifferent gaze of the aloof viewer disappeared within a short period of time. Terror, centred around Pony Masud, awoke inside them and soon they grew worried and anxious about themselves. They lost all sense of comfort, peace, assurance and safety and, astonished, they wondered about the impossible force that was Pony Masud: how did he come into being? Why did he come into being? Even the thinkers among the townspeople, those whose hide or hair had not, until then, been touched by the mad dog known as Pony Masud, opined that if someone was eighteen and if he, due to governmental indulgence, was granted power that superseded the powers of the district commissioner and the assistant superintendent of police, then many impossible, unthinkable events could be perpetrated by him. Those among the thinkers who were imaginative and aficionados of the ghastly, prophesied that the time was near when Pony Masud would stand on top of the town's central mosque in broad daylight, gnawing on a newborn's skull, and the DC, the ASP, the police and the BDR men would all clap and applaud.

But most of the people of Roop Nagar counted themselves among the faithful; they said that they did not worship the devil, they worshipped the great Allah, and therefore they had faith in the ultimate triumph of humanity. They said that in their minds, they harboured the faith that Pony Masud's destruction was inevitable; it was merely a matter of time.

'We could see it with our eyes closed,' were opinions that were heard, 'that the shrimp was definitely going to die.'

Nobody, however, vouchsafed their earlier assumptions about exactly how Pony Masud was going to meet his demise. But they stated confidently that no matter how, Pony Masud would most definitely have to face the harsh judgement of Allah, the great judge of right and wrong; Allah's wrath would descend upon him.

In this context, they spoke about the 'conduit', they discussed Pony Masud kicking the mysterious old darbesh who came in the guise of a beggar; they claimed that all the townspeople had heard the old man's curse loud and clear, and that they had been waiting for the divine sword hanging over Pony Masud's head to swiftly descend.

That morning, Masud had felt the desire to see his mother, so he had gone to his stepfather Brickly Mukhles' house; perhaps he had wanted to assuage the burning in his heart by gazing upon his dear mother's face. The people of Roop Nagar said that the boy certainly had a fire burning his heart, or else why would he turn out the way he did; but the people of Roop Nagar did not know *what* fire burnt Pony Masud's heart. When the news came that several BDR *jawans* had beaten Pony Masud to a pulp on Hili Road, near a village called Parulia, people remembered right away that the shrimp had gone to visit his mother that morning. He had felt the desire to see his mother as soon as he had woken up that morning because it had been preordained that doom would descend upon him that very afternoon. The eyewitness accounts from Parulia village were related thus: when the BDR jawans had wrapped Masud's body with a tarpaulin from their truck and thrown him onto the tarred highway, and were pounding him with their rifle butts, the only noise to exit the tarp was, 'Ma! Ma!'

When the skeleton of the Parulia eyewitness's account was overlaid with the flesh of the imaginings of the Roop Nagar's residents, the event of Pony Masud's becoming pulp at the hands of the BDR jawans acquired a realistic description:

The burning sun was pouring fire on everyone's heads at high noon; 'Oh, brother, the heat,' said the people of Parulia who, at the time, had been working the fields adjacent to the highway and watched as the police and BDR searched three cargo trucks that had come from the direction of Hili. And a magistrate stood beside a jeep with his hand on his hip, also watching. Right then a motorcycle drove in from the direction of Roop Nagar; and the eyewitnesses reported, 'There had been enough space to just go past the stopped trucks, so Pony Masud could actually have driven past the trucks onto his destination; there had been no obstacle.'

But why would he do that? How could Pony Masud operate outside of destiny's design? He had to stop his pony on that spot, because that is what the mysterious old man in the garb of a beggar had alluded to that morning. Therefore, Pony Masud stalled his Yamaha pony, balanced himself with one foot, and shouted out, 'Hey, what's going on here?'

The on-duty policemen and BDR soldiers had looked at Pony Masud in surprise when he shouted at them, while the magistrate stood there in silence, hand on hip. Pony Masud kept shouting, 'Hey, you spawn of pigs, what's going on here?'

A middle-aged BDR soldier told him, 'It's a checking.' His voice was somber, but he was raging inside after being called the spawn of a pig.

'What checking?' Masud climbed down from his ride and charged towards the BDR man shouting, 'What checking, you sons of pigs, what checking, eh? Checking on whose orders?'

The BDR soldier pointed towards the magistrate and said, 'Sir's.'

When the people of Parulia saw the scrawny young man slap the burly BDR man with the rifle and heard him shout, 'Did your sir take my order first?', they decided he was quite mad; and the people of Roop Nagar, when they heard this description, saw in their mind's eye that their Masud had turned into an ant that had grown wings and jumped into a pit of fire.

When he was slapped, the BDR soldier—whose last day on the job was that very day, who was going to retire the next day—slammed his rifle's butt into Pony Masud's belly so hard that the leaf-thin young man clutched his belly and doubled up and fell on the ground, and immediately the magistrate's voice was heard: 'Tie that thing up, right now, tie it up!'

So the police and the BDR soldiers surrounded Pony Masud and began to use their rifle butts and boots on him from every direction. A few of them pulled down a tarpaulin from a truck and wrapped Pony Masud in it; then they threw him onto the tarred road; some said, he was 'beaten to a pulp', and some say he was 'beaten like old batting to fluff it up.'

'We thought, that was it, it's over,' said the people of Parulia, 'the shrimp is dead. Can someone survive a beating like that and stay alive, yeah?"

But when the BDR took the crumpled up Pony Masud to the Roop Nagar District Hospital, he was still alive, although unconscious. The people of Roop Nagar were waiting for the moment when the doctors would pronounce him dead; the wailing of Pony Masud's mother imbued the hospital compound with the ambience of a house of mourning.

A loaded gun was found in the unconscious Pony Masud's pocket, and so the Roop Nagar police arrested him under the firearms act and surrounded the hospital. The MP for the ruling party, Abu Karim, instructed the district administrator to make all the paperwork regarding the case against Pony Masud disappear, and to have him released from police custody. He proclaimed that he was going to send Masud to Madras for medical treatment. However, the district administrator rejected his proposal; people said that the vigour in the district administrator's voice at that time was worth noticing. He told the MP of the ruling party straight to his face that Pony Masud had assaulted a member of the BDR force, so he was unable to shoulder the responsibility of a possible BDR revolt. The people of Roop Nagar were reminded of Khokon-the-Cripple and Laltu-the-Thug. They saw that the final curtain was about to be dropped on the era of Pony Masud. They waited for the moment when the physicians would pronounce Pony Masud dead. While the scene where Pony Masud's mother was grieving in the hospital compound was still going on, they spotted Pony Masud's actual father Majed-the-Principal and his stepfather Brickly Mukhles side by side, and they opined that those two men seemed like brothers in that moment, as if Laili Begum was their only sister. They said that at that moment they noticed an astonishing similarity among the faces and the expressions of all three of those people. A sort of sadness and tenderness had grown in their minds. As they waited for news of Pony Masud's impending death, pity, sorrow and tenderness grew in their minds, that was akin to the pity that had saturated their minds at the news of Khokon-the-Cripple's death, at the news of Laltu-the-Thug pissing blood after the police gave him a 'whaling', the pity that had arisen in their minds upon receiving the tragic news that Laltu would never be able to father a child.

But as they reminisced about Khokon-the-Cripple and the blind darbesh who had come in the guise of a beggar, they received the news that the doctors were unable to pronounce Pony Masud dead. At some point he had opened his eyes, looked at his mother's face, and in a hoarse voice, ordered his weeping mother, 'Don't cry, get me a glass of water.'

14

After that, the people of Roop Nagar philosophised: Pony Masud doesn't die! Does not die! When he recuperated, the district administrator fled Roop Nagar to rule over a different district. But he could have avoided that because Pony Masud went from the Roop Nagar District Hospital straight to the Dhaka Hospital for the Disabled in the capital city, and he never ever came back to Roop Nagar to stay.

The people of Roop Nagar didn't get to see the treatment and care he received at the Dhaka Hospital for the Disabled; they only learnt about it through word of mouth. Apparently, many influential people visited his bedside; they brought with them imported, overly priced fruits and other sick-bed foods for Pony Masud. Among these, pomegranates—known as *bedana*, and coming from faraway Pakistan—grew to be his favourite. The people of Roop Nagar heard that Pony Masud had raised the question of why this dearly beloved Pakistani fruit did not grow in Bangladesh. They laughed and said that Pakistan was Pakistan and Bangladesh was Bangladesh. But apparently Jabbar Ali Miya had said that Bangladesh was Pakistan's *baap*, i.e. father. The people of Roop Nagar had never ever heard of such a thing. They had witnessed Pakistan break apart and Bangladesh emerging from that break and considering that maybe Pakistan could be called Bangladesh's father or mother country. Then Jabbar Ali Miya asked the esteemed people of Roop Nagar, 'Where was the Muslim League born? In Punjab? In the state of Sindh? Or was it in our very own Bengal? And the fools who proposed the Lahore Resolution, who were they? Punjabis? Baluchis? Sindhis? Biharis?'

Anyway, Pony Masud called his mother's cellphone from the hospital and said, 'Ma, plant a pomegranate tree in the yard.' Laili Begum planted a grafted pomegranate tree in Brickly Mokhles' yard, but no pomegranates would grow on it.

The people of Roop Nagar heard that a minister had taken Pony Masud from the hospital and flown him to Bangkok. There, for a month, his treatment continued; some said it took three months. When he returned, nobody could tell that BDR members had pulverised his arms, legs and ribs with their rifle butts. Of course, Masud hadn't returned to Roop Nagar in a month or even three; so the townspeople hadn't seen him. In the next three years, they saw Pony Masud only once; he came to Roop Nagar for just two days, about a year and a half after the incident of BDR soldiers turning him into 'mashed potatoes'. He arrived in a Jeep, and the people of Roop Nagar heard that by then he owned not only a Jeep, but also a flat in the heart of Dhaka city. Of course, at first, the people of Roop Nagar found that hard to believe. Some of them asked the uniformed driver of Pony Masud's Jeep, 'Whose Jeep is this, Mr Driver?'

The driver had responded with some surprise, 'Why? It's *saar's*.'

'Which saar?'

'Why, my saar.'

'What does your saar do then, in Dhaka?'

When he heard this question, the driver of Pony Masud's Jeep went silent. The people jabbed the same question at him again. 'Aren't you going to say what your saar does in Dhaka?'

Pony Masud's Jeep driver remained silent for a few moments before answering. 'Saar has some business concerns.'

But his response didn't quench the small-town curiosity of the people of Roop Nagar. They dug even deeper. 'What kind of business?'

Pony Masud's driver was annoyed. His annoyance clearly showed in his eyes and his face; he lit a cigarette. The people of Roop Nagar noted that Pony Masud's driver smoked the 555 brand. They asked him, 'What brand does your saar smoke these days?'

Pony Masud's driver realised that these people were ragging on him, so he stopped paying attention to them and smoked his cigarette.

The people of Roop Nagar kept prodding him with constant questions. 'Did he get married?'

'Is he really close to ministers?'

'Does he have a house in Dhaka?'

Pony Masud's driver grew annoyed and asked in return, 'If he has a car, wouldn't he also have a house?'

At one point, as if on behalf of Laili Begum, the people of Roop Nagar grumbled to Pony Masud's driver as to why he no longer came to Roop Nagar; had he forgotten them? Didn't he feel the need to at least see the mother who had carried him in her womb? But Pony Masud's driver did not respond to their complaints.

The people of Roop Nagar saw that before the year had run its course, Majed-the-Principal's two-storied house had grown into a four-storied house, and a new building had begun to grow in the uninhabited plot of land beside his house that belonged to Noni Gopal. Pony Masud, or his father, had become owner of that plot of land earlier, when Masud was still an invincible warrior for Sheikh Mujib, when Noni Gopal, blind follower of the same man and who had only voted for his party's symbol, the boat, his entire life, who had owned Roop Nagar's once famous herbal drugstore, fled his motherland for India in the dark of night. At the time, the country was deep in Awami League's reign; before he left the country of his birth with his entire family, Noni Gopal had turned very bitter. One day, he had said about Awami League to Roop Nagar's esteemed people gathered at Jabbar Ali Miya's library, 'That party, in their minds, tell themselves that if the Hindus stay on in this country, we get their votes; if they flee, we get their land.'

Jabbar Ali had raised a mild objection. 'It's not a question of Awami League or BNP; this is a consequence of Partition. Before that, nobody could even imagine that it was possible to snatch someone's home, or their land.' When, two years after Noni Gopal left the country, and Awami League no longer occupied the throne and Pony Masud had again become a Soldier of Martyred Zia and had extracted two lakh takas as the price of the honour of the Hindu Kamini Sarker's four young daughters, Jabbar Ali had said, 'Just wait! There will be more to see!'

Noni Gopal's land was seized by Mujib warrior Pony Masud; a mall was built on it by the Soldier of Martyred Zia, Pony Masud. Majed-the-Principal named the mall 'Masud Shopping Complex', but the people of Roop Nagar referred to it as the Pony Market. One day, people saw that Majed-the-Principal was headed for his college in a blue Toyota Corolla. On top of which, an employee of the Roop Nagar National Savings Bureau leaked the news that Majed-the-Principal was purchasing savings certificates month after month after month.

Pony Masud's stepfather Brickly Mokhles' one-storied house (where Pony Masud's actual mother Laili Begum lived) quickly became two-storied; however, it grew no further because, according to what people said, at some point Masud stopped sending his mother money. Apparently, he often told his mother via cell phone, 'Whatever you've done till now, it's done. Now you should go back to Abba.'

But Laili Begum didn't leave Brickly Mokhles to go back to Majed-the-Principal's house; she couldn't because she loved Brickly Mokhles more than her life. Of course, Masud didn't place too much pressure on his mother. The people of Roop Nagar said that the boy had always been very tender about his mother; it just wasn't possible for him to be stern with her. But he did reduce communication with his mother, and at one point he stopped calling her cell phone. Laili Begum had her son's number, so she would call him herself; until one day she realised that there was no response from that cell phone. But it wasn't as if Masud had cut off all contact with his mother. He couldn't possibly go month after month without talking to his mother; he would call her himself. Laili Begum would be overjoyed to get a call from her son after a long gap. But he left no way for the mother to call the son. He would call his mother on the landline at Brickly Mokhles' house during the day time, when the possibility of Brickly Mokhles being home was low. Some days he got his mother, some days it was the housemaid; on the days it was the housemaid, he'd get angry and shout at her, 'Tell Ma that at this age she shouldn't be out taking the air in different neighbourhoods; she should be saying her prayers and reading the Book.'

Each time, the housemaid would inform Pony Masud that Laili Begum wasn't waiting around for her son to proselytise her but had already begun to say her prayers and keep fasts. Pony Masud kept calling back to say the same thing because he didn't believe that his gadabout mother had become a devout woman.

When the housemaid said, 'Why don't you give Khalamma your phone number? Khalamma wants to call you,' Pony Masud yelled at her and hung up.

15

When the number of terrorists killed during 'crossfires' with the RAB kept growing and growing, at one point, the conviction arose among many residents of Roop Nagar that Pony Masud's days were numbered.

At the same time, they also recalled an anti-crime drive called 'Operation Clean Heart' led by the army, during which, forty-three terrorists had died due to 'heart stoppages' while being interrogated. When the people of Roop Nagar began to think that number forty-fourth was going to be Pony Masud, the campaign was suddenly discontinued.

The people of Roop Nagar, therefore, vilified the alleged civil society and human rights organisations. They especially cursed the civil society: 'Those bastards eat foreign money and then shout, "human rights, human rights".' They said, 'Terrorists aren't human, what human rights should they get?'

People said that when the number of terrorists dying from 'heart attacks' while in custody of the combined armed forces crossed thirty, Pony Masud's mother Laili Begum began to perform her prayers five times a day. But prayers and the holy book could not restore Laili Begum's peace of mind. She began suffering from insomnia and anxiety. One day she went to the ruling party parliamentarian Abu Karim and asked, 'Nothing bad will happen to my boy, will it? My son is safe?'

Abu Karim lied to Laili Begum to console her. 'Is your boy even in Bangladesh anymore? I sent him off to India!'

The people of Roop Nagar didn't know if back then Pony Masud had escaped to India to save himself from Operation Clean Heart. But they knew very well that even if Pony Masud had fled to India for self-protection, he hadn't needed the help of Roop Nagar's member of parliament, because by then Pony Masud had grown quite close to a number of influential ministers as well members of the ruling party's Standing Committee; he no longer had any reason to pay attention to Roop Nagar's MP, Abu Karim.

But when Operation Clean Heart was discontinued, the people of Roop Nagar learnt that Pony Masud had not gone to India; he hadn't needed to go because during that period he had found shelter in a house on Minto Road where, after 11 p.m., many ministers, state ministers and deputy ministers came to visit.

But in the view of the people of Roop Nagar, this didn't mean anything. The real issue was that Pony Masud was a sinner, there was no limit to his sins, he would most definitely be punished, and he should be. Just because he had spared the people of Roop Nagar by leaving for Dhaka, didn't mean that everyone there had forgotten all the stories of the torment he inflicted. He had to be punished; he would find no absolution without repentance. But in Bangladesh, they said, the police and the terrorists were brothers, friends with the devil, and the staple food that magistrates ate was money. More to the point, 'In a country where MPs and ministers and leaders couldn't do without terrorists, who, in that lawless land, could punish Pony Masud?' They believed that Allah himself had sent RAB, and their 'crossfires' were the last hope. Let the curtains fall on Pony Masud's life to the sounds of a 'crossfire'.

But it is also astonishing, or perhaps it is not astonishing in the least, that while talking about Pony Masud, many people of Roop Nagar refer to him as 'our Masud', as if he were part of their households, not someone unrelated to them. But those who had had to bear his torture recalled him with much bitterness. Those who were unable to endure his torture and died were lying in their graves, cursing Pony Masud to fall prey to a RAB 'crossfire'.

The people of Roop Nagar had a very simple and uncomplicated faith regarding the Rapid Action Battalion's 'crossfires'. There was no doubt in their minds that RAB was catching terrorists and shooting them. This belief was rooted deeply in their minds because after each terrorist death by 'crossfire', RAB's explanatory statements disseminated to the public were more or less identical. The statements reported: RAB arrested this terrorist and, in accordance with his confession, took him to his locality in the deep of night, the purpose being that the terrorist would surrender the dens and illegal arms belonging to his accomplices to RAB. As soon as they got there, the accomplices, who were yet to be arrested, who were the very people RAB was there to capture in the first place, began to shoot at RAB officers. RAB fired back. The arrested terrorist got caught in the middle of this exchange and haplessly lost his life. RAB named such exchanges 'crossfire'. When each 'crossfire' incident was made public with pretty much the same story one after another, it wasn't hard for the people of Roop Nagar to understand that RAB was hiding the truth; it wasn't really 'crossfire', rather it was through 'direct fire' that they were finishing off these terrorists one after another and they were undoubtedly doing a good thing.

The people of Roop Nagar wanted to give RAB credit for killing terrorists but RAB was unwilling to accept any such credit. They claimed that they were not killing terrorists; the terrorists were all dying in crossfires. Some people in Roop Nagar joked that if the terrorists were dying in crossfires, then where was RAB's mastery? But that was merely a joke; the simple and uncomplicated people of Roop Nagar admitted to themselves without indulging in sophistry that all the credit for this innovative campaign to finish off terrorists was due to the RAB. And they hoped with body and soul that this very timely and extremely urgent step should continue; let all terrorists be finished off, let peace return to this country.

But there also existed a paradox in the minds of the people of Roop Nagar, which wasn't very easy to explain. They said that throughout their lives they had seen that what they wished for never took place. Disappointment moved about in the mysterious, solitary corner of their minds, whenever they desired something: 'Does what we want ever happen!' So sometimes it seemed that they hoped for nothing. Or they transformed their hope into despair. But when, due to the logical sequence of events, something positive did happen, they felt, or wanted to believe, that it was precisely what they had wanted.

Or when something of an opposite nature happened, they claimed that they had known all along that this was exactly what would happen. For instance, in the April of 1971, when Pakistani soldiers showed up in Roop Nagar and began to kill people, they had desperately wished for Allah's wrath to descend on those brutal attackers. Many of them had picked up weapons and decided that they would either finish off the Pakistani soldiers or drive them out and liberate the country. But in their minds, alongside that intent sat despair, like a brother. The common folk, who hadn't fought with weapons but nevertheless desired the fall of the 'brutish' Pakistani soldiers, possessed no deep faith that the country would indeed be freed. They thought, and some even said aloud, that all these 'troubles' would one day be 'sorted out'. Of course, what they wanted was for them to be resolved without liberation. It was their characteristic hopelessness that made them think like that; because what they desired never became real. But after the country was liberated, every single one of them claimed that they had known beforehand that the Pakistani army would be defeated, that Bangladesh would be liberated.

In reality, the people of Roop Nagar couldn't tell for sure whether, in general, what they thought they wanted really was what they wanted.

But it is perhaps certain that the people of Roop Nagar wanted RAB's campaign to be a total success. And so, for RAB to be successful, not a single terrorist, not even Pony Masud, could be given an inch of leeway and perhaps, in the end, even Pony Masud wouldn't be overlooked. But in the minds of the people of Roop Nagar, some uncertainty, born of despair, still remained.

They had heard that Pony Masud now roamed around Dhaka city in a four-wheeled pony, i.e. a car, and the windows of that car were tinted with a colour so that nobody could see Pony Masud from the outside, but Pony Masud could see everyone from inside the car.

Some of them said that Pony Masud's vehicle was a Jeep (which they had had the great fortune to see just once, and which was four times as pricier), and some said it was a terrifically expensive private car. But among those who visited Dhaka, nobody claimed that they had seen the Jeep or the car with their own eyes. When anyone described Pony Masud's vehicle, and the question 'did you see the car?' was posed, they would respond that although they had not seen it with their own eyes, someone else had. Nobody felt the need to hunt down this 'other person' to obtain their testimony because it wasn't as if they were unable to digest the food in their bellies without ascertaining this piece of information. The people of Roop Nagar loved to gossip and chat; Allah the Great had not given them nitpicky, investigative natures. They had heard that their Pony Masud drove around Dhaka city these days in a Jeep or a private car with black windows.

But who could guarantee that tinted car windows would grant complete protection? Instead, the concern that rose in the minds of many people of Roop Nagar was that the very glass might spell the end of Pony Masud. Apparently, the registration number for his car was no ordinary number. It was a number that allowed law enforcement officers to easily identify that the car was for the use of a foreign diplomat. In the judgment of the people of Roop Nagar, this was a crucial safeguard. Pony Masud was roving about right in front of RAB's nose in the guise of an ambassador; who could possibly catch him?

But he didn't stay in his car 24/7, day and night, of course; he went to various places for fun and entertainment, and at night, if not in his own home, surely he went to sleep in some house or other. RAB could capture him from any of these locations.

Therefore, although the name of the last terrorist to be arrested by RAB was misprinted in the newspapers as Pony Majid, in truth he was Pony Masud, the very own son of Roop Nagar's Laili Begum and Majed-the-Principal (and stepson of Brickly Mokhles as well); because at dawn Laili Begum had dreamt that her son's chest was riddled with bullets, and hot air was exiting his punctured lungs, and from that hot air the call of 'Ma, Ma!' could be heard. On top of which, that very morning that mysterious old traveller had appeared in Roop Nagar and pronounced, 'There's news!'

Therefore, most certainly there was news about Pony Masud.

The people of Roop Nagar remembered that in the earlier incident, when that old traveller had cursed or warned Pony Masud with 'you have misfortune written across your brow' and vanished, apocalypse had truly descended upon him. That the old traveller hadn't meant Pony Masud's death by the word 'misfortune' but had instead indicated his terrible suffering at the hands of the BDR, had become clear later on, just as it had happened with Khokon-the-Cripple, that 'a bamboo will make its way' hadn't meant that he would get a bamboo up his anus; it had meant that the bamboo would enter his belly and gut him.

Many people of Roop Nagar had no doubts that this time, when the mysterious traveller said, 'There's news', he had meant 'crossfire'. When they saw Laili Begum weeping in her crazed grief, they thought that Pony Masud's time was indeed running out. They thought that the mother had experienced precise premonitions about her son's forthcoming death. And that was why she was crying like that. It was only at a child's death that a mother wept in such a way.

When Majed-the-Principal returned to Roop Nagar in the afternoon after his urgent meeting at Atapara College, people spotted his Toyota Corolla and told each other, 'The principal doesn't know yet.' Some of them said, 'That fool doesn't read the newspapers, how is he supposed to get the news?'

Someone stopped his car, knocked on the window, and said, 'Saar, have you heard the news?'

'What news?'

When people heard Majed-the-Principal asking that, they became sure that he knew nothing. Some of them clucked their tongues and others said, 'Oh, the father doesn't know about the son yet!' But none of the people of Roop Nagar told Majed-the-Principal the truth; they felt apprehensive. They kept whispering among themselves, and within those whispers, one or two consoling or sympathetic sounds were uttered. Finally, when one of them advised Majed-the-Principal to read the day's newspaper, it struck him. He felt immediately that his son, his treasure, was done for. Because he knew quite well that the 'crossfire' campaign was running at full speed, and the fear that Pony Masud could fall prey to that campaign was not wholly absent from his mind. Gasping, he ran to Jabbar Ali's 'library'; the afternoon was dying, and the day's newspapers were almost all sold out. He grabbed copies of the two unpopular newspapers that still lay there and he held his breath as he read the entire news story about Ghora Majid's arrest by RAB. There was no description of who Pony Masud was; all it said was that RAB arrested him at 11 p.m. from a house in Gulshan, and there were thirty-one cases against him, twenty-five of which were for murder.

At first Majed-the-Principal didn't notice that the name of the captured terrorist was noted as Pony Majid; when Jabbar Ali pointed it out to him, he exhaled deeply and hugged Jabbar Ali to his chest, kissed his acne-scarred cheek noisily, and said, 'That isn't my son! That isn't my Masud!'

But when the other people present told him that nobody had ever heard of a top terror called Pony Majid, and that there were all kinds of errors in newspapers these days, Majed-the-Principal broke down and wept. He pulled out his cell phone and began to push buttons repeatedly, but he couldn't reach his son. He kept getting a message that the number he was dialling wasn't currently available.

In the evening, the people of Roop Nagar sat down to listen to BBC on the radio; eagerly, they crowded restaurants and hair salons that kept their radios on. But no news of a 'crossfire' was broadcast. People knew that the RAB-terrorist 'crossfires' didn't take place in daylight. Pony Masud (they assumed with certainty that Pony Majid was actually Pony Masud) had been arrested the evening before, and now he was in the custody of Azrael, the angel of death. The event was going to take place that night, most probably after midnight.

Therefore, the people of Roop Nagar spent an almost sleepless night. As soon as it was light, they rushed to Jabbar Ali's 'library' to buy or just look at the day's newspapers. When they got there, they saw that what they had thought would happen had come true: the terrorist arrested the day before was dead from a 'crossfire' with RAB, and his name had now been printed as Pony Majid aka Pony Masud.

The wash of tears from Laili Begum and Majed-the-Principal called forth a flood of grief in Roop Nagar; the town took on the air of a house in mourning. Laili Begum rolled around on the ground beneath the pomegranate tree in Brickly Mokhles' yard, while Brickly Mukhles stood in the veranda and stared at her helplessly, and Majed-the-Principal closed the door of his house and wailed and wept, 'Oh, ho, oh, ho, what just happened!'

People gathered in the yards of both houses, and a few of them tried to console Pony Masud's grief-ravaged mother and father, but they couldn't really find the language to console.

Someone said that both birth and death were in the hands of Allah, and one day everyone must die.

Someone said that the flesh made of earth would now return to earth.

In the middle of that, someone else said, 'Allah has taken back what is His.'

'That isn't condolence! That's a jab!'

'This fool is the spawn of Awami League!'

'Get that fool!'

A fight broke out in Brickly Mokhles' yard. Laili Begum stopped weeping and looked; she saw that two young men were pulling the legs of another young man asunder, and everyone was shouting, 'Rip him! Tear his legs apart!'

Suddenly, the phone rang in Laili Begum and Brickly Mokhles' bedroom. She jumped up, as if jolted by lightning, and rushed to the room.

Within moments Laili Begum's joyful shout came from the room, 'Son! Masud!'

The people of Roop Nagar went back to their homes. As they left, they told each other, 'Pony Masud never dies.' They accepted that not all dreams dreamed at dawn come true. And no eyewitnesses could be found who had seen the old traveller walk past Majed-the-Principal's house, muttering 'There's news!' and disappeared.